PLANNING FOR LOVE

Acclaim for Erin Dutton

"While there is fire and passion, [*Capturing Forever*] is a thoughtful romance, well written and well paced, it brings to life the reality of adult experiences and the strength of family despite the mistakes we all make."—*Lesbian Reading Room*

"In Dutton's highly entertaining contemporary [*For the Love of Cake*], well-drawn characters Shannon Hayes and Maya Vaughn discover romance behind reality TV...Dutton's love story never loses momentum."—*Publishers Weekly*

For the Love of Cake is "An enjoyable romance based in a reality show bake-off. A hot chef, a drooling contestant and a lot of cake...what's not to love? The main characters are excellent, their development well handled and their attraction and occasional rejection make for good reading. Thoroughly enjoyable reading. If you like a good romance this will hit the buttons, and if you like reality cooking shows you will have a double winner. As many others will probably say—it has hot women and cake, what else could it possibly need?"—*Curve Magazine*

With *Point of Ignition*, "Erin Dutton has given her fans another fast paced story of fire, with both buildings and emotions burning hotly...Dutton has done an excellent job of portraying two women who are each fighting for their own dignity and learning to trust again. The delicate tug of war between the characters is well done as is the dichotomy of boredom and drama faced daily by the firefighters. *Point of Ignition* is a story told well that will touch its readers."—*Just About Write*

"*Designed for Love* is…rich in love, romance, and sex. Dutton gives her readers a roller coaster ride filled with sexual thrills and chills. *Designed for Love* is the perfect book to curl up with on a cold winter's day."—*Just About Write*

In *Fully Involved*, "Dutton's studied evocation of the macho world of firefighting gives the story extra oomph—and happily ever after is what a good romance is all about, right?"—*Q Syndicate*

"*Sequestered Hearts* is packed with raw emotion, but filled with tender moments too. The author writes with sophistication that one would expect from a veteran author…A romance is about more than just plot and character development. It's about passion, physical intimacy, and connection between the characters. The reader should have a visceral reaction to what is going on within the pages for the novel to succeed. Dutton's words match perfectly with the emotion she has created. *Sequestered Hearts* is one book that cannot be overlooked. It is romance at its finest."—*L-word Literature.com*

"*Sequestered Hearts*, by first-time novelist Erin Dutton, is everything a romance should be. It is teeming with longing, heartbreak, and of course, love…as pure romances go, it is one of the best in print today."—*Just About Write*

By the Author

Sequestered Hearts

Fully Involved

A Place to Rest

Designed for Love

Point of Ignition

A Perfect Match

Reluctant Hope

More Than Friends

For the Love of Cake

Officer Down

Capturing Forever

Planning for Love

Visit us at www.boldstrokesbooks.com

PLANNING
FOR LOVE

by

Erin Dutton

2017

This Trade Paperback Original Is Published By
Bold Strokes Books, Inc.
P.O. Box 249
Valley Falls, NY 12185

First Edition: August 2017

Credits
Editor: Shelley Thrasher
Production Design: Stacia Seaman
Cover Photo by William Markus Photography
Cover Design by Sheri (graphicartist2020@hotmail.com)

Acknowledgments

This book began in my heart long before any of the words touched the page. In 2016, while writing and editing *Capturing Forever*, I was also busy planning my own wedding. After all of the excitement of ceremony, vows, cake, music, and family visiting had settled back down, I began writing this story. There are little nuggets from our adventure sprinkled throughout the book, but Rachel and Faith took over and really made this story their own.

Thanks to Sandy and Sheri for working with me on this cover and once again indulging my desire to make the design even more personal. Thanks so much to Will Meacham of William Markus Photography for capturing the photo from our special day (my nails have never looked better and probably never will again).

Thanks to Shelley Thrasher for once more walking me through the editing process—she makes it as painless as it can be, and I never fail to learn something new.

On a personal note, I need to thank our family and friends. We couldn't have asked for a more amazing wedding day, and having you all there with us made everything even more special. I'm constantly reminded of how lucky we are to have family that loves and accepts us.

And finally, thanks to the readers. Writing a book means a ton of solitary hours spent with these characters. So when the story is complete and I put it out there, it means so much to find out how it will be received by those who read it. Please keep reaching out with feedback, keep visiting us and chatting with us at events, and most importantly, keep reading.

For Chris—you're my favorite wife.

Chapter One

R achel Union parked her car by the curb in front of her best friend, Violet's, house. As she circled the front of her car, she studied Violet's house with a realtor's eye. She could already envision the photos she wanted to post with the listing. Violet would be married in eight months, and she'd asked Rachel to list the house in the spring, a couple of months before the wedding. Rachel would get her the best price she could and would waive her usual commission. Violet protested, but Rachel insisted, saying they could call it a wedding gift if she preferred. But honestly, she didn't expect to do much more than post some great photos. Given the growth in the area and how well Violet cared for the property, the place would practically sell itself.

The previous owner of the 1930s cottage had painted the brick, and Rachel was not a fan. But Violet hadn't minded, so she'd changed the color to suit her better. Rachel had to admit the medium gray looked great against the white trim and black shutters. Rachel and Violet shared a bit of a green thumb and had enjoyed sprucing up the landscaping together after Violet bought the place. A lawn service kept the yard neatly trimmed, but Violet handled the shrubs and the perennials that added a pop of color to the flower beds around the front of the house.

Rachel didn't recognize the luxury SUV in the driveway next to Violet's car. She'd come early to help Violet set up for the barbecue she and her fiancé were hosting and expected to be the first to arrive. She opened her passenger door and grabbed the bowl of potato salad, her specialty.

As she approached the house, she could hear music coming from inside, even through the closed door. She knocked once, and when Violet didn't answer, she fished her keys out of her pocket, certain Violet couldn't hear her.

"Why is the music so loud?" Rachel called as she pushed open the door. She stopped suddenly, and the bowl in her hand crashed onto the hardwood floor at her feet.

In Violet's haste to cover herself, she shoved the woman who'd been on top of her off the side of the couch. But the image of that woman, clad only in her underwear, rising over Violet, had already been scribed into Rachel's mind. She registered a lean body, messy blond waves, and a panicked expression as the woman flailed to the floor.

"You have potato salad on your feet," Violet said calmly. She grabbed a throw off the back of the couch and held it to her chest. As she smoothed her other hand over her blue-black hair, a slight tremor contradicted the serenity she seemed to project.

Rachel stared at her ruined shoes and then at the mostly naked form sprawled out on the floor. The woman groaned and rolled over. She swiped at her head, smearing a trail of blood that poured from a cut high on her forehead and ran down the side of her face. She paled when she saw the stain on her hands.

"Shit." Her eyes went glassy, and she looked like she might pass out.

Rachel toed off her shoes, somehow having the forethought to not want to track potato salad across the floor. When she reached the woman, she dropped to her knees, grabbed a shirt off the floor, and pressed it to her wound.

"Faith, are you okay?" Violet scrambled up, pulling the blanket more fully around her.

Faith? This was the wedding planner Violet had been so eager for her to meet?

"I'm fine." She tried to push Rachel's hands away.

"Hold still." Rachel's stomach turned queasy at the smear of bright red lipstick on Faith's mouth—Violet's signature color. But her instinct to stop Faith's bleeding took over, and she tightened her grasp on a very bare shoulder. As she avoided looking at Faith's lips, her eyes dropped to firm breasts and tight, light-pink nipples that appeared soft to the touch.

"Hey, this is my shirt." Faith's voice pulled Rachel's attention back to her face. The expression in Faith's eyes indicated she knew exactly where Rachel's gaze had been.

Irritated at herself for looking, and at Faith for catching her and for being so damn smug about it, she grabbed Faith's hand and pressed it against the shirt before releasing her and standing up. "Keep pressure on it. It's almost stopped bleeding."

Violet had pulled her clothes on and bent over to attend to Faith. "I'm so sorry. I was startled. Where did you hit your head?"

"The coffee table, I think." Faith stood slowly, bracing herself against the edge of the very piece of furniture that had split her skin open. "I should—um—" Faith gestured at herself with her free hand.

"Oh, yes, honey. Let's go to the bathroom and get you cleaned up." Violet took Faith's arm. Her easy use of the endearment cut through Rachel's shock at the whole situation, leaving anger surging in its wake.

"I can probably handle it myself." Faith glanced warily at Rachel, as if she could sense the shift in her mood. She made her way toward the hall bathroom, looking steadier already.

"I did this to you. The least I can do is help."

"She said she can handle it." Rachel grabbed Violet's arm and yanked her toward the kitchen. "I'd like to talk to you." She contained herself just until she'd dragged Violet out of the room. Once there, she released her and spun around to glare at her. "What the hell, Vi?"

"What are you even doing here? The party's not for two hours."

"That's your question? What am *I* doing? I came over early to help you set up. What are *you* doing?"

"Don't freak out."

"Don't—" Rachel took several steps across the small room, absurdly irritated that she couldn't get farther away from Violet just then. She'd always told Violet this damn kitchen was too cramped. "Are you kidding me right now? Your wedding planner?"

Violet blushed but didn't offer any explanation.

"I can't believe she hit on you. That is the most unprofessional thing I've ever—"

"She didn't come on to me."

"Then how did she end up groping you on your couch? I'm sure it's not the first time she's done this. I'm surprised she doesn't have some kind of reputation."

"She does. Why do you think I hired her?"

"What?"

"Sure, she's a great wedding planner, but that wasn't the only draw. Carly slept with her before her wedding."

Rachel stared at Violet, completely lost for words. How could she act so nonchalant?

"Please, don't make a big deal out of this. I was curious. I want to be faithful to Jack after we're married, so this was my last chance to find out what it's like to be with a woman."

"Curious?" Rachel scoffed, an odd, strangled sound that nearly turned into irrational laughter. "You want to be faithful *after* you're married?"

"Can you try not to be so damned old-fashioned for once?"

Rachel inhaled deeply, but that only increased her feeling of dizziness. Violet hadn't been seduced. In fact, this hadn't even been an impulsive act. Violet had contemplated and planned this scenario. "Why didn't you tell me you were thinking about this?"

"Because I knew you'd react like this."

"And what about Jack? Don't you feel even a little guilty about what you're doing to him?"

Before Violet could answer, Faith cleared her throat from the archway between the kitchen and living room. She'd managed to stop the bleeding from her head and had covered the cut with a Band-Aid. She now wore a clean T-shirt that Rachel recognized as one of Jack's. Rachel wondered for a moment what Violet would tell Jack about how it went missing. She carried her bloodied shirt balled up in her right hand.

"I—uh—I should go." Faith took a cautious step forward.

"Yeah, you should." Rachel strode to the front door and swung it open. Faith followed.

Violet trailed after them. "You can't go. I've already told everyone you were going to be here for the barbecue."

"She can't stay." Rachel stepped in front of Violet, cutting her off from Faith, willing her to see reason. Surely she understood she'd have to find a new wedding planner now.

Violet stepped around her and crossed to Faith. "Please, stay."

"I'm not exactly dressed for it now."

"I have something you can wear." Violet took Faith's hand and led her toward her bedroom, leaving Rachel standing in the kitchen.

At a loss as to what to do next, Rachel began to clean up the potato salad she'd spilled in the living room. She still hadn't completely processed what she'd walked in on. She wasn't sure she could spend the next several hours pretending everything was okay. But if she left, Jack would want an explanation, and she didn't think she could convince him she'd been so sick that she couldn't make it. So they would all have to paste on fake smiles and deal with the fallout later.

❖

Faith McKenna discreetly popped two more ibuprofen, though the ones she'd already taken had yet to ease her headache. After Violet had escorted her among the guests for the obligatory introductions, Faith had avoided both Violet and Rachel. She leaned against the railing of Violet's deck and watched as Rachel tossed back another shot of whatever Jack and his buddies were consuming. She had no frame of reference for how much Rachel usually drank, but she had to be nearing intoxication by this point.

After Faith had changed her clothes, she returned to the kitchen with Violet and received a proper introduction to Rachel, though Rachel avoided eye contact. The remaining time until guests began arriving had been tense and beyond awkward. Violet had bustled around the kitchen preparing food as if nothing had happened. Faith had tried to make casual conversation with Rachel in an attempt to gauge the level of her dissatisfaction. But Rachel ignored her, except when she was glaring at her.

Eventually, Rachel had taken a beer from the fridge and retreated to the backyard to sulk. Faith had offered to leave, but Violet insisted she stay. She said she would understand if Violet decided not to continue working with her, but Violet brushed the suggestion off.

In fairness, both Faith and Violet had known what they were getting into this afternoon. Since their first meeting, when Violet began flirting and giving her knowing smiles, Faith had suspected her reputation had preceded her. When she saw Carly's name on the wedding party list, she knew where Violet's information had come from. She'd slept with Carly a month before her wedding. But they'd parted on good terms, both knowing the rules and equally satisfied. She cut her gaze to the chairs gathered around a small fire pit, where Carly and her husband visited with Violet. Faith had been professional and polite earlier when she greeted them both—no issues.

Her plan—if she'd had one—with Violet was the same. Sex—one time—nothing more. Violet understood that. But given the visual daggers Rachel had been throwing her way all evening, the next eight months had just gotten a lot more difficult. If there was a way to plan a wedding and avoid the maid of honor, she'd have to find it.

Jack poured another round of shots. Rachel took one and raised her glass. She met Faith's eyes defiantly and tossed it back, wincing only slightly as she swallowed. Faith held her gaze, thinking it was a pity she hadn't met Rachel before this afternoon. She might have been able to resist Violet for a chance with her. She'd known right away that Rachel was a lesbian. At first she'd looked a little shell-shocked, but Faith knew the moment her mood changed. There was something enticing about the way her eyes blazed when she got angry. What would the shrink Faith's mother had dragged her to after her parents divorced say about the fact that Faith seemed to like her women mad?

But not just anger made Rachel attractive. She gave off a sporty, softball-player vibe that Faith sometimes went for. Her short brown hair was styled in a sort of messy-on-purpose way. She was taller than Faith by several inches—not too skinny—thick enough to have curves that filled out her khaki shorts and fitted polo shirt. Violet had said she was a real-estate agent, and Faith wondered if she wore dressy clothes for work. She would look hot rocking a power suit. She chatted easily with the guests, but when she did smile, she seemed only to use her mouth. Had catching Violet and Faith dulled a smile that usually lit up those intriguingly dark eyes?

Faith retreated to the kitchen for another bottle of water. She pulled it from the fridge and leaned against the counter for a moment, resisting the urge to press the cool plastic against her forehead. She'd removed the Band-Aid before the guests arrived and didn't want to risk the moisture reopening her wound.

Rachel came to a sudden stop as she entered the kitchen. Other than the slight closing of her eyes to reorient herself, Faith wouldn't have guessed she'd been drinking for the past couple of hours. "Are you still here?"

"I suppose it's been long enough to politely take my leave." She wanted nothing more than to go home, crawl into bed, and will away the pounding in her head. But the couple of times she'd tried to excuse herself, Violet had insisted she stay.

"It's way past time for you to leave. I'd say it was a pleasure, but since I don't expect to see you again, I don't need to be polite."

Rachel's confidence grated, and suddenly Faith wanted to push her. "I think that's up to Violet, and I don't see her urging me out the door." She gave an insolent shrug because something told her it would irritate Rachel even more. When Rachel's eyes narrowed, Faith felt a little thrill at being right.

"You have some balls, lady. I can't believe you think she's going to keep you on after what you did."

"I didn't do anything she didn't practically beg me for."

The slap was unexpected and so fast that Faith barely had time to register Rachel's movement before pain blossomed across her left cheek. Oddly, Rachel looked more surprised than Faith, even as she grimaced and clasped her palm in her other hand.

Faith brushed her fingers over her stinging skin, certain she now sported a blazing-red handprint. She blinked against the reflexive sheen of tears. She tried for stoic, but honestly, she'd never been slapped before, and it really hurt.

"I don't know two people more meant to be together than Violet and Jack. So help me, if you've jeopardized that—"

"Relax. She'll go through with the wedding. Most of them do." Faith kept her voice down, aware that another guest could come in at any time. Rachel had raised hers, and Faith hoped if she didn't respond in kind, Rachel might calm down.

Rachel laughed harshly. "That's supposed to make me feel better? That there've been enough others to create a pattern—albeit a positive one."

"She's going to marry him."

"You better hope so. Because if this falls apart, I'll make sure everyone knows why. And how many future grooms do you think will trust you with their brides then? Let alone the lesbians. I don't know if you chase only straight women, but in case you don't know, lesbians are brutal when they've been cheated on. I'll take out a full-page ad in the newspaper if I have to."

"Does anyone actually read the newspaper anymore?" Faith flinched. "Please, don't hit me again, I've already got a headache as it is." She rubbed her fingers against the cut on her head. "If you want to take another run at me, you'll have to wait until next time."

"It's funny you still think there will be a next time, once I've had a chance to talk some sense into Violet."

Faith had had enough of the drama. This kind of confrontation was exactly why she sought out attached women. If she were interested in arguing, she'd get herself a girlfriend. She put her hand up, not caring if Rachel took it as a sign of surrender. She purposely affected a condescending tone. "Just tell Violet to call me and let me know what you girls decide. I need to go home and lie down."

She was about to slip around Rachel and head for the front

door, when Jack stepped into the kitchen. He gave them both a half-drunk grin, and Faith returned it with her own tight smile.

"Hey, ladies." He winked at Rachel. "I was wondering where my drinking partner disappeared to."

Faith snuck a glance at Rachel. It was probably a good thing Jack was tipsy, or he might have been suspicious. Rachel had retreated to the other side of the small space and was alternating between glaring at Faith and giving Jack a pitying look.

"Can I get you a beer?" He leaned into the refrigerator and pulled one out for himself.

"Um—no thanks. I'm not drinking today," Faith said.

He glanced at Rachel, and when she shook her head, he let the refrigerator door swing closed. "Because you consider this shindig a work function? Or because of that?" He pointed at her head. "What happened there, anyway?"

"Just a little trip and fall."

"You should be more careful." His smile was so sweet and genuine that Faith understood why Rachel was protective of him.

"I should." She looked at Rachel and shrugged. "But I probably won't." She didn't often regret seducing the occasional bride here and there. They got what they wanted, and no one got hurt.

But she would feel bad if he found out what had happened. She'd liked him from her first meeting with Violet and him. His thick, black hair, dimpled chin, and blue eyes made him what some women considered classically handsome. He looked like one of those guys that might be full of himself, but in reality he was simply one of the top-ten nicest guys Faith had ever met.

He looked confused by her answer but flashed them both another smile anyway. "Okay. Well, I should get back out there. I'm manning the grill."

"Sure." Faith expected Rachel to grab the excuse to follow him back out, but she didn't. Without Jack's personality filling the room, tension rushed into the remaining vacuum. Faith glanced at Rachel, realizing she hadn't left the room because she would have to pass close by Faith to do so. Rachel stared at the floor—probably waiting for Faith to go.

"How's the hand?" Faith's cheek still tingled, and she was surprised Jack hadn't commented on what had to be a glaring handprint. "I've been told I'm hardheaded."

"It's fine." Rachel flexed her fingers.

Faith nodded, surprised by a rush of tenderness. She wanted to take Rachel's hand in hers. But Rachel didn't look so welcoming, and she couldn't absorb another slap.

"How can you just talk to him like you've done nothing wrong?" Seeing the anguish on Rachel's face made her feel guilty in a way she wasn't comfortable with. But Rachel didn't give her a chance to respond. "You know what, never mind. I don't even care." She pushed past Faith and headed for the backyard.

Faith blew out a breath and leaned against the kitchen counter. Any answer she'd given to Rachel's question would have left her sounding like a total jerk. For her, weddings were just business. Marriage didn't last. But, for the right price, she was happy to help her clients build the illusion.

❖

"Where did that delicious wedding planner go?" Carly asked as she reclined back on one of the lounge chairs.

Most of the guests had left, and Jack was out front showing off his motorcycle to Carly's husband. Rachel, Violet, and the other two bridesmaids, Carly and Marianne, had cleaned up a bit, then settled in on the deck. The humidity from the day hadn't abated, but nightfall had brought a cool breeze.

Rachel had stopped drinking a couple of hours ago, after Faith left, but sobering up wasn't making things any easier. Every time Jack threw his arm around Violet's shoulders and kissed her cheek, Rachel's stomach twisted with guilt. The first several times, she'd sought out Faith to see if she looked remorseful. But if Faith noticed the couple, she didn't show it.

"She said she had an early morning." Violet emptied the last of a bottle of wine into her glass.

"Didn't I tell you she was worth every penny?" Carly winked.

"Is she really that good?" Marianne asked innocently.

"Hell, yes. She went down on me like it was her job," Carly said unabashedly.

"Carly!" Violet said.

"Well, I guess it kind of was her job. I mean, it's why *I* chose her as my wedding planner."

"What? You slept with her?" Marianne's voice rose in shock.

Carly rolled her eyes. "A little louder, Marianne. I'm not sure my husband heard you. What I may or may not have done before I was married doesn't need to leave this backyard." She turned her attention back to Violet. "So you haven't had time to avail yourself yet?"

"Avail herself? She's not a complimentary champagne brunch." Rachel stood up, irritated—with Carly, but also with herself for defending Faith. She'd done nothing to deserve it. Most likely, she was exactly as cheap as Carly was making her sound.

"God, Rachel, don't be such a prude." Carly rolled her eyes, and Rachel was tempted to slap her face, too.

Violet gave her a look—pleading with her not to go off on Carly, which was exactly what she wanted to do. Why was she the prude for believing that a commitment should be honored?

She and Carly had never gotten along. Carly was judgmental and could be a major bitch. She was one of Violet's party friends— the group she rounded up when she wanted to go to the clubs downtown. Rachel didn't get that call because Violet already knew she wouldn't join in. She wasn't much for dancing and didn't like drinking to excess—despite how she'd spent this evening.

She'd had a few more shots than she usually would and had drawn some curious looks from their friends. But every time she caught sight of Faith at the party, she'd needed something to dispel the image of her and Violet together.

Rachel understood the attraction. Faith was hot. Her cut-off jean shorts left bare miles of creamy legs, but Rachel couldn't look at her without envisioning the black, lacy panties she knew were underneath. Even Violet's borrowed white blouse had accentuated her assets, hugging her waist and the swell of her breasts. Faith's long, blond waves belonged on a beach somewhere. And when Rachel had confronted her in the kitchen, she'd resented the calm in Faith's blue-gray eyes. Though it all added up to a pretty nice package, none of that negated Rachel's first impression of Faith.

When Rachel excused herself a few minutes later, Violet followed her to the front door.

"Will you still be my maid of honor?"

"Are you going to fire her?"

Violet shook her head. "I know you don't want to hear this, but it's not all on her, Rach."

"Are you going to sleep with her again?"

"I didn't actually—I mean, you walked in before we'd gotten—"

"Okay." Rachel held up her hand. "I don't need the details."

"What do you need?" Violet touched her shoulder, clearly taking her concerns seriously. "It didn't mean anything."

"Are you planning to follow through on your curiosity, or are you and Faith finished?"

"We haven't actually discussed it."

"If it happens again—I just don't know how I can stand up at your wedding and face Jack. In fact, I'm already not sure I can. You're really not going to tell him?"

"What good would it do? It won't change what happened. Knowing would only hurt him. Are you going to tell him?" Violet took a step back, as if distancing herself from Rachel's potential answer.

"I need time to process this. It was kind of a shock."

"I still want you to help me plan my wedding."

Rachel let a beat go by for the unspoken *with Faith*. "I just don't know, Vi."

"You're my best friend."

"I'll call you in a day or so."

She eased away and slipped out the door before Violet could say anything more. But what more was there to say? She climbed in her car and drove home almost on autopilot.

CHAPTER TWO

Rachel woke Sunday morning with cotton mouth and a mid-grade headache. She'd slept restlessly for the first half of the night, plagued by her dreams. She often carried her daily life into her subconscious. The only real surprise was usually how twisted her mind would get with whatever concern or stressor featured in that night's production.

This morning she was thoroughly confused. In her dreams, she'd walked in on Faith and Violet just as she had in real life, but they hadn't noticed her there. She lingered, unnoticed, and watched them together. Instead of calling out, she secretly watched as Faith touched Violet. With every confident stroke of Faith's hand, Rachel's own arousal grew. Violet enjoyed herself quite vocally, calling out and urging Faith on.

Rachel had awakened at the moment Violet's orgasm ripped through her. She rolled over and groaned, pressing her thighs together. Sure, having a sex dream about her best friend was a little weird, but she could get past it. The level of sexual frustration she was left with made her more uneasy—as did just how badly she'd wanted to be in Violet's place. Even her awareness that the scene wasn't real didn't erase how vivid it was or how much she'd wanted Faith's hands on her.

She debated taking care of her lingering arousal but decided she'd rather prove she didn't need to. The dream was as easy to explain away as her reaction to it. Faith clearly had no qualms about casual sex, and that made her attractive fantasy material.

She slid out of bed, delaying her shower until she got her urges under control. She followed the scent of coffee to the kitchen, thankful for the timer on her coffeemaker. She chased her first big swallow with two aspirin and half a bottle of water.

She grabbed the messenger bag that carried her work supplies and her coffee and headed out the French doors leading to the small patio that served as backyard space for her condo. She'd put a small metal bistro table on the concrete pad and often enjoyed her morning coffee there. She would have preferred a house on a little piece of land somewhere. But the compact floor plan and no-maintenance exterior fit her lifestyle better right now. A collection of various-sized flowerpots arranged on the patio was as close as she would get to a garden. But it was enough to grow her tomatoes, peppers, and a few herbs. She'd had a good little crop this past summer, but the pots now sat dormant.

While waiting for the caffeine to fire up her system, she flipped through her planner, reviewing her schedule for the week. Today, she'd meet up with an older couple looking to downgrade to a smaller home. Their three children were grown and now had families of their own. Since their kids had all stayed close, they rarely had overnight guests and no longer wanted to maintain their four-bedroom home. They wanted less square-footage but plenty of lawn for the grandkids to play on when they visited. She'd set up appointments at three homes to show them today.

Tomorrow, she had a closing on one of her listings. She'd worked hard with a difficult homeowner to sell that one, but her commission would make everything worthwhile. The latter half of her week remained somewhat open, but she expected to add a few more showings. She had several clients actively looking to buy right now. As she scoured the new listings every day, she would no doubt add a number of appointments.

After she'd showered and dressed, she called her mother from the car on the way to her first showing. Her parents lived in the same small town outside of Nashville where Rachel had grown up. Rachel phoned to check in a couple times a week and visited whenever she could.

After they exchanged greetings, her mother got right to the one topic Rachel didn't want to discuss. "How's the wedding planning going?"

Rachel cringed as Faith's face flashed through her mind. Maybe talking to her mother on the heels of the dream wasn't a good idea. "It's fine."

"You don't sound excited."

"I am. I'm so excited." She couldn't manage to inject any emotion into her voice.

"What's wrong?"

"Nothing. I'm just tired." She wasn't going to tell her mother what happened. But she was glad she'd made the call. Whenever she felt worried or anxious, hearing her mother's voice calmed her. "How's Dad?"

"He's good. He's already left for golf."

"Of course." Her parents were the type of retired couple who, instead of slowing down, only grew more active when they didn't have work to get in the way. They traveled a lot—often spending weeks at a time with Rachel's sister's family in South Carolina or visiting friends in New England. Her father played golf several times a week, and her mother had become part of a senior group.

"Honey, I know you probably have mixed feelings about Violet getting married, but you should be enthusiastic when you're with her."

"Why would you say that?"

"You and Violet have been single together for a long time—"

"I've dated." *Sporadically.*

"But it's been a while since you've had a girlfriend. And even longer since you were serious enough to bring someone home to meet us."

"Maybe I just don't want the two of you chasing off my future wife."

"Honey, if any of them had truly been your future wife, your dad and I wouldn't be able to dissuade her."

Rachel was losing control of this conversation and needed to bring it back quickly. She didn't want to dissect her lack of a love life. "Mom, I'm happy for Violet. And I love Jack."

"I know you do. But it's only natural that you might feel a little like she's leaving you behind."

Rachel didn't need time to consider that idea. Her "mixed feelings," if she had them, stemmed directly from Violet's actions, not from her own insecurities.

"I'm just saying, be careful not to cast any shade on her day. You'll find your princess in your own time."

Rachel laughed. "Thanks, Mom. I know."

Maybe she was the tiniest bit jealous of Violet and Jack. She did want to find that person she was supposed to be with for the rest of her life. She dated plenty, had even had a few long-term relationships, but for various reasons they didn't last. Sometimes the passion faded and they drifted apart, sometimes they just grew in different directions, and in one dramatic split, she'd been cheated on.

She couldn't pinpoint exactly when, but in the past few years, she'd left the urgency of searching for a partner behind. When her friends were bemoaning their single status and hearing biological clocks, she'd settled into near spinsterhood.

Not long after she hung up with her mother, she got a text from Violet—a tentative reminder that they were supposed to go look at venues the next day. The quick follow-up message made a vague promise about trying to be a good girl. Rachel wouldn't get more of an apology or commitment than that. She'd laid out her terms, and though Violet wouldn't address them again directly, the text represented her agreement that she wouldn't pursue anything more with Faith without having to come out and say it.

Rachel didn't like secrets, and she would probably always hate keeping this one from Jack. But she didn't doubt Violet loved him. And she believed they could have a long and happy life together. So what would she gain by telling Jack? He would be devastated. If he left Violet, they would both be miserable. And if he didn't, he would always have a kernel of distrust.

She replied that she would meet them tomorrow as planned. If Violet was intent on going forward with Faith as the wedding planner, Rachel should definitely be there to chaperone until after the wedding. After that, Faith would be out of their lives and no longer a temptation. She told herself the twist in her gut was guilt, and not a reminder that Faith might tempt her even more than she did Violet.

❖

From where Faith had parked at the far end of the strip-mall parking lot, she saw Rachel's blue sedan pull in. Inside the grocery store that anchored the strip, Violet was finishing her shift as store manager. After having met Violet, Faith wouldn't have guessed her profession. Retail management seemed a bit mundane for such a starkly individual person. But apparently, she excelled at the organization and people-management skills needed for the job. Their first destination wasn't far, so rather than Violet driving home then back this way, they'd agreed to meet at Violet's store.

Rachel maneuvered into a spot and immediately picked up her phone, never looking up to locate Faith. Faith couldn't see Rachel's features clearly from this distance. She already knew Rachel had a very expressive face. She'd seen both shock and disbelief when Rachel had walked in on them—then later, stark anger just a second before she'd surprised them both with that slap. Even sporting what Faith guessed was a nice alcohol buzz, Rachel let her emotions run as clear as water across her face.

Faith grabbed her tablet off the passenger seat and opened her calendar app. She forced her mind off Rachel, deliberately perusing her schedule for the next week. She opened the notes she'd taken after her first meeting with Violet and Jack. She couldn't have imagined at the sit-down how complicated this wedding could have become for her. But she'd tempted the fates so many times that she was probably due to get caught. And when she considered the potential fallout, things could definitely have been worse. That is—if Violet could convince Rachel to keep what she'd interrupted from Jack. She was pretty certain that's what Violet was trying to do.

She glanced up in time to see Violet come out of the store and head toward Rachel's car. Rachel stepped out and gave her a hug. When Faith realized that Rachel was parked next to Violet's vehicle, she started her own and drove closer to them. She rolled down her window and called out a greeting as she drew to a stop just in front of Rachel's car.

Violet smiled, and it seemed she was about to say something when her cell phone rang. She glanced at the display and then at the building she'd just come from in irritation. "I haven't even left the parking lot and they're bothering me," she said good-naturedly. "I'll just be a minute." She took a few steps away from them as she answered.

Rachel leaned against her car and folded her arms across her chest.

"Thanks for coming with us," Faith said.

"I didn't do it for you." Her tone was no more welcoming than her posture.

"Of course not. But I'm sure Violet appreciates it. And in my experience, it's always good for the bride to have someone to bounce ideas off of as we go along."

Rachel nodded stiffly, a challenge flashing in her eyes. Faith waited for the reminder that Violet had failed to consult her before acting on a very important idea. But Rachel didn't say anything.

After a brief, uncomfortable silence, Violet rejoined them. Since Faith knew where they were headed, she offered to drive them in her car, then bring them back later. Violet agreed and climbed into the passenger seat, leaving Rachel to get in back.

"Nice car." Now derision colored Rachel's words. Faith got the impression she was being judged for the luxury of her SUV.

"Thanks." She glanced over her shoulder and gave Rachel an overly sweet smile. She stroked the soft leather on the back of the passenger seat, enjoying the way Rachel's eyes narrowed when her hand skated too close to Violet's shoulder. She shouldn't egg on the tension between Violet and Rachel, but she couldn't help enjoying getting a rise out of Rachel. "I know it seems a bit indulgent. But I spend a lot of time in my car, so I like the bells and whistles. Also, given how often I shuttle clients around, it helps to make sure they're comfortable."

Rachel didn't respond.

"You are, aren't you? Comfortable?" Faith took her silence as agreement and continued talking. "So, we're off then. I have a couple of venues lined up based on what you told me you were into, Violet."

When tense silence filled the car, Faith replayed her last words in her head and cringed. Violet had expressed an interest in a sophisticated wedding—not opulent, yet still refined. She wasn't giving in to her mother's desire for a church wedding, so they were hunting for a venue that could handle the ceremony and reception seamlessly.

"The first place is an early 1900s plantation house, which has been in the current owner's family for over a century. The family moved into a smaller home that was constructed on another part of the property, and in the 1970s they began renting out the main house for events. The outside needs some maintenance, but it's gorgeous on the inside."

"I can't imagine being that connected to my roots," Violet said. "Faith, you don't sound like you're from the South."

"No. I'm originally from Philadelphia."

"Is your family there?"

"My father is. My mother lives in Kansas City."

"They're divorced?"

Faith nodded. "A long time ago." Her knuckles sharpened as she gripped the wheel tighter.

"Mine, too." Violet touched Faith's other forearm, which rested on the console between them. She glanced over her shoulder at Rachel, then drew her hand away. "Though my mom stayed with my dad until after my brother and I were grown. It was so weird when she started dating other people."

"Both my parents have been remarried. More than once actually." Faith forced a casual tone, but anyone who knew her well would read tension in her body language. She didn't talk to her clients about her family.

"Rachel's are still together. Can you imagine?"

She glanced in the rearview mirror and met Rachel's eyes. The image of Rachel growing up in an idyllic home and remaining close to her family into adulthood fit. Faith supposed she might have a different opinion of marriage if her own parents hadn't treated it as a means to hurt each other by continually trading up.

"And they're actually happy. Not just faking it like some of my other friends' parents."

Violet angled in her seat and looked over her shoulder. To Rachel, she said, "I love your folks."

"Yeah. Me, too." Rachel smiled back.

Rachel was one of those girls Faith had been jealous of when she was growing up. The kids who didn't have to leave home Christmas morning to go to the other parent's house before they even got to play with their toys. Those kids weren't forced to go on lame vacations with their mom's new husband and step-siblings, who were strangers. They acted like she was lucky because her dad bought her anything she wanted, and she never let on that he'd only done so to make up for not being around. She tallied up another reason not to like Rachel Union.

❖

"This isn't the place," Violet said as soon as she stepped out of the car.

"You don't think you'd like to look around a bit before you decide? She said it's better on the inside." Rachel closed the passenger door, already intent on touring the grounds. Two-story porches spanned almost the entire front of the house, but the tall pillars needed a fresh coat of paint—as did the whole house. There was plenty of established landscaping, but the shrubs and flowers felt like barely controlled wild vegetation as opposed to being well-planned and maintained.

"We can take the tour if it makes you feel better. But I already know."

Rachel looked at Faith for help, but Faith simply shrugged.

"This is the first impression your guests will have of your wedding. If you absolutely don't like it now, chances are you won't change your mind. Trust your gut."

"*Trust your gut.* That's what you're going with? This is the expert opinion she's paying you for?" She shook her head and grabbed Violet's arm. "Unbelievable. Come on. We made an appointment. You're giving it a fair shot."

Halfway through the tour, Rachel realized they were wasting their time. Violet had already made up her mind, and Rachel was the only one still interested. Inside, the home boasted beautiful wood floors and old moldings. Traditional styling and stately antiques filled the spaces.

The woman who led them around descended from the original plantation owners and clearly had a passion for the home. She talked about some of the weddings they'd hosted. In each room, she described elaborate parties befitting the Old South history of the home. In the backyard, she suggested an outdoor reception near three of the largest magnolia trees Rachel had ever seen, weather permitting, of course.

By the time they returned to the front porch, Rachel had to admit that, while impressive, nothing about the place fit Violet. She politely thanked the woman for her time, shook her hand, and followed Violet and Faith to the parking lot.

Back in the car, she met Violet's expectant gaze. "Okay. You were right."

Violet nodded smugly. "No settling. I'm going to have the perfect wedding."

"Yeah, perfect." Rachel had never known Violet to be so delusional. How could anything about this situation ever be perfect?

Leather creaked as Violet swiveled more fully in her seat and glared at Rachel. "Do you have something to say?"

Faith stared out the windshield, seemingly pretending she

wasn't listening. Rachel wanted to snarl back in answer. This entire day she'd been watching them both closely—searching for any sign that something was still going on between them. She'd been looking for hints of flirting or intimacy—some clue as to how things got as far as they did. She'd been tense and uncomfortable and now was a little bit pissed because it seemed like she was the only one not enjoying the day. Violet and Faith had been laughing and talking together like they hadn't been all over each other just days ago. She wanted to throw her frustration into the cabin of the car so they would both have to deal with it as well. Instead, she opted to turn toward the window and ignore them both.

CHAPTER THREE

I love it."

Faith grinned when she saw skepticism cross Rachel's features.

"I know, I know. Her gut." Rachel scowled.

Violet laughed as Rachel stalked across the parking lot. Faith fell into step with Violet as they followed. Violet slipped her arm through Faith's and winked. The way she glanced at Rachel's back made Faith think she might be more interested in riling Rachel than actually continuing anything they'd started on Saturday. She and Violet hadn't talked about their encounter after they'd been interrupted. Violet seemed content to go on with their business arrangement as if they hadn't almost had sex, and Faith was good with that. She never got attached to her clients, and Violet was no different. Keeping Violet's account was far more important to Faith's future than any physical relationship. So she would let Violet set the tone for their interactions going forward. She knew where she stood and didn't need a conversation, so if Violet didn't either, she would let it go.

"This is actually a great venue. The main structure originally housed the offices for a company that built barges, hence the amazing location." The building overlooked the Cumberland River as it snaked through downtown Nashville. It shared the east bank of the river with a football stadium and had clear views of the city across the river.

"I'm sure Jack will love the view. But I'm not sure a football stadium is what we want for this wedding," Rachel said. "I get that the original building might have had charm, but I don't love the renovations."

Faith paused near the entrance but didn't open the door yet. The building looked much more modern these days and at first glance might resemble a number of other multi-story office structures in Nashville. Personally, Faith liked the mix of modern and industrial. "I know what you're saying. But let me point out some pluses. It's close to downtown, so your out-of-town guests could stay in the city—"

"Which is more expensive."

"At least they have the option. And there's plenty of entertainment for them on the days surrounding the actual event. Also, given you're having a May wedding, the weather could be perfect for an evening walk across the pedestrian bridge from downtown to your wedding." She swept her hand toward the adjacent bridge that connected the stadium area to the center of the city. "That way no one has to worry about drinking and driving."

"Or there's Uber."

"You hate Uber," Violet interjected. "Let her talk."

"For the locals, or anyone from out-of-town who stays farther away"—Faith gave Rachel a pointed look—"there's plenty of free parking near the building. That's a rarity this close to the city." Before Rachel could argue further, Faith rushed on. "Violet loves the outside. Let's see the inside. Then we can talk about our impressions and any concerns we still have."

As they stepped inside, the events manager greeted them. Faith introduced Violet and Rachel, and they all moved immediately into the event space. As they walked, the woman spoke in general about the building, giving a little more detail than Faith had outside. The first room they stepped into was a large open space with high ceilings and full-length windows along two sides. Because the building faced away from the stadium, the views included mostly the river and the city skyline across the water. Glass, metal, and touches of stained wood made up the room, making it feel modern. Overhead, steel beams added to the industrial theme.

"One option for you is to reserve this room and the floor above us, which looks essentially the same. We can set one level up for the ceremony and one for the reception and move seamlessly between them. Logistically, because we're all open here, we can do a number of things and still have plenty of space."

She took them up in the elevator, and they stepped out briefly on the second floor, where the room mirrored the one below. Next, they went to the top floor.

"Another package allows you to use this area and the rooftop patio." She led them through another open-concept room and out onto the roof of the floor below. A heavy-duty tent-like structure covered part of the patio, and the other half remained uncovered. "The third choice is, of course, to reserve all of the spaces, giving you more versatility."

Violet walked to the edge of the patio and leaned against the metal railing. "I don't think we'll need the whole building. The wedding won't be that large. Unless my mother gets her hands on the guest list."

Rachel and Faith joined her at the railing, constructed of metal bars strung with heavy steel cable, which edged the entire roof.

"This really is a great view," Rachel said. "And since the ceremony is late afternoon, the reception will go into evening. I bet this looks amazing at night."

The events manager smiled and nodded. "Ms. McKenna said you're looking at a May date. We also have several patio heaters we can space out in this area if it's a cool night."

"I want it." Violet turned to face Faith and the manager. "The top floor and the patio. The lower rooms are great, but I want this view. And we purposely chose a mild time of year so we could have outdoor options."

"You don't want to look at any other places, or maybe run this by Jack first?" Rachel asked.

"No. He said whatever I wanted. Besides, you know he'll like this if we both do."

Faith glanced at Rachel, giving her a chance to object, but she just smiled and nodded.

"Okay, let's go downstairs, do some paperwork, and talk about a deposit."

The manager led them back to the elevator.

❖

While Faith drove them back to Violet's store, Rachel and Violet talked about the venue. Violet already had some ideas of how she wanted the ceremony and reception laid out. Violet texted a couple of the pictures she'd taken inside the venue to Jack. Instead of responding by text, he called. So, while they spoke, Rachel turned her attention to the side window, watching the city go by as they headed back to the store.

Rachel had to admit, after seeing the inside, she was sold on the venue as well. The exterior of the building lacked character, in her opinion, but the views were amazing, and she liked the flexibility of the space. The modern industrial vibe fit Violet and Jack much better than it would Rachel. In fact, the feel of the space wasn't that far off from Jack's urban loft-style condo.

At the store, Faith parked near their cars. Rachel and Violet got out. Faith rolled down her window and rested her arm on the sill. Violet touched her forearm.

"I need to check on things inside before I head home. Thanks for today, Faith. Jack loved the pictures I texted him. I knew he would."

"Sure. I've got copies of everything you signed today, and going forward, I'll be your contact person with the venue manager. You tell me what you want, and I'll get it for you. I'll send you and Jack an email tomorrow with some things to start thinking about in the coming weeks."

As Violet rushed toward the store entrance, Rachel lingered near Faith's door. She felt like she should apologize. She'd been irritable and more negative than was usually her nature. Sometimes, it seemed she couldn't help it. Just looking at Faith pulled her in two different directions. On the one hand, she couldn't ignore what

Faith and Violet had done. But her libido didn't care. She'd caught herself watching Faith more than once and finding her actions or mannerisms sexy. For example, she absolutely shouldn't have been so intent on the way Faith's hands moved when she slipped on her sunglasses as they stepped out onto the venue roof. And what was so special about Faith's profile as she leaned against the railing and looked out over the city?

Faith had been mostly pleasant and had remained professional. If anything, Violet had been the one who acted overly friendly. But that was her personality. She was a demonstrative person. That was a lie. Violet had been flirtatious and, at times, had crossed a line with Faith. Rachel had handled her frustration as best she could, but even with Violet her patience had a breaking point. She was tempted to tell Violet that, if she couldn't at least fake restraint, she was out.

"What's wrong?" Faith's question startled Rachel. While she'd been reflecting on the day, she had unknowingly braced her hand on Faith's car, keeping her from leaving.

"Nothing." Rachel shook away her analysis of Faith and Violet's interaction, telling herself she was just glad she was there to make sure they both behaved. "What's next?"

"We start looking at photographers, caterers, entertainment, and florists. It's early yet to book, but she should get an idea of what she wants. There's actually a wedding expo next week at the convention center. If Violet is free, I'd like to take her. It's a good place to see a number of vendors in one place. You're welcome to tag along, of course."

"I will. Tag along. Of course." Rachel didn't bother trying to cover up her sarcasm.

"This must be tough for you."

"What?"

"Babysitting us, when you so clearly hate me."

"I don't know you well enough to hate you. Though you've certainly done some things I don't like and can't respect."

"I suppose you'll get to know me better over the next eight months. Then you can hate me properly."

Faith's self-derisive tone caught Rachel off guard, and she didn't censor her next words. "Why do they do it?"

"You should ask Violet."

The teenage boy collecting the shopping carts from the parking lot came to the cart corral nearest them and began loudly pushing all the carts together.

Rachel stepped closer, both so she could be heard and so they wouldn't be overheard. "I'm asking you."

"I guess some of them see it as their last chance to satisfy their latent curiosity. Some have cold feet. And some are just a little freaky." When Faith looked up, her eyes were flat and so emotionless that Rachel wondered how someone could feel so little about something that put so much at risk.

"That doesn't bother you?"

"They're grown women."

"So you're okay with cheating."

"I'm not cheating on anyone. I'm single."

Rachel tried to ignore the little thrill she got at hearing that Faith was single. Wrong time and place for that nugget to sink in. She only had to summon the image of Faith half-naked on Violet's living room floor to chase away any excitement. "Seriously? You have no respect for the institution they're about to enter into?"

"What do you want me to say? I think people want to believe that, because you're married, you can get through anything. But in reality their relationships are just as fragile as anyone else's. Having a piece of paper doesn't mean anything."

"That's so romantic. You should put that on your business cards."

"Very funny."

"You're a wedding planner, for God's sake. Aren't you supposed to be all sappy and sentimental about marriage?"

"I don't really do sappy."

"How can you spend your career planning a day you don't even believe in?"

Faith shrugged. "It's good money."

"That's it?"

"You must have an idea how much weddings cost. It's just business."

"And occasionally sex, right?"

"I get the sarcasm, Rachel. And I don't appreciate the implication that I'm a prostitute."

"You're not?"

"No. But you're searching for a good reason to rationalize my behavior, and it's not there. Maybe I'm just the person you think I am, no more."

Was she looking for justification? If so, then why did she need to make Faith inherently good in her mind? After the wedding, she'd never see her again. And she wouldn't recommend Faith's *services* to any of her friends.

❖

Faith poured herself a glass of wine, then cut it with a bit of soda water. Her favorite wine vendor would cringe, but she didn't care. He was a wine snob anyway. She did as she advised her clients: don't worry about labels—drink what you like. She enjoyed a little spritz in her wine but didn't love the taste of champagne. In a pinch she'd been known to add Sprite to a glass of her favorite sweet red.

She wandered onto the large porch off the back of her farmhouse. Several boards creaked under her feet, and she added shoring up the decking to her long to-do list. Across a large expanse of grass she could make out the silhouette of the barn—a building that came with its own catalog of projects.

Whenever she started to worry that she'd made a mistake moving out of her apartment and buying this old property two months ago, she tried to think of the place as a blank slate. She had big plans for her new corner of the world, but she didn't have to institute them all at once. Patience would keep her sane until she could bring her vision to life.

While she discovered new challenges here every day, she'd also found plenty to like about country living. Her nearest neighbor was a quarter of a mile down the road. Apparently, cutting five acres of grass on her brand-new zero-turn riding mower provided the perfect peaceful frame of mind for wedding-design inspiration. She'd gotten some great ideas while riding the property. She hadn't wanted to spend the money on the mower upgrade, but the salesman had convinced her the machine would be worth the expense. He was right. Instead of lumbering around the property on the secondhand lawn tractor she'd been contemplating, she zipped through the chore in less than two hours.

She crossed the porch and sat down on the steps leading to the grass. At some point, she'd also have to go shopping for furniture. She hadn't had any outdoor space at her third-floor apartment except a tiny balcony, so her two folding lawn chairs sat forlornly at the far end of the porch while she set down her wineglass and tilted her head back. The sky was clear tonight. How long before she got used to taking a deep breath of fresh air and staring at a canopy of stars? She scowled. And when did she become so romantic? She would lose her city cynicism, living out here.

Thoughts of romanticism led her to examine her last conversation with Rachel. Not surprisingly, Rachel had traditional ideas about sex and relationships. Faith respected that viewpoint. What she hadn't expected was her own reaction to the disappointment in Rachel's eyes when she talked about Faith's behavior.

Her first impression, the day they met, was that Rachel was uptight. But after spending some time with her today, Faith decided she was more complex. She'd seen glimpses of humor, warmth, and kindness. Then Rachel would remember why she was mad at them and clam up.

Rachel clearly cared about Violet. She'd been snippy toward Faith all day, and that sometimes spilled over into her interactions with Violet. But when Violet so clearly fell in love with the venue, Rachel opened up to the idea and shared her excitement. Faith had seen an immediate change in Violet as well. Where she'd been edgy all day, she relaxed a little once she had Rachel's approval.

Faith needed to remember that as they went through the planning process. If Violet started to get nervous or full-on freak out at any point as the date drew nearer, she might need Rachel to help soothe her. Typically, a bride had one person she relied on more than anyone else in her life, and Faith could save valuable time by knowing who that person was ahead of time. Whether she liked it or not, she needed to keep Rachel Union close.

CHAPTER FOUR

This is all a bit overwhelming." Violet paused in the doorway to the convention-center floor. The huge area was filled from one side to the other with people milling among the rows of booths.

Rachel grabbed her shoulders and steered her in and to the side to get her out of the way of the patrons jockeying to enter around them. A group of women brushed past them, all talking at once about which vendor to see first. Two men, one young and one older—father and son, maybe—followed behind exchanging exasperated looks.

Right now, Rachel could feel their pain. Booths overflowed with flowers, and photo albums, and freebies designed to entice the customers that packed the aisles. The customers were mostly women, who, like Violet, had likely been dreaming of their wedding since they were children. Only for Violet would Rachel voluntarily subject herself to this afternoon.

"That's why I'm here—to escort you through it." Faith held out her bent elbow, and Violet looped her arm through. They fell in with the current of the crowd, and Rachel followed, letting herself get swept along like driftwood with no control over where she might land.

"I don't usually suggest wedding shows for my couples. If you don't know how to weed through the nonsense, you can leave more confused than you were when you arrived. But I wanted you to come to this one, because several vendors I think you might be interested in are here. We can see them all in one place here, and then you can decide who you might want a more extensive appointment with. I can steer you around the bullshit."

"Then I'll put myself in your capable hands." Violet winked at her.

"Give it a rest, Violet," Rachel grumbled.

Violet glared over her shoulder, then flipped her head around and kept going.

Rachel had to admit, it was convenient to have access to this many vendors. When Violet lingered at a booth Rachel wasn't interested in, she wandered ahead. Faith stuck with Violet, and they eventually caught back up to her. Before long, she had a collection of fliers and business cards stuffed in a tote bag she'd acquired at one of the booths.

They paused at a table assigned to a local baker, and she picked up a small plate containing three squares of cake samples. She'd heard of the bakery but had never tried any of their products. The vanilla cake was moist, as was a strawberry-flavored one, but the chocolate sample made her moan. The sweet icing contrasted nicely with the depth of the chocolate.

"This is amazing." Rachel turned to see Faith wearing a broad smile. "What?" She dabbed a finger against the corner of her mouth. "Do I have icing on my face?"

"No. You're good."

"You aren't going to try the cake."

"I've had it before. This bakery is on my short list of recommendations." She pointed to a photo album with pictures of some of their work. "Their cakes look great. They have a very talented decorator. She's creative and easy to work with. And, as you've experienced, they also taste good. They don't sacrifice flavor for style. That's an important balance in my book." Faith's eyes shone, and her hand gestures grew as she spoke.

"You've given a lot of thought to cake."

"It's my job."

"Sure. But I get the impression it's more than that." Rachel narrowed her eyes, allowing a bit of a smile to let Faith know she was teasing. "I think you secretly love cake. In fact, it must be very hard for you to resist these samples." She waved the plate teasingly under Faith's chin.

Faith gave her a full grin in return. "You got me. It's the real reason I became a wedding planner—so I could sneak pieces of cake at the receptions."

Arousal fluttered in Rachel's chest at Faith's playful tone. She held Faith's gaze, enjoying the intensity of Faith's focus for just a moment longer before she returned her attention to the booth. Many of the vendors offered a prize, special package, or discount of some sort as part of a series of drawings to take place later in the afternoon. A sign on the bakery table advertised a chance to win twenty percent off a wedding cake.

Rachel grabbed a pencil and slip of paper and began filling in her information. If she won, she could cover the rest of the cost and give Violet and Jack their cake as a wedding gift. They kept insisting they didn't need gifts since they already had two households stocked and would actually have to downsize when they officially moved in together. Violet had been engaged and lived with someone before. And when they broke up before the wedding, she was left searching for a new place. This time, she'd said, she wasn't giving up her house until she had more than just love keeping Jack around. Only two weeks ago, Rachel would have told Violet she was being ridiculous. Jack was devoted to Violet and she to him. Or so Rachel thought.

"Didn't you download the expo app from the information they gave us at registration?" Faith asked.

"Rachel doesn't do digital." Violet opened the app on her smartphone and turned the display so the woman behind the bakery table could scan the barcode on her screen. A beep confirmed her entry for the drawing. "Until three years ago, she still had a flip phone."

"Do you even know what you're signing up for?" Rachel folded her paper and dropped it in a box on the table.

"Doesn't matter. I'm hitting all the booths."

"And spend my time weeding through emails about my nonexistent upcoming nuptials? No thanks. I'm only giving *my* info to the vendors that have something we really want for your wedding."

Violet rolled her eyes and moved on to the next table. Rachel thanked the woman and grabbed a business card for the bakery before she followed. She might have found a new go-to for birthday cakes instead of her usual option—whatever the grocery store had left when she remembered to pick something up.

Violet was already getting her phone scanned at the next booth. Rachel wasn't interested in a teeth-whitening treatment to make her smile shine for the big day, so she moved into the aisle to leave room for the other women crowding close to the table.

She walked among the booths, taking note of several clearly gay-friendly businesses that included same-sex couples in some of their advertising. She spotted a real-estate agent she knew and stopped by his booth to chat. He'd booked the space to see if he could drum up any clients that might be looking for their first home together. He'd had some interest but couldn't tell yet how many were serious or if the expo would prove worth his time. Rachel left him her card, and he promised to let her know how it went.

She imagined such an event would yield similar results to an open house—mostly lookie-loos and very few serious buyers. She held open houses only selectively and not nearly as often as sellers wanted her to. But, she tried to explain, there were much more effective ways to gain exposure.

If the seller still occupied the home, an open house could be a security nightmare. As the selling agent, she couldn't possibly keep an eye on everyone wandering through the home, and an open house allowed people in that weren't chaperoned by their own agent the way individual showings were. She'd had multiple clients report theft the next day.

She searched for Faith and Violet, and when she found they still had one more row of vendors to visit, she headed for the snack bar instead. She grabbed a cold drink and wandered outside to enjoy the moderate mid-September day. There, she sat on a concrete wall and watched people come and go until Faith and Violet exited. Violet suggested lunch but Faith declined, citing an appointment with another client.

Rachel and Violet hit a nearby sandwich shop, where Rachel patiently listened to Violet talk about the inspiration she'd gotten from the expo. As Violet described several different ideas that didn't seem to gel, Rachel understood what Faith meant when she said the expo could be overwhelming. But as they talked and reviewed their brochures, Violet discarded several of her plans. They discussed which vendors could most likely meet Violet's needs. Rachel made notes on the back of one of the fliers she'd collected. She wished Faith had joined them so she could share these thoughts with her.

❖

Faith woke early Wednesday morning and decided to take advantage of a rare free mid-week morning. She had to meet a couple for a tasting with one of their top three caterers that afternoon. She put on some old clothes and headed for the barn. She'd bought the property with the hopes of turning the barn and the lawns around it into a charmingly rustic wedding and party venue. She'd spent years building her reputation as an event coordinator, and this was the next step in her plan. Investing so much of her savings in the project made her extremely nervous, especially since it would be a while before she would even be in a position to make a profit here. She had enough put away to carry the mortgage until she could begin renting out the property. But keeping a full load of clients and finding time to do some of the physical labor was wearing her out.

Over the past several years, she'd seen farm and rustic weddings gain popularity. She could only help her current business by being able to offer a venue alternative where she could control the rates and overhead. She hadn't quite been ready to take the leap when she happened across the listing for this property. She'd called the agent for a showing anyway and fell in love right away. That night, before she could change her mind, she sat down with her agent and wrote an offer. A part of her hadn't expected the sellers to accept, so when they did, she scrambled to make the timing work with her apartment lease, set to expire in just a few months. She moved into the house before doing any projects inside. She planned to deal with the mostly outdated interior as long as she could so she could focus on the exterior.

Since then, she'd set aside all her extra funds for renovations. She hoped to save some money doing whatever work she could herself and contracting out only the bigger, more complicated projects. Her first chore included hauling away the junk that had been collected in the barn for decades.

As soon as she walked inside the barn, she heard a tiny noise, almost like a squeak. She followed the sound, hoping she wouldn't find a mouse or, worse, a possum. The barn no longer held much hay, but there were probably still critters around. She didn't want a close encounter with one. The way they scurried and darted gave her the willies.

When she pushed open the door to one of the remaining stalls in the back of the barn, the squeaks got louder and appeared to be coming from under an overturned wooden crate. She squatted and peered through the hole left by a couple of missing slats in the box. She saw fur but couldn't clearly make out the creature in the darkened corner. She pulled out her cell phone and clicked on the flashlight feature, prepared to bolt if anything darted.

Inside the crate, the smallest kitten she'd ever seen squinted against the glare of her light. She shaded her phone with her hand, muting the intensity of the light. The little green eyes blinked back open. A strip of gray ran down to its nose, bisecting its otherwise white face.

"How did you get in there? Where's your mama? You're too young to be all on your own." Faith lifted the crate away carefully. The kitten crouched down as if not sure what to make of Faith, but it studied her boldly. She stood and backed away. "If you're thinking about sticking around, you've picked the wrong home. I'm not a cat person."

She pulled on work gloves and tried to ignore the little fur ball. She began dividing the debris in the front section of the barn into several piles, then carried whatever needed to be disposed of to the utility trailer she'd parked outside the door. Once she'd filled it, she would haul it to the county dump. It would probably take more than one trip just for the stacks of stuff inside the barn. The kitten followed her on every trip out to the trailer and back. And when she paused to survey her progress, it rubbed up against her leg.

"I guess if you want to live in the barn, I won't stop you. But you're on your own for food. I hope you've got some hunting skills." The kitten made a noise—not quite loud enough to be called a meow. "I personally haven't seen a lot of mice around here, but you're welcome to whatever you can find." The kitten made another sound, and Faith rolled her eyes. "Now I'm having a conversation with a cat."

She went back to work. As she sorted through old farm tools, she set some aside that were in good enough shape to consider for decor around the barn. She also salvaged six mismatched dining chairs. With some sanding, a coat of paint, and some new upholstery, they would add a unique touch in the reception area of the barn. She'd hoped for a big, old table to pair them with, but by the time she cleared out the largest of the furniture she hadn't found one. She'd have to locate something suitable someplace else. Maybe she would try the flea markets or talk to some of the neighbors about where to find the best bargains on farm-style furniture. She didn't want to overpay, so she'd avoid the antique stores if she could help it.

Her new friend trailed her around the barn until she took a break. When she sat on one of the old chairs and downed a half a bottle of water, the kitten sat down and stared at her.

"Stop looking at me, swan." She tried to sound stern as she spouted the silly line from that Adam Sandler movie. The cat was kind of cute. He or she—she didn't know and wasn't about to check—didn't break her stare. "So, that's your name now. Swan. If I'm going to talk to you, I have to address you somehow."

A couple hours later, she and Swan had cleared most of the barn.

As she headed for the house to shower and dress for her afternoon meeting, Swan followed. She closed the back door and left him—she'd decided on masculine pronouns—sitting at the bottom of the porch steps. She checked when she left and he was gone, but she suspected he'd just returned to the barn.

CHAPTER FIVE

I think you're really going to like this house," Rachel said as she unlocked the front door of a newly built home in a rapidly growing subdivision. "There's still some new construction going on a couple of streets away, but this area has already been finished so it shouldn't be too noisy."

She stepped inside, then moved to the side to wait for her clients to come in as well. They were a middle-aged couple with two young children, ready to trade up from their previous starter home. He worked in IT and she was a schoolteacher.

Just off the foyer, the house boasted an open floor plan, encompassing living, dining, and kitchen areas. The neutral paint color left everything looking a little bland, but the lighting and kitchen fixtures had been upgraded.

"It's in your preferred school district and not far to the interstate, so your commute would be about the same as what you have now."

She hung back as the couple toured the house, only offering important tidbits and answering questions. She didn't subscribe to high-pressure sales techniques. In her experience, a buyer knew when they found the right house. Her job was to get them inside the good-quality homes that most closely matched their dream and let them decide which one they wanted.

For this couple, this house got close. They wanted a pool or a yard that would accommodate adding one. This house didn't have one, and the patio was plain and barely developed. And as they stepped into the backyard, her clients commented on the lack of existing outdoor entertainment space.

"That is the one drawback of this house. I have one more to show you today, and it's in the same area. It does already have a pool, but it's a little smaller and needs some updating on the inside. I wanted you to see this one to compare the two." Clients expected their agents to magically whip up a house that had everything they wanted and just happened to be in their budget. But ticking all of the boxes could be difficult, especially in a tight buying market. Rachel's goal was to find something that would take the least work and additional money to make it into what they wanted.

A few minutes later, as she pulled away from the curb to lead her clients to the other listing, her phone rang. She glanced in her rearview mirror to make sure the little red sedan fell in behind her.

"Hey, Vi," she said after she pushed the button on the steering wheel to answer the call.

"Hey. What are you doing tonight?"

"Catching up on work, probably. What's up?"

"Faith is taking Jack and me to check out a band we might want for the wedding. They're playing a bar in East Nashville. Come with us."

If Jack was going along, Rachel didn't need to chaperone. "I have a ton of stuff to get done at home."

"Come on. Have a couple of drinks and listen to some music. This is the fun part of wedding planning. And I know Jack would love to see you."

She hadn't been around Jack since the afternoon of the barbecue. But spending time with the three of them together made her nervous. Seeing Jack would probably only make her angry at Violet. Despite continuing to stay involved with the planning, she hadn't totally forgiven Violet. Maybe the band would be loud enough that she wouldn't feel obligated to make conversation and pretend she wasn't totally uncomfortable. "Okay."

"Cool. We're meeting Faith downtown. Do you want us to pick you up?"

"No. I'll drive myself. I'm having coffee with a new client tomorrow morning, so I can't be out late."

❖

Faith hurried into the bar, scanning for Violet and Jack. She found them at the bar buying drinks. She wound her way through the bodies already packed into the area. The popularity of the band, Stark Raven, had grown over the past year, and it was getting harder to book them. But Faith knew their drummer's sister, so if Violet and Jack wanted them, she would call in a favor.

When Violet spotted Faith, she threw an arm around her neck and pulled her in for a hug.

"Sorry I'm late." Faith spoke into Violet's ear to be heard above the din of the crowd. She'd been working in the barn, and the day had gotten away from her. After she'd rushed through a shower, she knew she wouldn't be on time. She threw on some slim-cut jeans, then layered a denim blouse over a white T-shirt. She wouldn't exactly fit in with the hipsters that had taken over East Nashville, but she wouldn't stand out either.

"That's okay. You're here now." Violet released her and she shook Jack's hand.

"Has the band played yet?" She didn't hear any music coming from the back room.

"They've done one set. But said they'd be back on in ten," Jack said.

"And?"

"We love them. Can we book them for the reception?"

"If you want them, I can make it happen."

"You're awesome." Violet grabbed her in another hug. Faith smiled at Jack over Violet's shoulder and eased away.

"Do you want a drink?" Jack tilted his head toward the bar. The five-o'clock shadow Jack had last time she saw him had now morphed into a full-on beard. With his flannel shirt and his undercut hairstyle, he could blend in to this crowd.

"Not yet. Thanks."

"We have a table near the stage. Rachel is there if you want to sit down." He pointed toward a separate room at the back of the bar.

"Sure." She navigated through the bodies again, which seemed to have multiplied since she arrived.

In the back room, she searched the tables close to a small raised platform that passed for a stage. Rachel sat at one of them, talking to a pretty woman who stood next to her and bent close enough to be heard. When the woman smiled and Rachel returned the gesture, Faith experienced an unexpected pang of jealousy. Rachel's expression was open and friendly. And because she'd caught Faith and Violet together, she would never look at her as freely as she did this woman.

Faith tried to imagine what conversation was taking place between the two. Was the woman hitting on Rachel? Or maybe they already knew each other? The woman placed her hand on the back of the chair next to Rachel and inclined her head. Did she want to join them? With only three vacant chairs, Faith would be without a seat after Jack and Violet returned. Rachel said something to the woman and shook her head.

When the woman walked away, Faith approached. Rachel's posture stiffened when she saw Faith.

"Hey." Faith lifted her chin toward the woman, who had joined a group of people at a nearby table. "Friend of yours?"

"What? Oh, no. She wanted to take one of these chairs for her friend. I wish Violet and Jack would hurry back. Empty seats are becoming a hot commodity around here."

"Oh." Faith tried to ignore the flow of relief at Rachel's explanation. "Thanks for saving them, then." She slid into the chair next to Rachel, leaving the two across from them for the soon-to-be newlyweds. They had to turn away another would-be borrower before Violet and Jack returned.

The band came back on, and their proximity to the stage eliminated any conversation. Faith had seen them play before and always enjoyed their energy. The lead singer passionately covered the whole stage during the course of a performance. Faith snuck glances at Rachel and found her eyes glued to the lead guitarist. Faith couldn't blame her. The girl was hot. Her dark hair had been twined into a braid down the center of her back. Her sleeves were rolled up to her elbows, and her hands and fingers moved with confidence over the strings. She wasn't just a gimmick; she could flat-out play. When the band finished, Rachel shot out of her chair along with the rest of the crowd and applauded.

As they sat down, Faith leaned closer so Rachel could hear her. "You look like you're having a good time."

"Why wouldn't I? They're a great band." Rachel's cheeks were pink, and Faith wondered if they'd be warm to the touch.

"Can I get you another drink?"

"No, thanks. This is my last. I have an early showing tomorrow."

"How did you get into real estate?"

"I suppose for the same reason you got into wedding planning. The money's good."

Faith raised her eyebrows and smiled, but didn't comment.

"I was an administrative assistant at a title company. I used to talk to some of the agents between closings. The market was on the way up, and they were starting to make real money again. I thought, 'I can do that.' So I got my license and here we are."

"I bet you're good at it."

"I do okay."

"I would buy a house from you."

Rachel laughed.

"What?"

"I'm guessing that's the first time you've tried that line out on a woman."

"You'd be surprised."

"Really?"

Faith shrugged. "I would buy a house—I would buy furniture—I would take investment advice. It's all a variation on the same theme—appealing to a woman's pride in her work."

"I see."

"So, if not real estate, what was the dream?"

Rachel took another sip of her drink. "I don't suppose I had one. I grew up in the same small town both of my parents have spent their whole lives in. It's an hour and half outside of Nashville, but it's a world away from the city. Just moving here seemed like a big step after high school."

"You didn't want to go to college?"

"My parents didn't have a lot of money. My older sister always wanted to be a doctor, from the time we were little. They were helping her get through college by the time I graduated. And she still had medical school ahead. I know they would have supported me and helped any way they could. But I saw her passion for it, you know? And I didn't have that for anything at the time. I figured if I ever found it, then I would follow that path."

"That makes sense. Probably more so than the four years I wasted bouncing from one major to another. My dad paid for college just to prove to my mom that he could. I had no idea what I wanted in life. But I was young and selfish and didn't care if I wasted his money." She held up her hands. "I know. You think I'm still selfish."

"Hey, Faith, should we go ahead and book Stark Raven?" Violet yelled across the table.

"Yes. I can go talk to them now, if you're sure."

"We are," Jack said. "Those guys are awesome. I played a little bass guitar when I was in high school."

"Okay. Hey, do you want to come back there with me and meet them?"

"Yeah." He jumped out of his seat.

"Let's go." She clapped a hand onto his shoulder. "Maybe don't talk about your glory days playing bass, though."

He laughed and followed her toward the side of the stage, where the band had started packing up their gear.

❖

Rachel and Carly followed Violet through a maze of white dresses. Marianne hadn't been able to get off work to meet them. They pulled out and examined gowns of every shape and style encased in clear plastic bags, making sure they saw every option before making a decision. Violet had selected four to try on.

"What about this one?" The perky bridal-shop attendant, who had giggled when she introduced herself as Lola, pulled a dress off the rack and held it up. Violet nodded, and Lola draped it over her arm.

"I think I'm ready to try these on."

"Okay. I've got you set up right over here." Lola led them to the back of the store, where mirrors lined every available surface. A row of dressing rooms had been hidden behind the mirrored walls on either side. Lola opened one that had Violet's name written on the outside in purple dry-erase marker. She hung the new dress inside, along with the ones Violet had already selected. When Violet moved inside the little cubicle, Lola followed her in. "You're going to need help with those zippers. You girls wait here so you can *ooh* and *ah* appropriately."

Rachel grinned at Violet's "help me" look, but she wasn't about to get in Lola's way when she was on a mission.

She and Carly sat in the chairs just outside the room. Sooner than she expected, the door opened again. Rachel suspected that if she'd gone in with Violet, she would still be trying to figure out the elaborate laces she'd seen up the back of this first dress.

The strapless dress hugged Violet's torso, and then the skirt fell in a cascade of taffeta—at least that's what Rachel thought it was. She wasn't well-versed on wedding-gown materials. Violet stepped into an alcove of three-way mirrors and turned both ways, studying herself over her shoulder.

"I'm not thrilled with the strapless." She grabbed it near the top and hefted it up higher. "I feel like I'll be tugging on it all day long." She looked at Rachel as if seeking her opinion.

"It's pretty. But it's just the first one. Try another."

Violet nodded, and she and Lola disappeared into the fitting room.

Carly angled toward Rachel. "I can't wait to see what we're wearing. I know you don't think all of this is as exciting as I do, but you should try to pretend for Violet's sake."

Rachel glanced at the dressing-room door, which was definitely close enough for Violet to hear them. Maybe Carly thought the rustle of taffeta would drown them out, or she just didn't care. Rachel had suspected for some time that Carly thought *she* should have been the maid of honor. "I'm thrilled for Violet. I'm so glad she and Jack found each other. And it's going to be a beautiful wedding."

"Just because you lesbians can't get married—"

"Actually, we can." Did this girl live under a rock?

"Okay, but that's not real."

"It is." Now Rachel kind of hoped Violet could hear them.

"You know what I mean, like a big church wedding."

"Violet's not getting married in a church. And yes, if I wanted to, I could get married in a church. Just maybe not your church."

Carly sighed. "Why are we arguing about this? You don't even have anyone to marry."

Rachel clamped her jaw shut tight, stood up from her chair, and turned away. Violet came out of the dressing room while she was still contemplating slapping Carly. Apparently, slapping Faith had awakened a violent side of Rachel she'd never known about.

"I love it." Carly jumped up and pressed her hands together in front of her. "It's beautiful."

"Rach?"

The dress fit Violet well. But the traditional style didn't suit Violet's personality. She looked like any other bride in the catalog on the table nearby.

"It is nice. But I don't know if it's *the one*."

Carly huffed. "There is no *one*. That's your problem, Rachel. You're too old-fashioned."

"Oh, that's my problem, huh? Well, thank you so much for pointing out my shortcomings, Carly. Forgive me if I don't want to use you as my moral compass."

"What the hell is that supposed to mean?"

"I know all about your—"

"Rachel!" Violet's voice broke through. When Rachel spun around, Violet glanced pointedly around the room at all the other patrons, who were now trying to act like they hadn't been listening to the argument. "Sit back down and behave yourselves while I go put on another dress."

Rachel sank back into her chair. Carly flopped down beside her, pulled out her cell phone, and tapped angrily on the screen. Rachel ignored the urge to try to see who she texted so vehemently. No doubt she was reporting to Marianne what a bitch Rachel was. Well, she didn't care. Carly's opinion of her didn't matter.

Rachel picked up a magazine and flipped the pages, not really registering their content. She couldn't help wondering what Faith could find attractive enough about Carly to sleep with her before her wedding, too. Her bottle-blond hair had been overprocessed a couple of dye jobs ago. She wore too much makeup, in Rachel's opinion. Her small waist appeared even more so in contrast to the size of her fake breasts. But, Rachel admitted, Carly had a confident carriage that she envied.

Before Rachel could figure out why she cared what drew Faith to a woman, Violet stepped out of the dressing room and paused, her expression nervous.

"Oh, Vi." Rachel's throat felt tight with emotion, and her eyes were suspiciously moist.

"What? Is it bad?" She looked between her reflection and Rachel's face, obviously concerned.

Rachel shook her head, struggling to regain her ability to speak. "It's perfect."

"Yeah?" A huge grin transformed Violet's expression.

Rachel nodded. "It really is, isn't it?"

Rachel stood and walked around Violet, getting a better look at all sides.

"I kind of love that's it shorter than the others."

"It's tea-length," Lola said.

The fitted top of the white dress flared at the waist into a full skirt that ended just below Violet's knees. The retro style fit Violet, and after she'd styled her dark hair and done her makeup to match, she would be stunning.

"Right, and it has the feel of that strapless one, because it's solid here." Violet swept her hands over the heart-shaped silhouette that covered her breasts. "But I don't feel like it might fall down, because of the cap-sleeves here." A layer of lace with a rounded neck came up over her shoulders.

"It's got a vintage feel that is so—you," Rachel said.

"I already know how I want my hair." Violet twirled around, stopping when she caught sight of Carly's frown. "You don't like it?"

"It's just not as pretty as the last one. You looked like a princess. And I could loan you my diamond necklace as your something borrowed."

"I don't think diamonds go with this one. No necklace, just some drop pearl earrings."

Rachel smiled, glad Violet didn't let Carly's opinion bring down her excitement about the dress. This one was clearly a better fit for Violet.

"This is it. I don't have to try any more on," Violet said to Lola.

While Violet changed back into her street clothes, Rachel wandered through the shop, mostly to get away from Carly's incessant texting. Rachel hadn't taken her phone out since she'd shoved it into her pocket as she left the house this morning. Of course, her parents didn't text, and aside from her clients, Violet was the only other person who cared where she was or what she was doing.

When she heard Violet exit the dressing room, she returned to the mirrored area. Violet's smile reflected happiness so pure that Rachel wanted to tell her she was just as beautiful in her cropped jeans and printed blouse as in the dress she'd just tried on. She would be radiant on her wedding day. The bit of tarnish on that thought when she remembered catching Violet and Faith made her sad.

"Well, now that the bride is all taken care of, do you have any plans for the bridesmaids yet?" Lola had passed Violet's dress off to an assistant to be bagged up until her fitting.

"I'm thinking tea-length as well. Maybe a halter neckline. Something with a vintage look to coordinate with my dress."

"Color?"

"Navy blue."

"Let me pull a couple of selections, and we'll have you two try them on." She looked Rachel and Carly up and down. "Sizes?"

"Eight," Carly said.

Rachel shrugged. "Do they fit like regular clothes? Maybe a twelve."

Lola looked disappointed that Rachel didn't know her dress size. She shuffled off without asking anything further, clearly deciding she could figure it out just as well as Rachel could. Violet nixed two of the four selections Lola brought over, and then Rachel and Carly went into dressing rooms to try the other two.

"Do you need help?" Lola crowded behind Rachel as if she might follow her inside, clearly having decided she was the more helpless of the two.

Rachel stopped, impeding her progress inside the tiny room. "I'm good. I'll holler if I need anything."

Chapter Six

Rachel took her time changing into the dress. But once she had it on, she ran out of reasons to stall. There wasn't even a mirror in the room so she could check herself out first. Apparently, that was how the salespeople forced you out of the cubicle to humiliate yourself in front of your closest friends and family.

After a deep breath, she flung open the door and stepped out. Carly had already moved into the three-way mirror alcove and was busy admiring herself from every angle. Rachel lifted her gaze to Violet's face and was mortified to see Faith standing next to her with a strange expression.

"Well?" Rachel focused on Violet, but she could feel the heat creeping up her exposed chest and throat.

"Turn around." Violet made a twirling motion with her finger in the air.

Rachel obliged and caught sight of herself in the mirrors. The dress had the same fitted upper as Violet's dress, but instead of the lace embellishment, a simple halter-neck strap would keep her from tugging to cover her breasts all night. The skirt flared suddenly at the waist as well, falling to a symmetrical hem in a shape that reminded Rachel of a poodle skirt.

"It's great," Faith said.

Rachel spun back around just as Faith's gaze traveled back up her body. Their eyes met, and there was no mistaking her expression now. Rachel's stomach flopped at the admiration in Faith's gaze.

"Well, of course you'll need the right bra." Lola stepped in front of her and started pulling at the bodice, much closer to Rachel's breasts than was comfortable.

She'd tried, at first, to leave her bra on, but the black straps stood out obtrusively against her pale skin. So she'd taken it off and shoved her breasts as deeply as she could into the cups. She glared at Violet, trying to convey just how much she owed her for letting Lola feel her up.

"I don't know." Faith moved next to Lola. "If it were altered a little." She let her hands hover near Rachel's shoulders but didn't touch her yet. She met Rachel's eyes again. "May I?"

Rachel nodded, her throat suddenly dry. Faith grasped the halter, just behind her neck, and pulled it tighter.

"If you bring it up here, she might not need a bra at all."

Lola considered Rachel's cleavage far too long before approving. "That would work." Seeming satisfied, she transferred her attention to the fit of Carly's dress.

Faith let go of the strap and smoothed it over Rachel's shoulders. Rachel shivered as Faith ghosted her hand over her skin. She stared at Faith's mouth, noticing for the first time that her upper lip was slightly fuller than her lower one. Faith winked at her, then said so only she could hear, "It's not my first time shopping for dresses."

"I didn't know you were into bridesmaids, too," Rachel bit back to cover her rising arousal. Once more, she called upon a memory sure to douse the flames—Violet's lipstick rubbed messily across Faith's mouth.

Faith blushed but didn't move out of Rachel's personal space.

"What are you even doing here?" Rachel covered her discomfort with an accusatory tone.

"I just finished up with a client at the flower shop down the street. I remembered Violet saying you ladies would be here this afternoon, so I decided to check in—see how the shopping was going. I hope that's okay."

Before Rachel could answer, Violet said, "Of course it is." She fluffed the skirt on Rachel's dress. "Rach, you don't have to try on that other one. This is it. Carly hates it. But she doesn't like mine either. Oh, Faith, come let me show you my dress." She grabbed Faith's arm and pulled her away.

By the time Rachel had changed back into her jeans and T-shirt, Violet had unbagged her dress and held it up against her. Judging by Violet's grin, Faith was fawning appropriately over her choice. As Rachel joined them, Carly called out for Violet to come over to the bridesmaids' dress racks. As soon as Carly had changed back to her own clothes, she'd headed over there in search of a better choice for them. Violet rolled her eyes and strode across the shop, clearly only pacifying Carly.

"You really did look great in that dress." Faith's tone was casual, but her gaze was anything but. Her eyes swept over Rachel like a caress. Rachel tilted her head, stretching her neck against the very visceral memory of Faith's hands on her shoulders.

"That's nice of you to say, but I know better."

"You don't think so?"

"I'm uncomfortable, and I have no idea what kind of shoes to wear with it."

Faith laughed. "I know it's not really your thing. But it definitely could be worse." She nodded toward Carly, who was trying to sell Violet on a hideous bridesmaid dress with a big bow on the ass.

"Oh, God. I'm not a quitter, but I would have to withdraw as maid of honor." The banter between them helped distract her from the sexual awareness shimmering through her nerves.

"Maybe that's Carly's devious plan."

"You picked up on that, too, huh?" They shared a smile that warmed Rachel's insides.

"She strikes me as one of those quid-pro-quo women."

Rachel raised her brows, holding back her comment about how Rachel knew what kind of woman Carly was.

"Thanks for passing on the cheap joke." Faith gave her a saucy smile. "I've seen the type. Let me guess. Violet was her maid of honor?"

"Yes."

"So she expects it in return. That's why she picked Violet. She figured she was a shoo-in."

"Yes. Because I'm the last person you would want as your maid of honor. I don't know the first thing about what I'm supposed to do. Wait—does that mean Violet expects me to get married and ask her to be mine?"

"Nah. Violet's not like that. She picked you in spite of your inadequacies."

"Thanks." Rachel playfully punched Faith's arm.

"I said no, Carly, and that's final. I like what I've already picked out." Violet's voice carried through the store. Even Violet could only handle so much of Carly's overbearing personality.

"And that's why she's not maid of honor," Rachel whispered.

Faith exaggerated a grimace.

"Wrap it up, ladies. The bride is getting hungry," Violet called, and they all met at the front of the store. "Faith, come to lunch with us. We're going to Lotus."

Rachel purposely didn't look at Faith, but she imagined she could feel Faith's gaze pass over her before she answered. She tried to keep her expression blank, which wasn't hard since she didn't have any idea if she wanted Faith to join them or not. She couldn't seem to ignore the part of her that wanted to spend more time with Faith. But she wouldn't forget who Faith was long enough to trust her.

"Okay. I've got some time."

"Lotus gets busy during the lunch hour. While I finish up the paperwork here, why don't you guys go get us a table?"

"I'll wait with you," Carly said quickly. "Then you can ride with me to lunch. Parking over there can be a bitch. We'll have one less car that way, and I can bring you back here after."

"Okay. Rachel, do you want to go with me then? You know, because of the parking," Faith asked.

She didn't really want to, but it would be rude to say so. She could always catch a ride back with Carly and Violet after lunch. That way she wouldn't have to be alone with Faith any longer than necessary.

❖

Faith slid behind the wheel of her SUV and waited for Rachel to climb into the passenger seat. She'd had an appointment with a client at the florist's, that had been true. Since she didn't have any afternoon obligations, she should have gone home to work in the barn afterward. But she'd been unable to pass the bridal shop without popping inside. She just wanted to check on Violet—strictly business. She chuckled aloud at the obvious lie. Her visit to the dress shop had everything to do with the woman sitting next to her.

"What's so funny?" Rachel said as she closed her door.

"What?"

"You laughed."

"Oh, nothing." She fumbled to change the subject. "Well, we've got another thing checked off the list. Some women think the dress is the most important piece of the wedding."

Rachel scrunched up her nose.

"You don't agree."

"I can't see myself in some big puffy white dress."

"Yeah. I don't envision you in one either." Faith laughed when Rachel narrowed her eyes. "Hey, don't act all offended. You said it first. That wasn't a comment on your appearance, but you're not the wedding-dress type."

Rachel bit her lip as if deciding if she was offended. Faith pulled into traffic, hoping that keeping her eyes on the road instead of on Rachel would distract her from the sexy way Rachel's expressions changed.

"Okay, Ms. Fancy-wedding-planner. What would you dress me in for my big day?"

"That really depends. What's the setting?"

Rachel shrugged. "I don't know. I never planned on being able to marry."

"Never? Not even as a little girl playing with your dolls?"

"Nope. I didn't play with dolls much. And I knew pretty young that there wasn't a groom in my future."

"Okay. Well, a lot of lesbians go the pantsuit route. But I can definitely see you in a three-piece suit—something classy and gray, tailored for the perfect fit." Faith didn't dwell too long on the image of the person who might be standing beside Rachel at said ceremony. "If you're interested in a beach wedding, I'd put you in all white—still pants—but something loose and flowy, no jacket—maybe a vest, though."

"Just off the top of your head, huh?"

Faith nodded. "I'm pretty good at this."

She found a spot on the street less than a block from the restaurant. They walked side by side until they met another couple on the sidewalk. Faith moved closer and fell a step behind to make room to pass, and her hand bumped Rachel's. As their fingers touched, she thought Rachel's closed a little but then told herself she'd imagined the near grasp of their hands. Hell, was she really waxing poetic about some chick-flick moment she'd fabricated? She hoped the others joined them before she completely lost her mind.

They asked the hostess for a table for four and were seated at one of the last empty booths in the dining room. The hostess left a stack of menus and told them their waiter would be right over.

"What about you? What are you wearing to your wedding?" Rachel asked as she opened her menu and studied Faith across the table.

"If I were the marrying kind, I would definitely be built for a wedding dress." Faith winked at her. "Something sleek and simple. Nothing poufy or overdone."

"If?"

"It's not for me."

"Is it the monogamy you can't handle?"

Faith winced. "I probably deserved that one."

"Even if I understood the lure of casual sex with lots of women, don't you think you'll eventually want to settle down?"

"God, I hate that phrase, *settle down.* Does that sound like something you would want to do? It's like accepting that there's just nothing else out there."

"Okay. It's not a great term. But the concept of finding someone to share your life with—someone you couldn't imagine being without—you don't want that?"

Faith tilted her head, trying to picture the scenario. She wasn't heartless. Of course she understood the lure of finding a partner. She wasn't opposed to being in a relationship. She'd dated a woman in college for almost a year, and another for three semesters. But both relationships had fizzled out. She didn't believe human beings were built for longevity. "I've been on my own for a while now. I like things the way they are."

"After this, after Violet's wedding, you go back to your usual pattern? Well, I guess you could still be doing that now. She's not your only client, is she?"

"She's not." Faith picked up her water glass and took a sip. She hadn't slept with anyone since her aborted encounter with Violet a month ago. She'd certainly gone a month without sex before, but not too much longer. Typically, whether with a client or someone she met casually otherwise, the opportunity would present itself, and she'd take it. She'd had the chance. She'd turned down two women since the afternoon of Violet's barbecue. She refused to examine why spending time at home working in the barn held more allure than the sexy near strangers.

"Yeah, well, I'm not going to ask if you're screwing any of them, if that's what you're thinking." Rachel's expression hardened.

Faith glanced at the door, checking for Violet and Carly. She weighed the smart-ass comment Rachel no doubt expected in response. Despite her current lack of activity, she could easily prove herself to be the rake Rachel expected her to be. Instead, she met her gaze and became as honest as she could. "If I'd met you when I met Violet, I would have hit on you instead."

"Oh, what, so it's my fault you and Violet—"

"That's not where I was going with that."

"What, then?"

"If I had—hit on you—"

"You make it sound so romantic."

"I'm not sure what flowery turn of phrase you need, but my question is, what would you have done?"

"I wouldn't have known your reputation then."

"Probably not." Faith wished Rachel didn't know—firsthand—who she was. She'd never been ashamed of her life, and she wasn't now, necessarily. But a part of her wanted a clean slate with Rachel.

"So what's your definition of hitting on me?" Rachel rested her elbows on the table in front of her. She gave Faith a flirtatious smile that made Faith wonder who was supposed to do the seducing in this scenario. "What does a Faith McKenna pass look like? Same endgame? To get me in bed?"

"Maybe." Faith let her eyes slide slowly down Rachel's neck and chest. She swept her gaze over Rachel's breasts, not long enough to be creepy, but just so Rachel knew she noticed them. "Whatever the ultimate goal—getting my hands on you would have been a major component."

Rachel blushed and looked away. Faith reached across the table and trailed her fingers along Rachel's forearm, pleased at the immediate rise of goose bumps on Rachel's arm. Rachel might act like she was only interested in stability and monogamy, but she could be tempted, that much was clear.

"I'm usually pretty honest about my intentions."

Rachel covered her hand and stopped the caress, but she didn't pull back. "So am I. I'd have said I'm not the one-and-done type."

"Then I would have had a very tough decision to make."

Rachel released her hand and leaned back into the booth, restoring some space between them. The light left her eyes, and Faith knew she'd dismissed the whole scene as just another play on Faith's part.

"You know, I don't typically go dress shopping with my brides. That's something they usually arrange on their own."

"So why did you?"

"I wanted another chance to see you."

"You don't think you'll get enough of me in the next six and a half months?"

When Violet and Carly entered the restaurant, Faith was saved from admitting that the idea of seeing more of Rachel over the coming months both scared and excited her.

❖

As Carly and Violet reached the booth, Rachel excused herself to the restroom. She spent a few minutes in the stall, then even longer obsessively washing her hands while staring at herself in the mirror. Why was she flirting with Faith? *What does a Faith McKenna pass look like?* She'd momentarily lost her mind. Even while Faith had unapologetically admitted she was only interested in fast and physical, she still tempted Rachel. But she wasn't yet delusional enough to convince herself she could do casual. Though she wasn't drowning in jealousy of Violet and Jack, her mother had been right about one thing. Rachel wanted permanence. She wanted someone to wake up with and go to bed with, and a woman who would look at her like Jack and Violet looked at each other.

She shook her head at her own reflection. Now was not the time for over-the-top sap. She needed to get back out there and join her friends for lunch. She'd been in here for so long they probably thought she was having intestinal problems.

She washed her hands again and waved them under the hand dryer, too impatient for much more, then headed back to the table. Carly now shared one side of the booth with Faith, so Rachel tapped Violet's shoulder.

"Scoot in."

"Everything okay?" Violet asked.

"Yeah, why?"

"You were gone for a while."

Rachel's face flushed hot immediately. One side of Faith's mouth quirked, and humor danced in her eyes. "I'm fine. I—had to take a phone call." She threw out the white lie rather than admit she'd been talking to herself in there.

"New client?" Violet asked eagerly. "Please, tell me about it. I want to talk about something besides my wedding."

Rachel laughed. "Starting to get stressed?"

"Starting?"

"We have lots of time left, Vi." Rachel expected Violet to freak out a little when the date drew near. But over six months out was early to be getting overwhelmed.

Faith smiled. "Don't worry, Violet. I've got it all under control. That's what you hired me for, right?"

Carly laughed. Violet glared at her, and Faith gave her a curious look. "Violet is the most organized person I've ever met. Wedding planning is not what she needed you for."

"Damn it, Carly," Violet muttered.

Rachel avoided looking at Faith and, in doing so, found Violet glancing away as well.

"What? Come on. It was a joke." Carly giggled and grabbed Faith's forearm where it rested on the table. Faith stiffened, but she didn't pull away.

The awkward silence went on for a moment longer, before Rachel decided a complete subject change couldn't be any worse. "I do have a new client that's being very difficult. I've already found him three near-perfect houses. But every time I do, he changes his demands."

"What's his deal?" Violet gave her a grateful look.

The tension between them hadn't eased, but Rachel soldiered on. "Either he can't commit to buying, or he's just that susceptible to whims. He'll come to me with something he saw on HGTV last weekend, and suddenly his new house has to have whatever it is, too. And he's not open to purchasing and then customizing. Turn-key only."

"I know the type," Faith said. "Reality television messes with my business, too. They don't understand the difference between their budgets and those of the people on those shows."

Violet chimed in. "I'm so glad my customer service comes in small doses. I don't have to think about people again once they leave the store."

"Mostly, I like dealing with people—especially families. I love helping them find a new house to make a home. I like to think about them making memories there. But it's about the challenge, too.

Poring through listings and searching for the ones to show is like solving a puzzle."

Apparently tired of being left out, Carly touched Faith's arm again and said, "I'm so glad our clients just basically have to do what we tell them." Carly was a paralegal for a criminal-defense attorney. "I mean, if they don't want to go to jail, they better listen to us."

Rachel stared at Carly's hand on Faith's arm and was swamped with pettiness. Carly's boss was one of many defense attorneys in town, and certainly not as important as she tried to make him seem. And the way she prattled on now, making herself seem like the brains behind the whole operation, made Rachel want to push her hand off Faith.

"Rach?" Violet said quietly, close to her.

Rachel jerked her eyes from Faith's arm. Confusion swirled in her head. Was she feeling spiteful because she didn't like Carly or because she didn't like Carly touching Faith?

"Where'd you go?" Violet bumped her shoulder against Rachel's.

"I'm right here in this room." She gave Violet a reassuring smile. She'd never gone farther than across the table. And, she feared, she could be getting too close. She could find Faith attractive, but being truly attracted to her was unacceptable.

CHAPTER SEVEN

Faith pushed a grocery cart through the aisles at Violet's store. She passed through this area often on her way to meet clients. The store was right off the interstate and easy to get to. Violet patronized her business, so she figured she could return the favor.

Today, she stopped for a few staples. The complete lack of food-delivery options was one disadvantage to living so far out of the city. The first couple of weeks after she moved was rough, but once she started learning how best to cook for one and utilize her leftovers well, the adjustment wasn't that bad. So once a week she made a detailed grocery list and stocked up. This weekend, especially, she didn't need an excuse not to venture too far from home. She'd planned a full weekend that included working on her property, updating her website, and sending out emails to current clients and prospective new ones.

She headed for the pet-food section, an aisle she could usually skip completely. One of the wheels on her cart had a wobble, but she'd put up with the rhythmic noise this far and didn't feel like going back to the front to exchange it. She scanned the shelves, trying to discern the difference between the various kinds of cat food. Were there really that many flavors? And didn't kittens need a different type than adult cats? She picked up two random cans and tried to compare the labels.

She was still engrossed in what was apparently the biggest choice of her day when she heard Rachel's voice behind her. "Wedding-planning business not what it used to be?"

"What?" She turned. Rachel carried a shopping basket in the crook of one elbow.

"You're buying cat food." Rachel pointed at the cans in her hand. "You don't strike me as a cat person—"

"Oh, I so am not."

"So, that was a joke about you eating cat food because it's cheap and business isn't good." Rachel gave her an awkward smile.

"Nope. Not a cat person, but also not eating cat food. Gross. Somehow I've acquired a cat—or rather I share my property with one. He—I've decided it's a boy—he's just a kitten really."

Rachel laughed.

"What's so funny?"

"You should see your face. I wouldn't have thought I'd see you go so mushy about—well, about anything really."

"Hey, I have a heart."

"And a soft spot for kittens, apparently."

Faith hadn't expected to care about him either, but the little fur ball had grown on her. Her every-cat-for-himself mentality had lasted barely a day before she broke down and fed him some tuna. After watching Swan fumble around the barn, she couldn't imagine him ever being stealthy enough to catch his own dinner. But, even though he followed her to the back porch every night, she refused to let him in the house. When she ran out of tuna she'd picked up some cheap cat food, but the damn thing was apparently a picky eater. Or he'd had a taste of the real stuff and now was too good for anything else.

She dropped several different flavors in her cart, then grabbed a bag of dry Kitten Chow. She resumed walking down the aisle, pleased when Rachel fell into step beside her.

"What about you?" She peered into Rachel's basket. "What are you buying today?" The basket was filled with frozen dinners, prepared food from the deli, and bagged salads.

"Yeah. I don't really cook." Rachel's self-deprecating grin was charming.

"I'm learning how—because of necessity. I recently moved

out to the country, and no place delivers out there. So now I'm in survival mode."

"What have you conquered so far?"

"Over the summer, I mastered steak and baked potatoes on the grill. This winter, I'll probably take it inside and figure out how to make comfort food." She rounded the corner and headed for the meat section.

"My mom makes an amazing pot roast. Do you want me to get you her recipe?"

"Whoa, are we already to sharing secret family recipes? You're moving a little fast for me." She winked at Rachel.

"Huh. I didn't think I *could* move too fast for you."

"Good point. But I'm not sure I should use your mother's recipe until after I've met her." Faith had no idea what made her even joke about such a thing. She tried to cover her discomfort by leaning into the meat case and acting like she needed to examine several packs of chicken breasts before she could choose one.

"Funny. Like that's going to happen. Just my luck, she'd probably like you, and I'd have to hear about why I don't bring around that nice wedding planner again." Rachel glared at her. "You're probably one of those women who's good at charming parents, aren't you?"

Faith shrugged. "I haven't met a girlfriend's parents since college. But I do okay with mothers of the bride."

"Oh, God, don't tell me you sleep with them, too."

Ouch. Faith pressed her lips together against the urge to snipe back. She didn't want to create a scene in the grocery store.

"I'm sorry. Wow. That was a bitchy thing to say."

"Forget it." Faith turned away and hurriedly pushed her cart toward the front of the store. Apparently, the friendliness she'd thought they were enjoying had been one-sided.

"Faith, wait."

She didn't slow down. She'd made it almost to the front of the store before Rachel caught up with her. Violet was behind the customer-service desk helping one of her employees with a transaction, and again Faith squelched the desire to let Rachel know what she thought of her snide comments.

"Hey, come on. Wait a minute." Rachel grabbed her arm and Faith stopped. She forced herself not to glance down at the warm fingers on her skin. Instead, she met Rachel's eyes. Rachel looked embarrassed and sincere. "That was wrong. I'm really sorry. And while we're on the subject, about what Carly said at lunch yesterday—"

"Don't worry about it. It's not a big deal."

"It is. I mean, of course Vi knew about—well, she'd heard from Carly—but that doesn't mean it's why she hired you." She gestured toward Violet. "You see how busy she is. She really did need a coordinator. And Carly certainly shouldn't have said—"

"Look, let's just agree that Carly has a big mouth all the way around and leave it at that."

"Okay."

"I should get going." Faith nodded toward her cart. "My cat's probably hungry. And you've got frozen foods."

"Yeah, sure. I guess I'll see you around."

They filed into checkout lanes next to each other, but Faith faced the cashier and resisted the urge to glance back at Rachel. She did see Rachel go to the service desk to talk to Violet after her transaction was complete. Faith swiped her credit card, loaded up her bags, and headed for the door. She returned Violet's wave but didn't stop to talk on her way out. If Violet thought her behavior was strange, Rachel could explain if she wanted to.

❖

"I think Rachel has a thing for our wedding planner." Jack sipped carefully from a mug of steaming coffee.

Rachel's hand jerked halfway to her mouth, and a piece of French toast fell off her fork onto her plate. She steadied her hand and speared the bite again. He nudged her with his elbow, and she regretted sitting beside him in the booth. She'd met him and Violet for breakfast at a diner down the street from her office. It was one of the few places left in the midtown area that hadn't turned into a tourist trap.

"What makes you say that?" Violet found something interesting in her own coffee mug and began stirring it much more than necessary.

"Why else do you think she's at every meeting with Faith? She can't be that into weddings."

"When it involves my closest friends—why wouldn't I be?" Rachel threw her arm around Jack's shoulder.

"Hey, I don't blame you. She's attractive. But I thought she was straight."

Rachel laughed.

"What?"

"Not straight, my friend." Rachel removed her arm from his shoulders and returned her attention to her breakfast.

"Come on. You think every hot woman is a lesbian. It's not wishful thinking?"

"No." She picked up her apple juice, trying to appear more casual than she felt. Violet was avoiding her gaze, no doubt out of guilt, but Rachel had her own reasons for not wanting to discuss Faith.

He paused with his mug close to his mouth, his elbows resting on the table in front of him. "I thought at first you two didn't like each other. There's some tension there, right? But is it just like— foreplay, or something?"

Rachel coughed and somehow managed not to spew apple juice across the table.

"Eat your breakfast, Jack," Violet said.

"What? Did I say something wrong?" Jack asked. Before Rachel had time to assure him that they were good, his cell rang. He glanced at the display. "This is my boss. I need to grab it." He slid out of the booth and moved to step outside in deference to the hum of conversation around them.

As soon as he was gone, Violet put down her fork and stared at Rachel.

"What?" Rachel maintained eye contact, though it made her uncomfortable.

"So, do you?" Violet sounded nervous.

"Do I what?"

"Have a thing for Faith."

Rachel forced a laughed, then hoped Violet didn't pick up on how fake it sounded. "Are you kidding me?"

"Well, you do seem awfully interested in my meetings with her."

"I'm interested in making sure you don't screw her again."

Violet's expression frosted over and Rachel sighed.

"Vi—"

"That's the only reason you want to be involved in the wedding?"

"Of course not."

"I pissed Carly off in order to make you my maid of honor."

"Well, nobody asked you to," Rachel snapped. Between her conversation with Faith at the grocery store and this one, she was screwing everything up. "I'm sorry. I think I'm just a little sick of Carly."

"What does Carly have to do with you and Faith?"

"There is no me and Faith."

"Good. Because that would be weird." Apparently satisfied that the subject was settled, Violet returned her attention to her fruit salad.

Rachel stuffed a bite of bacon into her mouth. So she couldn't get involved with Faith because it would be weird for Violet— as if the reason Violet would be uncomfortable was perfectly acceptable. Not that she wanted anything with Faith. But if she did, why should Violet be a concern for her? Violet apparently hadn't given any thought to anyone else's feelings before she went after Faith.

"I'm sorry. This wedding has me stressed." Violet glanced toward the door, where they could still see Jack outside on the phone. "And I feel guilty about what happened. Every time I look at Jack's sweet face, I feel even worse. He loves me so much,

Rach. And what's worse, he trusts me. And I feel like shit." She teared up.

Rachel darted a look toward the door. Was she really going to do this now? "Do you think you're going to tell him?"

Violet shook her head. "I can't break his heart just to make myself feel better. I'll have to spend the rest of my life making it up to him, even if he doesn't know why."

Rachel didn't know what to say. If she were in Violet's place, she'd probably have to confess and hope they could rebuild the trust. But if she talked Violet into telling the truth and Jack left her—this decision had to be up to Violet.

"What's with all of the serious looks over here?" Jack asked as he slid back into the booth next to Rachel.

"Just wedding stuff." Rachel hated the lie, but she gave Violet a reassuring look just the same. In six months all of the wedding stress would be over. Then Violet and Jack could concentrate on their marriage, and Rachel's life could return to normal—without Faith in it.

❖

"This was a bad idea," Faith muttered as she pulled a tray of homemade sweet-potato chips out of the oven.

She liked to meet with her clients once they got inside six months until their wedding, just to go over the checklist—talk about what had been done and what decisions remained. Typically, she'd pick a centrally located restaurant and schedule the meeting during an off-time so they could linger over dessert and coffee. When Violet mentioned that she'd invite Rachel along, Faith suggested they come out to her house instead. Eventually, she'd planned to set up the barn for earlier meetings with her clients so they could check it out as a venue option. She'd been telling herself to see this as a dry run—a chance to show off the place. Sure, she was a long way from having it ready for an actual event, but she needed to get comfortable talking it up.

"Sure. It's just business." She pulled out the fresh bread she'd baked earlier that morning. She'd sampled a couple of slices, and though it wasn't as soft as some she'd had, it wasn't bad for a first attempt at baking. When they were ready for lunch, she would toast the bread and serve it with lemon cashew chicken salad and the sweet-potato chips.

Ten minutes later, she opened the front door to Violet, Jack, and Rachel. She stepped back to let them in and tried not to be nervous. When she lived in her apartment, she'd hosted clients, fellow vendors, and friends many times. But since moving to the country, she hadn't invited anyone into her new home. She hoped they would overlook the country-blue flowered wallpaper she hadn't gotten around to pulling down in the foyer.

Violet embraced her as soon as she stepped through the door. When she released Violet, she shook hands with Jack. But when she turned toward Rachel, she didn't know what to do. Trying to cover the moment of awkwardness, she stepped forward and gave Rachel a quick hug—which ended up being a one-armed half-embrace, and she was certain they both looked uncomfortable.

"Come on back to the kitchen." She led them through the home, bypassing a tour of her private spaces. She needed to get back on comfortable, professional footing.

"Nice place," Jack said.

"Thanks. A few renovations in the house were done before I bought it, like the kitchen. But I've been concentrating my efforts outside in the barn, so I still have a lot to do in here."

Someone must have told the previous owners that kitchens sell houses. Because it was clear that a large chunk of their reno budget had gone into that room. Faith watched Rachel look around the kitchen, she presumed with a realtor's eye, and wondered what she thought.

Huge windows along the back wall flooded the kitchen and dining area with plenty of natural light. The light-gray kitchen cabinets contrasted nicely with the white quartz countertops. The large, open kitchen had great flow for cooking, and Faith loved having the big farm table only steps away. She preferred this type of set-up instead of a formal dining room.

"Make yourselves at home." She served them lemonade and sweet tea, then took a few minutes to toast the bread. Once she had transferred everything to the table, they settled in around the table.

She flipped open the cover on her tablet and stood it up next to her. As they ate, they reviewed the decisions Violet and Jack had already made.

"This chicken salad is amazing—the lemon makes it pop with flavor," Violet said, as she scooped up a forkful. She'd passed on the bread, citing a pre-wedding low-carb diet.

"You weren't kidding when you said you cooked." Rachel popped a sweet-potato chip in her mouth.

"Thanks. But I can't take credit for this recipe. I had something similar in a restaurant downtown. I thought it would make a nice, light lunch."

"Good call." Jack grabbed another piece of bread off the plate in the center of the table.

Violet set down her fork and pulled a piece of paper from her purse. "I've been looking over the vendor list you gave me. There are probably a ton of good caterers in town and I don't want anything out of the ordinary, so that will be easy. But when it comes to the pictures, I want the best." She flipped her hair over her shoulder and grinned. "Jack and I are going to look amazing, so I want the perfect photographer to immortalize the day. All our friends will be jealous when I post the pictures online."

"Okay. Have you checked out any of the websites?"

"I have. But tell me, who do you think is the best in town?"

"That's easy. You want Casey Meadows. She's a friend, but she's also amazing at what she does. I can give her a call and see if she's available, if you'd like."

"If she is, I'd like to meet with her."

"Okay. How about next week?" Faith made a note in her tablet.

"I'm out of town next week. But go ahead and set it up. Violet can say yea or nay." Jack draped his arm across the back of Violet's chair.

"We can wait until you get back—"

"No. If she's really that good, I want to get a deposit down as soon as we can." Violet looked expectantly at Rachel.

"I have showings all day Monday and a closing on Wednesday. But otherwise, I'm all yours."

Faith nodded and noted those times as well. She tried not to dwell on the way Rachel said *all yours*. She reminded herself that Rachel was being generous with her time for Violet. "I'll text you both when I have an appointment set up."

They finished their meal, and Faith stacked their plates in the sink. Rachel carried two glasses into the kitchen and handed them to her.

"So this is what you gave up food delivery and modern conveniences for, huh?"

Faith laughed. "Yeah. This, the barn, and the lawns outside."

Rachel leaned over the sink to look out the window, which put her very close to Faith. "Can I see the rest of it?"

Faith hadn't realized before how long Rachel's eyelashes were. She felt like she was staring, so she averted her eyes. But she found herself looking at the hollow between Rachel's collarbones and the open vee of Rachel's plaid button-down shirt. She cleared her throat and took a step back. When she spoke, she directed her words to Violet and Jack as well. "The yard's a bit soggy because of the recent rain, but everything's dry and tight inside the barn. I'll show it to you if you'd like."

Violet glanced pointedly at her heels. "I'm not really a barn girl, and I am not walking out there in these."

"I can fix that." Faith opened a closet near the back door and held up a pair of black rubber boots.

"No, thank you." Violet's look of repulsion was amusing.

"The previous owner left them. I know they aren't high fashion, but they'll keep your feet dry."

"I want to see it." Rachel stepped out of her shoes and held out her hand for the boots.

"Jack?"

"You ladies go ahead. I'll keep Violet company." He gave

Rachel a strange grin and a wink Faith couldn't decipher. Both Rachel and Violet looked annoyed with him.

"Am I missing something?" Faith asked while Rachel tugged on the boots.

"Yeah. Jack's a dick." Rachel headed out the back door.

Violet shrugged, and Jack waved her toward the door with a flick of his fingers. She shook her head and followed Rachel.

CHAPTER EIGHT

Rachel clomped out to the barn in the too-big boots, struggling to keep up with Faith's quick strides.

"Is this payback for all the times some taller woman outpaced you before?" she called.

Faith laughed and slowed down. "Sorry. I might be a bit excited. No one's been here but me since I bought the place. I mean, contractors for bids and such, but that's not the same thing."

As they walked, she explained where she would add a walkway leading from the parking area to the building.

"Flower beds, low-level LED lighting, blah, blah, blah." Faith grinned. "I'm not a landscaper. I'll probably hire someone to do the design. Something eye-catching here at the front though."

"Because of the client's gut and all that."

"Exactly. You saw yourself how a first impression can sour a tour."

"Or make it."

"Right. So, I've gone back and forth on the entrance." She waved at the large, plain panels hinged to swing outward. "I'd love to have some new panels made, something different—wood tones, maybe. Then I could mount them on rails so that when the weather is right we can slide them back and bring the outdoors in. I'd do a set at both ends for airflow."

"That sounds amazing."

"Yes. But I sacrifice some in efficiency on heating and cooling in the other seasons. The other option is to lose these doors, frame it out, and put in a set of double doors with custom glasswork."

"I don't think you can go wrong either way."

"Thanks. Now for the inside." She swung open one of the large doors.

"It doesn't look like much now. But try to picture it." Faith walked to the center of the barn and turned slowly as she spoke. "After I clear everything out of here, I'll have polished concrete floors poured. Then I can start building out the inside. I'll leave most of the center area open so it remains flexible for table placement. Along that wall, I'll add a small stage for the bands or DJs. And there's plenty of room for a dance floor. I'm going to add restrooms over there. And I'll enclose that corner and construct a full kitchen for caterers." Her voice rose and her hand gestures grew bigger the longer she spoke. Her eyes glowed as if she were actually seeing the space the way she imagined it.

When she moved outside a smaller side door and into the yard, Rachel followed. "The early evening weddings will be the best. The sun sets just over those hills and washes this side of the barn in a beautiful orange glow. I need to keep that in mind when I decide what color to paint it. After dark, strings of lights overhead, you know, the ones with those big old-fashioned bulbs, will illuminate this outdoor area as well as the inside of the barn."

"Wow. You are enthusiastic."

Though the air was crisp, the clear blue sky offered no cover from the full midday sun. Faith squinted, revealing tiny lines at the corners of her eyes. "Sorry. When I get going on this stuff, you just need to tell me to shut up."

"No. I think's it's great. You clearly love it. And you light up when you talk about it. It's invigorating."

Faith smiled, and Rachel had a sudden urge to step forward and wrap her arms around her. She wanted to be closer to this Faith—the one who had a long-term vision for this piece of land.

"I do. I'll continue doing wedding planning. But I want this to be an all-purpose venue for weddings, birthdays, fund-raisers, you name it."

Rachel searched for the image of Faith with Violet to offset the allure of Faith's passion for this project. When the vision wouldn't crystalize, she fell back on light teasing. "So this is how you get them, huh?"

"What?"

"You bring a woman here and describe the perfect wedding and just charm the pants off her, right?" She was joking—sort of. Faith had already told her she hadn't shown the place to anyone else yet. But then why did a streak of jealousy shoot through her gut when she thought about Faith glowingly describing her plans to some other woman? She could easily picture Faith smoothly taking said woman in her arms and kissing her until her legs melted.

Faith looked for a second like she was offended, but then her expression lightened. "Are you feeling charmed, Ms. Union?"

"No. I didn't mean me. I was referring to your other women."

Faith flicked her eyebrows up briefly, humor dancing in her eyes. "Your use of the word *other* might lead one to believe that you want to count yourself as one of my women."

"I think you took that off the table when you slept with my best friend." Rachel called on contempt to cover her discomfort with the direction of her thoughts.

"Well, if you want to get literal, I didn't. You interrupted us."

"You were practically naked with her. I don't need to discuss semantics to know that means I won't be acting on—" She cut herself off when she realized what she was about to reveal.

"What exactly won't you be acting on?" Faith's voice deepened, and she took a step closer. "I'm not alone, then? There's something here." She waved a finger in the increasingly small space between them.

Rachel shook her head slowly, struggling to keep Violet in the forefront of her mind. "There can't be."

"But it's already there." Faith stroked her fingers against

Rachel's cheek and along her jaw. "I want to kiss you. I can't believe Violet hasn't caught me staring at your mouth yet."

"Faith," Rachel whispered, wishing the words sounded more like a warning and less like a plea.

Faith's fingers brushed Rachel's earlobe as she feathered them down her neck. "Nothing more is going to happen with Violet. I promise. But I'm also not going to kiss you until you truly believe that." She spoke as if she had no doubt that day would come. She inhaled and nodded slightly, as if fortifying her decision. Then she eased back, not fully, but enough to let Rachel know she wouldn't push this moment. "So, you think you know everything you need to about me. What's your story?"

"What do you mean?" Rachel drew in her own full breath, trying to shift her mind from the near seduction to this new line of conversation.

"You're all about monogamy and commitment, but you aren't in a relationship."

"I'm not."

"Just by the law of averages, you must meet some eligible lesbians in real estate."

"I guess."

"No one satisfies your high standards?"

"Don't be an ass just because I won't let you kiss me." She gave Faith a coy smile to take some of the edge out of her words. "There's no big story. I've dated, been in a few relationships. Nothing stuck."

"But you're not giving up on the fairy tale?"

Faith's skeptical tone irritated Rachel.

"I try to have realistic expectations. I've watched my parents struggle from time to time. I know happily-ever-after isn't effortless. But I do believe, with the right person, it's worth putting in the work."

"Yeah? Maybe that's why my mom and dad keep marrying the wrong ones."

Faith's lips tightened and she turned away. Rachel followed her back through the barn on their way toward the house. Faith paused in the middle of the open space and looked around. Rachel tried to see the space through Faith's eyes. Faith had a clear vision of what she wanted, and Rachel admired her passion. The barn was still in the demo phase, and until Faith started some construction, the final images would remain only in her head. But Rachel could already see the work that had been done.

"What if I've taken on more than I can handle here?"

"Well, if you want to get rid of it, I'd be happy to list it for you."

Faith glanced at her. "Standard commission, of course."

"Absolutely. I don't do friends and family discounts."

When her comment earned a small smile from Faith, she couldn't hold back an answering grin. "Is that what we are—friends?"

"Sure. It sounds better than acquaintances. Or don't you have friends either?" Rachel wasn't sure why she'd suggested they could be friends. She'd never had so much animosity with any of her other friends. Looking back at their interactions, one wouldn't think they even liked each other. But she was learning that Faith was more complex than her first impression. At least, trying to be friendly might make the next six months more bearable.

"I have a few friends."

"Good. So we'll shoot for that."

"Okay. I'll try not to sleep with any more of Violet's wedding party, if you think that will make it easier." Faith winked.

"Great. I wasn't going to say anything, but I really think that would help."

As they exited the barn, a ball of variegated gray-and-white fur flew around the corner and stopped suddenly. The kitten looked up at Rachel with blue-gray eyes that seemed familiar. The black "eyeliner" around its eyes made the color even more striking.

"Oh my God, aren't you adorable?" She squatted down and held out her hand. The kitten came over and started rubbing his head against her fingers immediately.

"His name is Swan."

"Like from the Adam Sandler movie?"

Faith smiled. "Exactly."

"I get it. He has a very intense stare." Swan purred loudly. "He's a charmer."

"He thinks so." Faith started back toward the house, as if to prove she could dismiss the kitten.

Rachel stood and followed her. "You're saying he's not? Have you forgotten I've seen you agonizing over gourmet cat food?"

"I wouldn't say agonizing." Faith met Rachel's disbelieving look and chuckled. "Okay. But if he's intent on living in my barn, I can't let him starve." Faith stopped at the steps of the porch and turned around to give him an exaggerated glare. "You're not going inside."

Swan had tailed them all the way to the house. Under Faith's gaze, he sat down and stared back. Despite their eye contact, both seemed relaxed, and Rachel got the impression this was part of their normal routine.

"Let's go, Rachel. I think I have some of that delicious chicken salad left." Faith gave Swan a gloating look before climbing the stairs to the back door.

"That's just mean." Rachel couldn't look at Swan again as they went inside. She wouldn't be able to resist those big eyes.

❖

Rachel sat next to Violet on a couch in Casey Meadows's photography studio. Violet swiped and tapped her way through samples on a tablet. Rachel had checked out Casey's work on social media and on her website. She agreed with Faith's recommendation. Casey took beautiful pictures. She tried to focus on the tablet screen and Violet's comments on the samples, instead of on Faith.

Casey had gone to get them some drinks while they looked over the samples. Faith wandered around the studio, the soles of her sneakers shushing across the floor. She touched every light stand and tripod she passed. She dragged her fingers over the surface of a long table pushed against a wall, tripping them over a camera and a closed laptop.

"You know that stuff is probably expensive," Rachel said.

"She's fine." Casey came in and set three bottles of water and a Diet Coke on the table near Faith. "I'm used to her putting her hands on everything she sees." Casey winked, and Faith gave her a sarcastic smile.

Rachel stood and crossed the room. She accepted one of the water bottles from Casey. A framed photo from Casey's wedding held a place of honor over a work table among some other shots. Rachel leaned in to get a better look.

"My son took that one. But the others are mine."

Casey and her wife, both wearing white, held each other and smiled at the camera. Casey was cute—blond—great smile—probably just Faith's type. Casey's wife was gorgeous as well. Maybe Faith would be more drawn to the curvy brunette.

"Was Faith your wedding planner?"

Faith spun around and gave Rachel a warning look.

Casey glanced between them, then said, "No. It wasn't one of Faith's galas. We had a very small ceremony and reception. Just close family and friends."

"Hey, I can do small." With a pointed glance at Rachel, Faith crossed the room and sat down right next to Violet. She scooted closer and studied the photo on the tablet.

Rachel pretended not to care how little space remained between Violet and Faith. She glanced back at the photo, then at one beside it that included a college-aged man and an older man who resembled Casey's wife.

"That's my son and my father-in-law."

"You have a beautiful family."

"Thank you."

"How old is your son?"

"He would tell you he's *almost* twenty-one."

Rachel nodded, having a faint recollection of that time in her life. "That's really the last time you want to be *almost* an age, isn't it? I'm thirty-seven, and I wouldn't say that I'm almost forty."

"You can't be. You barely look old enough to be thirty."

From across the room, Violet scoffed. "Don't bother. She doesn't appreciate her baby face and perfectly unlined skin."

Rachel smiled. "I'm starting to, the older I get. The women in my family age well, I guess."

"Casey, your pictures are great. I really hope you're available for our wedding, or I'm going to be very mad at Faith for bringing me here and teasing me." Violet set aside the tablet.

"Of course, I checked the date with her first. What kind of wedding planner do you think I am?" Faith stood and moved aside so Casey could sit down beside Violet. "I'll let you two talk about the creative stuff. Casey, when you get ready to talk logistics, let me know and I'll jump in."

Faith had barely crossed the room before Casey and Violet were having an animated conversation about wedding photos. Rachel turned back to the photos on the wall, but she sensed Faith's presence beside her.

"What the hell was that?" Faith spoke quietly, but her voice was hard.

"What?"

"I don't appreciate the implication about me."

"What do you mean?"

Faith grabbed her arm and pulled her into the hallway outside of Casey's studio, where they couldn't be so easily overheard. "You know exactly what I mean."

She did. And maybe she'd overstepped, so soon after they'd agreed to be friendly for the duration of the lead-up to the wedding. But the idea of Faith with either Casey or her wife had caused her to react without thinking. She jerked her arm free. "The *implication* that you did something with Casey—something that I know for a fact you've done with more than one other bride? I think that's more a truth than an implication."

"Casey is a friend. And you're being disrespectful."

Rachel laughed harshly. "Oh, it's so funny to hear you talking about respect."

"Shit, Rachel. Regardless of what you think of me, I'm not an animal. I don't sleep with every woman I meet. You should be careful. You're starting to sound jealous."

"I'm not. I'm just wondering how small and *close* the whole wedding-services community is." She felt petty, even as she said it. But she couldn't stop judging Faith. Before, she'd been offended for Jack and all the intended spouses. Now, she also disapproved, because she felt Faith was better than such shallow behavior.

Faith stared at her and tilted her head. Rachel had expected an angry retort or some sort of acerbic comeback. Faith's friendly smile and flirty wink surprised her.

"Well, that depends on what *services* you require." There was the expected sarcasm, but her words didn't have their usual bite. Her eyes sparkled with humor, and she seemed to be enjoying the snippy exchange. Her expression grew more serious but remained soft. "We do travel in the same circles professionally. She's a friend, never anything more. She's also the photographer I recommend first. She not only takes beautiful pictures, but she always has new ideas instead of just following the trends. Violet's pictures won't be the same as the ones of every other wedding this year."

"Okay. If you say she's it, I'm in."

"That was easier than I expected."

"It doesn't hurt that I've already seen her awesome portfolio." Rachel considered the range of emotions between them in the last several minutes. After Faith's initial gut reaction, she'd settled down and taken Rachel's barbs with patience. Perhaps Rachel needed to respond in kind. "So, should I wait until tomorrow to call you and apologize for being a bitch? Or just get it over with now?"

"I accept. But you're welcome to call me tomorrow, just to chat, if you want to." Faith's natural flirtation was back, and Rachel envied the way she so easily sloughed off Rachel's earlier slight.

"Hey, guys," Violet said as she stuck her head out of the studio doorway. "We're ready for you in here."

Faith nodded, then turned back to Rachel. "I guess we should get back to business."

Rachel didn't want to be disappointed that their time alone together had come to an end. As Faith went inside, she passed too close to Rachel, her shoulder brushing Rachel's breast in what she was sure was a deliberate move. Rachel intended to glare at Faith, but she didn't even turn around to gauge Rachel's reaction, so she ended up staring at her blue jean-clad backside. When she pulled her eyes away, she found Violet's curious gaze. She scowled and forced her mind back to wedding planning.

CHAPTER NINE

"Where is my damn cake?" The angry bride paused with her dress pulled halfway up her torso. She'd just stepped into the center of it as Faith passed on the news that the bakery delivery was running late. She clutched the dress in one hand and shook her other balled-up fist in the air. Despite her size and the exposed miles of white fabric and lace, she was still a formidable sight.

Faith's clients tended to fall into one of two categories. Either they were content to let Faith handle everything, or they micromanaged every detail. Only a few wound up on the spectrum in between. This particular bride had been persistent and detail-oriented from the start.

"Don't worry. The cake will be on the table at the reception, and no one will know it was late." Faith glanced up from the text she'd just received from the manager of the bakery.

"I can't believe they're cutting the delivery so close. I won't recommend them to any of my friends." The bride pulled the straps of her dress up over her shoulders and turned so that her mother could zip the back.

She spun around and waited for her mother's reaction. Faith paused and granted them this moment. Her mother gave a subtle nod, and the bride visibly relaxed.

"You look beautiful, honey." Her mother's eyes welled up.

"Okay, no tears. We don't have time to touch up that makeup." Faith set her phone aside and stepped in. She took the bride's hands in hers. "You're about to marry the man you love. We have planned an amazing day—*your* day. And I won't let anything go wrong. Okay?" She waited while a cycle of emotions ran across the woman's face. When she settled on happiness with only a touch of remaining anxiety, Faith smiled. "Let's go get married."

Faith walked the bride, her wedding party, and her parents down the hallway to the area they would stage in until it was time to enter. She turned to the mother of the bride. "Mom, this is where you leave us. I have an usher waiting to escort you to your seat."

After a quick hug, made a little awkward by the care taken not to wrinkle the dress, the mother hurried into the sanctuary. A few minutes later, Faith sent the bride down the aisle on the arm of her father. She stood behind the last row of pews and watched the ceremony, slipping out for a moment to confirm that the cake had indeed been set up in its place of honor.

She spent the next two hours guiding the flow of events as the wedding guests moved from the ceremony to the reception. The bride and groom had chosen to get married in the same church his family had belonged to for three generations. Conveniently, the church had an adjacent reception hall large enough to accommodate their lengthy guest list.

After dinner, the cake-cutting, and toasts, the dancing got underway. Faith finally allowed herself to sip the glass of champagne the father of the groom had foisted on her. She never ate at her weddings, but she did allow herself one glass of wine or bubbly. She considered that her chance to toast the couple she'd been working so closely with for months.

"Job well done," the groom's father said as he raised his own glass. Faith had liked him from the first time she met him. He had a quick smile, which made his thick, gray goatee twitch. His wavy hair, a shade more silver than his facial hair, swept back from his broad forehead.

"Thank you. Your son and daughter-in-law were a joy to work with."

He laughed, his sizable belly jumping. "I've met the girl. You don't have to snow me." When she started to protest, he held up a hand. "She's sweet and generous, and I'm very glad my son found her. But she's a handful."

Faith watched the couple glide across the dance floor with the ease of two people who'd danced with each other many times before. The bride gazed at the groom and he smiled back. He said something that made her laugh, then twirled her away and back again.

"Well, he seems to know how to handle her. They're great together." She clinked her glass against his.

❖

"Oh, my God, this is the best thing ever." Rachel popped another bite of shrimp-stuffed artichoke into her mouth. "I didn't mind that you guys went to the florist on your own, but I would have been pissed if you'd done this without me."

Violet nodded, not speaking around her own mouthful, and Jack gave her a thumbs-up. Faith didn't look as enthusiastic as she took a bite, then placed half of the appetizer back on her plate.

"The artichoke is a popular appetizer for almost any season. It's nice if you pair it with a cheese and olive plate." Wes, the manager of the catering company, pushed the appetizer plate aside, then set down a couple of salad choices for them to try.

As soon as they'd arrived at the catering company, they'd been escorted to a room with a view of the kitchen through a wall of large windows. Wes had invited them to sit at a dining table set for four. He'd filled water glasses as they unfolded their napkins and placed them on their laps.

After trying the salads, Jack pointed his fork at one of the plates. "Definitely this one."

"I agree." Rachel liked the simpler of the two salads—a straightforward tossed salad garnished with sunflower seeds and a light vinaigrette.

"I don't know if that one is fancy enough. I like the beet salad with whatever kind of cheese this is," Violet said. "What do you think, Faith?"

Faith wrinkled her nose. "I don't love the dressing on the beets."

"That's a citrus dressing. We could try something different, but that one is typically well received." Wes seemed partial to the beet salad as well.

"Your call, Vi. It's all salad to me," Jack said.

Violet set her fork down with conviction. "I want the beet salad."

Wes made a note on his tablet, then gestured to his kitchen employees to bring in the entrée samples. They all tasted a salmon dish, chicken, and a vegetarian selection of some type of mushroom and squash. Rachel didn't care for the salmon, but the other two choices tasted okay to her. So far nothing had topped that artichoke appetizer.

"I like the chicken. What kind of cheese is on top of the portobello?" Violet took another bite of the vegetarian dish.

"That's a quenelle of warm goat cheese."

"I'm in for the chicken, too." Rachel enjoyed the roasted chicken served on top of a red potato cake. The chicken wasn't dry, and the potatoes were creamy and well-seasoned. "But you probably need a vegetarian option, too. Don't you have a several guests who would appreciate that?"

"Once the guest list is finalized, we can send Wes numbers for both main courses." Faith hadn't tasted either of the entrées.

"Are you not hungry?" Rachel asked.

Faith shook her head. "This is my second tasting today. And my fourth this week. Believe it or not, no matter how delicious, you *can* have too much wedding food."

"You have that many clients at the same stage of planning?"

"Five weekends in a row. Spring is a very busy time for weddings. The temperatures are just right for outdoor weddings."

"Wow."

"I'll take the work where I can. It'll get a little crazy for a few weeks as you all reach the home stretch. But I usually find that all the enthusiasm the couples have is contagious, and I manage just fine."

"I know we're inside six months, but that seems so far away still." Violet continued to pick at the two entrée choices.

"It'll go by faster than you expect," Faith said.

"Yeah. If you think about it—next week is Thanksgiving. Then once we survive the holidays, you really have only five months." Rachel felt unprepared for the upcoming holidays. Between work and helping Violet, she hadn't even started her Christmas shopping yet. Typically, she would be finishing up by next week.

"Speaking of Thanksgiving, are we still celebrating early with your folks?" Violet put her hand on Rachel's arm as she spoke.

"Yes. I think Mom is already baking the pies."

"Faith, what are you doing Sunday?" Violet asked, ignoring Rachel's glare.

"I—uh—nothing really."

"We're having dinner with Rachel's parents. You should come." She finally looked at Rachel. "What? You know your mom won't mind. She loves when you bring people over."

Rachel glanced at Faith, trying to gauge from her expression whether she was seeking permission or looking for an out. She couldn't imagine Faith spent this much time with her other clients outside of the normal planning business. Maybe she'd prefer not to but didn't want to be rude to Violet. Well, Rachel wasn't concerned with making things easier for Faith.

"My parents are going to my sister's for Thanksgiving, so we're having a small dinner with them this weekend. I say small, but she makes enough food for an army. There'll be plenty. She'd just have less to box up and force on us when we leave."

"I've seen your grocery list. I don't know if I should deprive you of a home-cooked meal, even if it is leftovers."

So she was hoping to decline, then. Rachel shrugged. "Your call."

"Hey, that was a joke. If you're sure it's okay, I'd love to come to dinner. What can I bring?"

"Just your appetite. Maybe skip a few more tastings. Mom knows they're leaving the next day for a week in South Carolina, but she still cooks like they might be snowed in for weeks."

"I'm certain I can summon a sufficient appetite for you—for dinner." Faith grinned, indicating the slip was deliberate.

Rachel's face flushed hot. Violet was too wrapped up in self-satisfaction at having issued the invitation to notice the much-too-intimate exchange between Rachel and Faith.

❖

"Are you mad that I invited Faith?" Violet asked from Rachel's passenger seat. Rachel had picked up Violet and Jack on her way out of town. Violet always complained about the monotony of the hour-and-a-half drive out Interstate 40 to reach Rachel's childhood home. Rachel didn't enjoy the drive as much in November as she did at other times. The colors of autumn had faded to brown, and the trees were mostly bare, skeletal remains of Rachel's favorite fiery season.

"No. Why would I be?"

"Sometimes you two seem to get along, and other times it's as if you can't stand each other."

Rachel shrugged but didn't take her eyes off the road. "We're not besties. But I'm okay sharing a meal with her."

"I almost invited her to ride up with us, but I figured that'd be pushing my luck."

"That's never stopped you before, dear." Jack met Rachel's eyes in the rearview mirror and grinned at her.

Rachel pictured Faith in the passenger seat beside her, instead of Violet. Apparently, her imagination put Violet in the backseat, if not out of the car altogether. What would she and Faith talk about during the drive? She didn't know much about Faith, other than her profession. Maybe they would tell each other about their childhoods or talk about their hobbies. Now that she'd begun to see new layers to Faith, she suspected there was even more to learn.

She shook the fantasy free. Layers or not, Faith wasn't the woman you took home to meet the parents. And she didn't need to delude herself into thinking otherwise. Maybe Faith would get lost on the way there and decide to turn back. No. Rachel had given her the correct address, and the directions getting off the interstate were so simple Faith's phone map likely wouldn't screw it up.

She resigned herself to being polite and took comfort in knowing that her mother would probably handle most of the small talk. Her mother loved meeting Rachel's friends. She worried about Rachel living in what she thought of as a big city. She took comfort in knowing Rachel had people she could count on if she needed anything. Rachel would let her mother think Faith was one of those people if it meant getting through this day unscathed. But she couldn't afford to let herself believe it.

Thirty minutes later, she turned into the U-shaped driveway in front of her parents' house. The white house with black shutters was traditional and modest, but well kept up. The lawn was neat, and the shrubs had probably been recently trimmed. Her father was a man of routine and typically took care of the landscaping on Saturday mornings. When she was growing up, her mother would visit yard sales while he worked outside. After she returned, she'd show him her treasures and describe her plans for him to restore the outdated items she'd found. Unfortunately, the hand-me-down clothes she bought couldn't be transformed into something unrecognizable. So when Rachel went to school in them, an older girl realized they used to be hers. Rachel was picked on at a time when she was already self-conscious around other girls because she was gay. Rachel had gotten a job babysitting her neighbor's hellions, and the next year she paid for her own, brand-new, wardrobe for school.

Faith's SUV pulled in right behind her. Rachel inched to the right of the drive, expecting Faith to follow. She got out and walked back to Faith's car.

"You weren't kidding about growing up in the country." Faith circled her car and opened the passenger door. She lifted out a bouquet of flowers and a plastic storage container.

Violet looked pointedly at the container.

"You'll see." Faith gestured toward the front door. "Shall we? Rachel, it looks like I'll be meeting your mother, after all."

Violet looked at Rachel. "What does that mean?"

Rachel shook her head. "It's just a joke." She moved in front of Faith and headed up the walk to the front door.

❖

Faith hung back and let the others go into the house ahead of her. From Nashville, Rachel's parents lived in the same direction as Faith's home—just farther out. For her, the drive took a little over an hour. Not long after she got off the interstate, she realized she'd caught up to Rachel's car. She'd slowed and stayed patiently behind Rachel, who apparently drove more cautiously than Faith did.

Inside, Rachel's family home felt warm and inviting. They walked into a family room, filled with an oversized sofa and love seat. Family photos graced every wall. None of it resembled the formal living room and framed art in Faith's mother's house. Here, Faith felt like she could just come in, sit down, and be welcomed.

"Come in the kitchen and meet Sharon." Violet steered her toward the next room, behind Rachel.

The kitchen smelled amazing. Faith detected turkey, some kind of baking bread, and aromas she associated with homemade stuffing and yams. Here again, the finishes were older and clearly well-used, but the space was clean and homey. Nearly every inch of the Formica countertops was covered with some type of casserole or other dish. A basket with a cloth napkin folded over its contents hinted at the bread Faith smelled.

"Hey, Mom." Rachel crossed the kitchen and hugged the older woman fussing over a pot on the stove. The woman half turned, while continuing to whisk, and smiled. She was shorter than Rachel, but Faith saw a resemblance around her warm, brown eyes. Her hair was the same length as Rachel's, but curlier and more carefully styled.

"Hi, sweetie." She gave Rachel a one-armed hug. "Come on in, kids. I'm watching my gravy so I can't greet you properly."

"Where's Dad?"

"He's tinkering in the garage. Something's wrong with his truck."

"Sharon, this is Faith, our wedding planner." Violet looped her arm through Faith's and pulled her forward. Rachel's eyes followed the motion, lingering on Violet's hand.

"It's lovely to meet you." Sharon glanced back at the pot, and apparently satisfied, she moved it off the burner.

Faith eased her arm free, stepping forward to cover the reason for her separation. "Mrs. Union, thank you for including me. These are for you." She handed over the flowers, then held out the plastic storage container. "These are my favorite brownies. I don't like to show up empty-handed, but I wasn't sure if you'd planned for dessert. If not, these are great. If so, I don't want to impose on your menu, so maybe you could take these along for a snack on your trip."

"Why, thank you. Please, call me Sharon." She beamed at Faith. "Rachel, get a vase. Those will make a lovely centerpiece for the table. I did make dessert, but judging from the way the girls are looking at these, I'll have to share some of them."

Rachel pulled a clear vase from a lower cabinet. Faith stepped close and handed her the bouquet. As Rachel arranged the flowers in the vase, she asked quietly, "Who are you?"

Faith winked. "Your mom likes me already."

CHAPTER TEN

When dinner was ready, Faith, Rachel, and Violet helped Sharon transfer everything to the dining-room table, while Jack went to the garage to get Rachel's father. When they returned she introduced him to Faith, and they all sat down. Sharon said grace, and they began passing dishes overloaded with food. Rachel's parents sat at either end of the table. Rachel took her usual place to her father's left, and Faith sat down beside her, their thighs bumping together as they settled into their chairs. Rachel glanced across the table at Violet and Jack and wished there'd been a way for her to sit next to one of them instead. This close, everything almost felt real. She could easily imagine touching Faith's arm during casual conversation. But she and Faith weren't a couple, despite the cozy scene at this dinner table.

"Did you figure out what's going on with the truck, Sam?" Sharon asked.

"Not yet, but we're taking your car tomorrow anyway. It'll keep until we get back in town."

"It's time to trade that old thing in, Dad."

"Nonsense. They don't make trucks like that anymore."

"It's a 1979 Ford pickup. He's been driving it since I was a kid." Rachel spooned green-bean casserole onto her plate.

Faith lifted her own plate. "That looks delicious. Load me up."

Rachel plopped a spoonful on the edge of her plate so heavily that it tilted, and Faith almost dropped it. They both reached for it at once. Rachel's fingers got there first, and then Faith's hand covered them.

"Sorry. I've got it." Faith's fingertips tickled the back of Rachel's hand in what had to be a deliberate caress. Rachel jerked her eyes up to Faith's face and found her staring back intently. She wore light makeup, almost undetectable, except around her eyes where her charcoal eyeliner and mascara made her light eyes seem electric. She flashed on the image of Swan's eyes and laughed out loud.

"What's so funny?" Faith asked.

Rachel eased her hand free slowly, so as not to upset the balance of the plate again. "I just realized you and your cat have the same eyes. I didn't see it without the eyeliner. But—when I say it out loud—it sounds ridiculous."

"Yes, it does." Violet's voice broke the spell between them. "You have a cat?"

"A barn cat." Faith gave Rachel a strange look, then cleared her throat and shifted her eyes to Sam. "I think it's great that you're holding on to your history. And you're right. Vehicles these days are all plastic and cheap paint jobs."

"The body's in great shape. I had to put a new engine in her several years back, but she's been running like a champ until this week." Sam grabbed a roll and handed the basket to Violet.

"Enough car talk," Sharon said, "Tell me about the wedding planning. How is it going?"

"Mom is obsessed with weddings because she and Dad didn't have one. They ran off together and eloped."

"Rachel says that because it sounds more romantic than saying we went to the courthouse, which is more accurate."

Faith laughed. "It's never too late for a wedding. You could renew your vows."

"Oh, that's a great idea. Maybe I'll hire you to plan the ceremony."

Rachel coughed, nearly choking on the sip of water she'd just taken.

"You okay, Rach?" Violet asked, a huge grin on her face.

"Yeah, I just—" She struggled to clear her throat. "Mom, I don't think you need a wedding planner." More specifically, *this* wedding planner. "If you want to have a party, we could plan something together."

"We could finally have the big shindig we couldn't afford back then." She turned to Faith. "Her father and I didn't have much money. But we did have quite the secret back then."

"This is where she says, when my sister came along less than seven months later, they were too happy to care if anyone bothered to do the math." She glanced pointedly at her mother. "Now who's embellishing the story to make it sound more romantic?"

She looked at Faith, expecting to find her usual cynicism in her expression. But instead, her features softened with something Rachel couldn't identify.

"Faith, will you spend Thursday with your family?" Sharon asked.

"No. My parents both live out of town. I sometimes visit one of them on Christmas. But Thanksgiving's not a big holiday for us."

"Well, we're glad you joined us today." Sam raised his water glass in salute.

"Thank you."

The rest of the dinner conversation stayed light, meandering from talk of holiday traditions to whether any of them thought Nashville would have bad weather that winter. The past several years, the area had moved away from the typical ice storms and into higher-than-usual snowfall. The mild autumn they'd been having had begun to give way to cooler temperatures. Typically, they would get several warmer days, when the sky was clear and sunny, well into December and sometimes January.

After dinner, Rachel began stacking their empty plates. When her mother stood to help, Rachel waved her off. She gathered a fistful of silverware and put it on top of the plates.

"You know the deal. I can't cook, but I can wash dishes. That's my contribution to dinner."

"I'll help." Faith gathered several glasses and headed for the kitchen before Rachel could argue.

"Me, too." Violet picked up a bowl of leftover food. "Sharon, you go relax. Jack and Sam can keep you company. We girls will handle this."

Rachel ran a sink full of hot, soapy water while Faith and Violet cleared the table. She loaded what she could in the dishwasher, but she would scrub most of the larger serving dishes in the sink.

"The table is clear. What should I do with the leftovers?" Violet asked as she set the platter of turkey on the counter.

Rachel pointed to a lower, corner cabinet. "Rubbermaid containers are in there. It should all fit in the fridge. Mom will probably try to foist most of it off on us when we leave."

"I'll dry." Faith picked up a towel and moved to the sink.

Rachel dipped her hands into the water and began the familiar task of scrubbing dishes with baked-on food. When she was growing up, her mother had wanted to teach her to cook, even tried to foster an interest in baking. But Rachel just didn't enjoy it. Sharon said she wasn't going to walk away from the table with no effort put into the meal. So she sent her to the sink. Rachel suspected Sharon thought she'd hate washing dishes so much that she'd start participating in the meal prep. But she actually found the chore somewhat peaceful. Plenty of evenings she stood at the sink, looking out the window at the sun setting in their backyard. Even as an adult, she enjoyed this as a time of reflection on her day and planning for the next.

"Are either of you going Black Friday shopping next weekend?" Faith dried a bowl and set it aside. As she took the next one from Rachel, their fingers brushed. Rachel's tingled, but if Faith was affected, she didn't show it.

"Jack and I are. And I've almost convinced Rachel to meet us."

"Do you have a lot of family to buy for?"

"Jack has three siblings that all have kids, from toddlers through teenagers. I'll buy for a few friends and family, then help him shop for his family."

Rachel laughed. "He's really bad at it. His family was happy when he started dating Violet, if only for the upgrade in birthday and holiday gifts."

"We're going to hit up some of the hot deals early. One of his nephews is dying for some new video game. Then later in the day, I want to register for some wedding gifts while I have Jack with me."

"I won't be out and about too early. If I meet you, it'll be mid-morning," Rachel said.

"Do you want to join us, Faith?" Violet asked before she ducked her head into the fridge to load in a stack of leftovers.

"No, thanks. I'm not much for shopping."

On one hand, Rachel wouldn't mind spending part of her day with Faith. But she wasn't in the mood for the awkwardness that came along with spending time with Jack and Violet as well. That's why she wasn't thrilled with Faith's inclusion today. Though nothing more had transpired between Faith and Violet, she still watched them closely when they were together. Having Jack around, as well, made her nervous.

Faith added, "I have a busy week preparing for a mid-December wedding. Then, starting Thanksgiving Day, I'm forcing myself to take a long weekend off from planning. If the weather holds up, I'll do some work around my place."

"If you change your mind, you've got my number." Violet winked. Rachel tensed, and the gravy boat she'd just finished washing slipped from her fingers and plopped back into the water. She winced and fished it out, turning it over to inspect for cracks. She'd be in trouble with her mother if she broke her favorite gravy boat.

"Is it okay?" Faith leaned over to look for herself.

"Yes. Mom would have killed me. It's part of a set that you can't even buy anymore."

"You'd be scouring eBay, huh?"

Rachel nodded. She exaggerated carefully transferring the gravy boat into Faith's waiting towel.

"You good?" Faith asked quietly.

"Yep." Rachel turned away and began putting the dried dishes into the cabinets. She didn't want Faith's concern. She knew she'd overreacted to Violet's flirty comment. Violet was a grown woman. If she wanted to jeopardize what she had with Jack, Rachel couldn't do anything about that. And despite her own confusing attraction to Faith, she had no claim on her.

❖

Rachel steered her car into Faith's driveway and slowed to a stop. She stared at the house, shaded by two large trees, confident she hadn't gone far enough up the drive to alert Faith yet. She'd spent the first half of the week working up to a closing on Wednesday. The sale had been a last-minute surprise when she'd been ready to tell her client not to expect too much action on the listing over the holidays. Her client had already turned down two low-ball offers from buyers trying to capitalize on the natural real-estate lag. This last offer had been marginally higher, but apparently enough so to tempt the homeowner. They'd countered, and the buyer accepted the terms.

She'd spent Thanksgiving alone, turning down an invitation to join Violet and Jack at his family's table. She granted herself a lazy day and loved every minute of it. She opened a bottle of wine, well before noon, took a long bath, then caught up on some reading. In the evening, she indulged her guilty pleasure and watched two romantic comedies on cable, back-to-back. She'd had a much-needed day to decompress and think about no one but herself.

She could hardly complain about having a busy summer in real estate. But since Violet and Jack got engaged, she'd spent much of her free time making sure Violet was calm and comfortable. For someone who was so together professionally, Violet tended toward anxiety when it came to her personal life. Jack had helped level her out since they'd been dating. But the engagement had flipped a switch, causing Violet to need reassurance from someone other than her fiancé. Rachel had gladly stepped into that position for her closest friend. But when this wedding was over, she would suddenly find herself with all kinds of free time and nothing to fill it but work.

She'd finished Black Friday shopping with Violet and Jack just an hour ago, turning down a late lunch with them. As she drove, she headed in the opposite direction from her place. Now, she blamed her inactivity yesterday for her lack of desire to spend another day at home alone. So after a long drive in the country, she found herself close to Faith's property.

Ignoring the voice in her head that told her to back out of the driveway and go home, she advanced up the drive and parked next to Faith's car. Showing up here without calling was probably a mistake. But the gravel crunching under her tires had likely already signaled her arrival, so it was probably too late to leave. She got out and was about to head for the house, when she heard a noise coming from the partially opened door to the barn.

She detoured that way, and as she reached the door, she called, "Hello?" She paused just inside, letting her eyes adjust to the dimmer interior light.

"Hey." Faith stood at the far end of the space holding a sledgehammer. "All done shopping?"

Rachel nodded.

"So what are you doing here? Not that I mind."

Rachel shrugged. "I went for a drive and ended up here. What are you working on?"

Faith lifted the sledgehammer slightly. "I'm ripping out the rest of the old stalls. It's the last bit of demo before I can finally start building in here. Do you want to help?"

"Sure."

"You're going to get dirty." Faith gestured to Rachel's jeans and hoodie. "I probably have some old clothes you can put on."

"An old T-shirt would be great. These jeans are fine." She didn't want to ruin her sweatshirt. But also, given the moderate temperature today, she'd likely get overheated in such a thick layer.

Faith nodded and headed to the house. While she was gone, Rachel wandered around the barn, recalling Faith's vision for the space. She'd half joked about being in over her head, but she clearly had a passion for this project. She actually had a good idea here. As a wedding planner, being able to also offer venue space could allow her to help her clients control their costs. And having space that could be used for events other than weddings gave Faith another source of income and contacts for future business.

Faith returned and handed Rachel a red T-shirt. Rachel glanced pointedly at the open space, then back at Faith. She made a circle with her finger, indicating Faith should turn around. Then, she stripped off her hoodie and pulled the shirt over her head. It smelled clean and the fabric was soft, probably from many washings.

"Okay."

Faith turned back around, donned clear safety glasses, and held out a pair to Rachel. "You'll need these." Then she lifted the sledgehammer. "Do you want the first swing?"

"Yeah? I'm honored." Rachel stepped forward and took the heavy tool. She pointed at a panel on the end of the first stall. "Here okay?"

"Have at it." Faith folded her arms over her chest and grinned.

Rachel's first swing didn't do more than rattle dust off some of the boards. "Wow. If I wasn't such a secure lesbian, that would be embarrassing."

"Try again."

Her second attempt knocked loose a couple of boards. Faith picked up a pry bar. For the next hour, they tore apart several of the stalls. Their conversation centered around the progress of the demolition—what projects Faith would do herself and which she would contract out. She didn't plan to do any of the electrical herself. She'd hired a plumber to get the pipes in the right location and by code, but she would install the sinks and fixtures herself. And she'd need help with some of the carpentry. She'd also already talked to a caterer she knew about consulting on the design of the kitchen. She wanted it to be the most efficient it could be for the type of people who would use it most—who better than a caterer to help?

When Rachel's arms started to burn and the hammer got too heavy, she switched with Faith for the crowbar. They piled the salvageable wood to one side. Faith had plans to reuse it in building the furniture for the space. Faith pulled the trailer up to the back of the barn, and they loaded the pieces that were too rotted or damaged.

After one trip back from the trailer, Rachel paused to watch Faith work. Faith swinging a sledgehammer was a surprisingly arousing sight. The sleeves of her T-shirt had been cut off, and her arms and shoulders showed more strength and definition than Rachel expected. She'd pulled her hair back into a ponytail, but several sweat-dampened strands clung around her face. Each swing seemed full of barely controlled energy, as if she put all of herself in the motion.

As Rachel approached, Faith stopped and turned around. As she did, she moved into a slash of late-afternoon sunlight streaming through a window. She squinted. Rachel stood close enough to see the freckles sprinkled under Faith's eyes and over the bridge of her nose.

"With the right decorating choices, this place will be an appealing venue." Rachel spoke more to distract herself than to start a conversation.

"That's what I'm hoping for. I don't want to clutter it with too much of the rustic stuff that some folks use. I won't hang a bunch of metal signs and such. I'm going for more elegance. I want it to be a blank slate against a backdrop of quality wood finishes and interesting lighting. Then, as a planner, I can work with them to personalize the space for each event." Faith leaned on the sledgehammer and studied Rachel for a moment. Rachel broke their eye contact under the guise of looking around the interior of the barn. "I imagine that's much the same thing you do when working with clients who want to sell their homes."

"Yeah, absolutely. You want people to walk in and envision their life playing out here as opposed to seeing yours."

"You get it." Faith seemed very happy with her understanding. "I do."

"Okay. Let's call it a day. Remember, this is still technically a holiday weekend. We can't work too hard."

"Thanks for letting me help. The physical activity felt good. I don't get too much of that in my line of work. Maybe I should start flipping houses so I can get my fix."

"Or you could just come over here and help me with this beast of a project. That's a lot less risky than investment real estate."

"True. You've already taken all the risk here. It's stress-free for me." Rachel smiled.

"Come on in the house. You can shower and I'll give you some fresh clothes."

"I should just get home."

"Suit yourself. I'm offering a hot shower with an amazing blackberry-scented soap, but if you'd rather drive home dirty..." Faith walked out the door, calling over her shoulder, "Thanks for your help today."

Rachel followed her outside and hesitated when she reached the gravel parking area. Faith kept going toward the house. Rachel glanced at the safety of her car, then at Faith's back and the dark oval of sweat that dampened her T-shirt. The fact that she could so easily imagine Faith stripping off that shirt and stepping under a steamy spray should have chased her into her car. But instead, she headed for the house, too.

"Well, since you have blackberry soap, how can I refuse?"

"Exactly."

Faith showed her to the guest bathroom. Rachel followed her in before realizing how small the space was. Faith pulled a large towel from a cabinet under the sink and left it on the counter.

"I'll get you some clothes." Faith took Rachel's shoulders and moved around her, their bodies brushing as she passed. "The bathrooms in these old houses are small. I've got plans for the house, but they're all back-burnered until things are done in the barn."

"That makes sense." When Rachel's voice came out raspy, she cleared her throat. She was sure she smelled sweaty, and here she was getting all bothered by the slightest contact with Faith.

"So don't worry. When we're finished out there, I have plenty of projects in here to give you your physical fix."

Rachel nodded, thinking only of the one way she wanted to get physical with Faith. They could start right here in this room—or in the shower. She wished Faith would hurry up and leave the bathroom. Faith shuffled for the door as if she could read Rachel's mind. After she left, Rachel reached into the shower and gave the knob a quarter-turn toward cold.

Chapter Eleven

Faith took a quick shower in the master bathroom, lingering for only a moment under the lukewarm spray. She threw on some flannel pajama pants and a long-sleeved T-shirt. She left her feet bare because she liked the cool feel of the hardwood. The floors were still in decent shape, and she hoped she could save most of them. She'd seen a home-improvement show where the host feathered new boards in with the old to hide the difference between them.

She went to the kitchen, and Rachel walked in a moment later. She'd put on her own hoodie along with the sweatpants Faith had left out for her. Her damp hair looked like she'd simply dragged her fingers through it a couple of times.

"I left your T-shirt folded on the sink."

"Thanks. I'll get it later. Would you like a drink? I've got lemonade, soda, or water."

"Fresh-squeezed?"

"Is there any other kind?" She pulled a pitcher from the fridge.

"Wow. I was joking. You're really taking this whole perfect, country-farm thing seriously, aren't you?"

"So was I. This is from the frozen stuff. But it's my favorite kind." She poured two glasses and handed one over to Rachel. "It's a nice evening. Would you like to sit on the back porch?"

Rachel glanced at the front door as if she'd already decided to leave. But she visibly set that urge aside and nodded. "Sure."

Outside, Faith grabbed one of the folding chairs from the corner and pulled it toward the center of the porch. "Have a seat." She went back for the other chair and placed it beside the one Rachel was already settling into.

They sipped their lemonade in silence. The sun, now half-hidden by the horizon, painted oranges, yellows, and purples across the sky. Sometimes she couldn't believe she had this view every evening.

"You were right about the sunsets. The weddings out there will be amazing." Rachel lifted her glass toward the lawn in front of them.

"It's at least a thousand-dollar view."

"What?"

"I'm kind of hooked on those reality shows where people are shopping for vacation homes. And if one of them overlooks the ocean, they always say it has a million-dollar view. Mine's at least worth a grand, don't you think?"

"At least." Rachel laughed and glanced toward the barn again. "This isn't what I pictured you doing on a Saturday night."

"What do you mean?"

"It's a bit more low-key than I imagined."

"Because you think I'm a player?" Faith didn't need an answer; she saw the confirmation on Rachel's face. "Maybe I just get so much action while I'm working that I don't need to troll the bars for more. That is what you thought I'd be doing on a Saturday night, isn't it?" She'd intended to come across as sarcastic and bitchy, but she heard a bit of hurt creep into her tone. Rachel still judged her as a person based on one act. And Faith was tired of her superior attitude. "You think I'm one of those women who goes to a bar alone every weekend and leaves with a different woman? Hell, the bartenders even take bets on which poor, vulnerable woman will fall victim to my charms."

"I'm sorry. That was rude. I didn't intend to offend you." Rachel looked taken aback, but her apology felt more automatic than sincere.

Faith laughed harshly. "You don't know a thing about me."

"You're right. I'm sorry." Rachel reached across the expanse between them, but Faith flinched away. Rachel gave a small nod and folded her hands in her lap. "So tell me about yourself. I know you grew up in Pennsylvania. And your parents are divorced."

"You really want to start there?"

"Not if you don't want to."

"It's okay. Though I might have to add some vodka to this lemonade by the time we're through." Faith paused to take a sip. She didn't necessarily relish rehashing her childhood. But she wanted to alter Rachel's perception of her. Rachel had seen her at work, and she'd already had the tour of her homestead. Her love life was off-limits, so that left only her family.

"I was fourteen when they divorced. Mom has remarried twice, and Dad has had three wives after Mom." She watched Rachel try to cover her initial shocked reaction. "Not exactly Sharon and Sam's story, is it?"

"Well, I'll admit, it's not the world I was raised in. But it does sound like neither of them gave up looking for their soul mates."

Faith chuckled. "I love that you want to find the positive in my train wreck of a family. But my dad is a typical midlife-crisis story. Every wife is younger than the last. And my mother can't stand to be alone." Faith set her glass down on the floor beside her. "The funny thing is, every one of Mom's husbands has tried to act like a stepfather—or maybe they just wanted to assert their authority. None of them were bad guys, I guess. But I wasn't looking for another dad.

"Is it any wonder I don't believe in forever? My parents have mastered throwing away a relationship that isn't glowingly perfect. Not only that, but they could barely figure out how to be civil to each other after the divorce."

"I get it. But can't they be an example of what not to do in a relationship, instead of the blueprint for your future?"

"Hey, this little session was for information only, not so you could fix what's broken in me." Faith smiled to let Rachel know she was mostly joking.

"I'm not trying to fix you. But if I can help you see things from another angle, what's the harm?"

"All right." Faith stood and took Rachel's empty glass. She

needed some distance from the compassion in Rachel's eyes. "Can I get you anything else?"

"I'm good."

Faith stepped inside and placed their glasses in the sink, then returned to the porch. She walked to the wide steps leading to the yard and sat down on the top one. Then she lay back and stared at the sky. "I'm still getting used to how many stars I can see on a clear night. I keep finding myself out here looking at them even though I wouldn't know the Big Dipper from the little one."

"It happens quickly, too. After the sun sets, it's dark out here without the streetlights." Rachel sat down next to her and reclined back as well, bracing herself on her arms behind her. She tilted her head back and Faith had to look away. She longed to take Rachel in her arms and kiss her. She'd never held back such a strong impulse, and she struggled to do so now. She'd promised Rachel she wouldn't kiss her until she was ready, but she wasn't sure she'd be keeping that vow tonight.

"I'm not real big on examining my emotions. I prefer to act." Faith navigated back toward their previous conversation. She rolled to her hip, facing Rachel, and rested on her elbow. Rachel's expression was serious—her brows drawn in and her mouth a firm line. "I don't imagine you do anything without thinking and analyzing all of your feelings first."

"How do you manage to make that sound like a bad thing?"

"Just for a minute, try acting without thought." She skated her hand up the outside of Rachel's arm, barely touching her. Rachel closed her eyes briefly and leaned her head to the side, the tension melting away from her face. When she opened her eyes, they fixed on Faith's mouth, and Faith could already imagine the caress of her lips there. "Just feel. And react."

"I can't." Rachel sat up and turned toward her.

"You can." She rose as well and sat cross-legged facing Rachel. She traced back down Rachel's arm and lightly tangled their fingers together. Rachel let their joined hands rest between them, and Faith took that as encouragement. "Look at me."

Rachel lifted her gaze, her eyes soft and more vulnerable than

Faith had seen them before. Faith stroked her cheek with her other hand, then pushed into the soft hair at the nape of her neck.

"Stop thinking so hard. What do you want?"

"I'm not some naive bride you can—"

"What do you want?"

"I don't want—"

"Yes, you do." Faith had barely uttered the challenge when Rachel surged forward, claiming her lips.

Faith caught Rachel against her and allowed their momentum to take her backward until she was flat on her back with Rachel on top of her. Rachel was an active kisser—a fact that both surprised and delighted her. Rachel held her face between her hands and controlled the slant of their mouths together. Faith grasped her waist and followed, trying to keep up as she alternated between bruising kisses and soft caresses.

Faith stroked her hands down Rachel's back, but when she touched bare skin under the hem of her sweatshirt, Rachel froze. She planted her hands on either side of Faith and levered her upper body away, causing her hips to angle harder into Faith's. Faith smothered a groan as the pressure against her center inspired a rush of pleasure—stronger than she expected. She'd barely touched Rachel, and she wanted her so badly already. And if the tension growing in Rachel's body was any indication, this encounter was about to stop before it even got started.

"This is a bad idea." When Rachel fumbled to get off Faith, she planted her knee high between Faith's legs. Faith reflexively pressed herself harder against Rachel's thigh. She grabbed Rachel's hips and held her still.

"Wait."

"No, I'm—I shouldn't have—" Rachel jerked back and Faith let her go. Rachel clumsily rolled away from her and sat with her back to Faith. Faith could feel her growing guilt filling the space between them.

"Rachel, don't—"

"We can't do this."

Faith sat up and stared at Rachel's rigid back. She'd pulled her knees up to her chest and wrapped her arms around them. Faith wanted to touch her, but instead she pressed one fist against her mouth. "Why not?"

"You promised not to sleep with any more of Violet's wedding party."

"You don't really want to be maid of honor anyway."

Rachel's strangled laugh carried only a hint of amusement. "How can you joke about this?"

"Hey, you did it first." Faith stood and circled so she could see Rachel. She leaned against the porch railing and folded her arms over her chest. "What did you come out here for?"

"I don't know."

"That's a lie."

"I didn't come here to sleep with you."

"Maybe not." She knew Rachel wasn't the kind of girl she should be messing around with. But the attraction she'd felt for Rachel before had just gone atomic with their kiss. "I think you were just as curious about the chemistry between us as I was. And that kiss was amazing."

"I can't just forget what happened with Violet."

"I didn't know you then. Tell me you can forget that kiss."

"Come on. I know what this is. Meeting me didn't change what you were looking for."

Faith ignored the part of her that suddenly wanted to apologize for something she'd never worried about before. But Rachel wasn't asking her for apologies, only honesty. "Nothing more has happened with Violet. I don't flirt with her. I'm not leading her to think it's an option."

"I should go." Rachel stood.

"Wait." Faith scrambled to her feet, but Rachel was already off the porch. By the time Faith reached the bottom of the steps, Rachel was yanking open her car door. Faith stopped. She wouldn't chase Rachel down the driveway. She had more pride than that.

❖

Faith looked up when a chime sounded to indicate someone had entered the bakery. She'd arrived ten minutes early for her cake-tasting appointment and had been perusing the display cases. A part of her hoped Rachel would arrive early as well. She hadn't seen or spoken to her in the two weeks since their kiss. She'd sent a couple of texts with no response. She'd decided to be patient and not give in to her urge to seek her out further. It helped that she'd known she would see her during the various stages of wedding planning. Hopefully, they would arrive soon because she'd already placed an order for three dozen cookies. She would keep a few for herself and take the rest to a holiday party one of her preferred vendors had invited her to that weekend.

"Here they are," Faith said to the proprietor of the shop as Violet walked through the door with Carly behind her. Carly? She'd expected Rachel, but now she couldn't recall if Violet had told her Rachel would be with her or she'd just assumed that.

Edward, the owner of the bakery, worked behind the counter, as well as helping out with the baking. His wife was the decorator and his brother handled the books. Several small bakeries in town had made Faith's vendor list, but Edward's had been one of her favorites since they first opened the shop two years before. Faith made the introductions, and they were led to a small bistro table by the side of the counter. One of the baker's assistants placed a plate of cake samples between them. Each small square was filled with a different flavor and had a dollop of icing on top.

Edward briefly explained each of the combinations.

Violet picked up a chocolate sample with raspberry filling and took a bite. "Mmm. This is just as good as I remembered from the wedding expo."

"Today, we're going to narrow down design and flavors. Did you bring any pictures of cakes you've seen and liked—ideas you have for your wedding?" Edward asked.

Violet pulled out her tablet and unlocked the screen. She opened her photo app and turned the screen toward him. "I like several of these. But I'm open to suggestions."

Edward swiped through the photos while Faith looked over his shoulder. Most of her choices were very ornate, and all kept to a monochromatic white-on-white palette.

"We can definitely work with these. Are there elements of any of them that you especially like? Maybe we can combine them and come up with something totally original for you," Edward asked.

Violet turned the tablet back in front of her, and within seconds they had their heads together excitedly talking design. Faith stood and walked to the large window at the front of the shop. She stared out at the people walking by, still vaguely listening to Violet and Edward talk.

"Which flavor is your favorite?" Carly came to stand beside her. She held a square of vanilla cake with caramel buttercream. "This is the same bakery we used for our wedding. Do you remember my tasting?" She winked at Faith.

"I'm partial to the chocolate and peanut butter." Faith ignored the second part of Carly's inquiry. Carly had flirted dangerously with Faith during her own tasting appointment, in front of her then-fiancé. Faith was ashamed to admit that, at the time, she'd probably been even more aroused knowing they would get away with it. She'd already decided by then that she would sleep with Carly; all that remained was when.

"Married life is boring." Carly curled her lips into a seductive smile.

"You should take up a new hobby." Faith glanced at Violet, wishing she could get her alone and ask where Rachel was.

"I'd rather revisit an old hobby." Carly gave her another shot.

"It's not going to happen, Carly."

"Why not?"

"You're married."

"You didn't care when I was engaged. What's the difference?"

The difference was Rachel. As soon as the thought materialized, she shook her head as if trying to free the idea from her mind. She and Carly had enjoyed each other. But she didn't want to sleep with her again. She latched on to a reason that had nothing to do with not wanting to touch anyone but Rachel. "I don't do repeats. Too complicated."

"No exceptions?"

"None."

"Well, you're boring, too." Carly stuck out her lower lip. She probably thought she was being cute, but Faith wasn't swayed. In fact, the exaggerated pout just made her seem bratty.

Faith turned back to the table to find Violet and Edward had moved on to the cake flavors. They'd settled on a three-tiered cake, and Violet wanted a different combination for each layer. Faith sat back down at the table and half listened while they finished. When Edward had all he needed, he disappeared into the back of the bakery.

"I'm finishing this." Violet picked up the remaining cake sample.

"While we're sitting here, let's go over a couple of things on the checklist." Faith opened her own tablet. "Have you started looking at designs for invitations?"

"Not yet. Jack and I need to find time to sit down together. Our schedules aren't exactly lining up right now."

"If you're sending Save the Date cards, you'll want to get them in the mail right after the new year. The invitations should go out two months before the wedding. If you order them in the next month, they'll be printed in plenty of time. So, get Jack in a room, pick out an invitation package, and order them. Then start finalizing your guest list so that when the invitations arrive, you can prepare them to go in the mail."

"Got it. What else?"

"We're getting down to the small things. I know it seems like there's still plenty of time, but I promise that after the first of the year, those last several months will fly by. You two could talk about what kind of wedding favors you want for the reception. Have you picked out the wardrobe for Jack and the groomsmen?"

"I have ideas about what I want him to wear, but I need to get him to the shop to try some things on for me."

Carly shifted in her chair, clearly bored now that she wasn't involved. "If we're done with the cake, I'm going to take off."

"See ya." Faith didn't bother acting like she was torn up. She was starting to wonder why she'd ever found Carly attractive to begin with. Carly gave Violet a hug and swished away. Faith's eyes drifted toward her trim waist and shapely backside. Oh, yeah, that was it. But now, despite how intimate they'd been once, she felt nothing for Carly and, in fact, was a little annoyed by her. By contrast, just thinking about kissing Rachel made her heart rate accelerate. She needed to see Rachel again.

"I don't think you should sleep with her," Violet said.

"What?" Faith turned to her, still toying with the memory of Rachel stretched out on top of her.

Violet raised her eyebrows and nodded toward the door. "Carly. I don't think you should get with her again."

"Oh, no. I'm not planning on it." She didn't want to talk about Carly anymore. She wanted to know where Rachel was, but she couldn't find a smooth segue to the question, especially now that they were talking about sex.

She packed up her things and walked Violet to her car. She waited while Violet put her bag in the backseat. And when Violet leaned in to hug her, she found her moment.

"No chaperone today. I get a hug." She released Violet after a quick, casual embrace.

Violet laughed as she pulled back. "I guess so."

"Did Rachel have a showing?"

Violet slid behind the wheel of her car, rolled down her window, and closed the door. "I don't know. She just said she couldn't make it."

Faith nodded. She tapped the top of Violet's car. "Drive safely."

After Violet pulled away, Faith strolled down the block to her car. She didn't know for sure that Rachel was avoiding her. Maybe she really was busy. Her life probably didn't revolve around where Faith was and what she was doing. And Faith would do well to remember that her world didn't have a thing to do with Rachel Union.

Chapter Twelve

Rachel lifted the lower section of her artificial Christmas tree out of the box and set it in the tree stand. She crawled underneath and tightened the stand around the center post. After adding the other two pieces, she plugged in the light cords. She turned the lights on and checked to make sure all of them worked. For the next ten minutes, she moved around the tree, fluffing up the branches that had been mashed down while in the box. After she finished, she picked up her mug of cocoa and stood back to study the tree. She fussed with a few pieces. The fake tree had held up well in the five seasons she'd been using it. Her parents would have a real tree, but Rachel preferred the convenience of artificial. By the time she decorated it, stacked some wrapped gifts under it, and lit an evergreen-scented candle, she wouldn't see a real difference. She was too busy to go hunting a tree and dragging it into the house. And she despised stepping on the dropped needles in her bare feet.

She'd just opened a box of ornaments when her doorbell rang. She called, "It's open."

Violet strolled in, carrying a white paper bag. She dropped her large purse by the door.

"Is that what I think it is?" Rachel asked.

Violet held up the bag. "Homemade doughnuts from your favorite place down the street."

Rachel rushed across the room and flung her arms around Violet. "I love you." When she pulled away, she took the bag with her. As she unrolled the top of it, the smell of grease and yeast hit her. She pulled out a still-warm doughnut and savored a bite.

Violet laughed. "Did you just whimper?"

"Maybe." She shoved Violet playfully. "Leave me alone. This is my only source of pleasure these days."

"Speaking of pleasure. We missed you at the cake tasting."

"I need to cut back on sugar anyway."

"She says as she devours a doughnut."

Rachel held out the bag with the open top toward Violet. "Want one?"

"No thanks. I still have a wedding dress to fit into. And I ate cake the other day."

Rachel shrugged and set the bag aside. She would probably dip her hand back into the bag later. She pulled a couple of ornaments from the box. "Are you going to help me decorate this tree?"

"Listen, Rach, Faith said something about you being our chaperone, and it got me thinking about everything that's taken place these past couple of months. I wanted to talk to you about what happened with Faith."

"What do you mean?" She set down the ornaments and turned toward Violet. Did Faith tell her they'd kissed?

Violet gave her a disbelieving look. "I know you haven't forgotten what you walked in on."

"Oh, right." She should have breathed easier, but she didn't want to talk about Violet and Faith any more than she wanted to talk about herself and Faith.

"I need to say something, and I think you need to hear it. What I did with Faith—"

"You don't have to—"

"Yes. I do." Violet took Rachel's hands and held them loosely between them. "It was a mistake. I love Jack. But I got scared. I want to spend the rest of my life with him. And I guess I started thinking, what if I've missed out on something. Am I okay with all of the things I haven't done yet?"

"Violet—"

"But I've realized that I am. Jack is the most loving, patient, amazing guy ever. He's also exciting and passionate, and just as adventurous as I am. And I can't believe I ever risked losing him because I was afraid that getting married meant letting go of my spontaneous, a little wild side."

"I'm glad you've realized that. I would hate to think you were going into this marriage with doubts."

"I have none." Violet laughed and swiped at her damp eyes. "Good. We've cleared that up. It seems like you and Faith have been getting along lately, and for the first time, this wedding-planning thing has been fun and less stressful."

Rachel nodded, feeling guilty. She'd avoided the bakery outing on purpose. Now she would have to put her own emotions aside and become involved again.

"We really did miss you. In fact, Faith even asked about you."

"She did?"

"She didn't seem thrilled that I brought Carly along instead. Though Carly was happy. I think she wants to sleep with Faith again."

"Does her husband know that?" Rachel forced a casual tone despite the jealousy wringing in her gut.

"I don't think so. And we're not going to tell him. Besides, Faith didn't seem interested."

"No?"

"Carly was flirting hard, and Faith barely looked at her."

Rachel turned away so Violet wouldn't see the smile she couldn't hide.

"I don't think she sleeps with anyone more than once." Violet chose an ornament and hung it on the middle of the tree.

Rachel picked up her phone and scrolled through her music until she found her favorite Christmas album. She turned on the Bluetooth speaker on her bookshelves and pressed Play. Faith probably hadn't been thinking about Rachel at all. Violet's reasoning made more sense. Faith wasn't thinking about that kiss. No doubt, she would move on to the next bride or bridesmaid, if she hadn't already. If she knew what a big deal Rachel had made the whole incident in her mind, she'd probably laugh at her.

"You're still coming Wednesday night, right?" Violet and Jack were hosting a dinner party, including his boss and several of his coworkers. One of the single guys said he didn't have a date. Jack didn't think it was a big deal, but Violet begged Rachel to come so she would have an even number of guests. Then he called Jack and said he'd asked someone after all.

"I don't know." She'd thought she'd be off the hook when the dude found a date.

"You have to. When that idiot found a date, I invited Faith to even things back up."

"Uninvite her." Dinner with Faith, even a pseudo-date, was probably more than she could handle right now.

"I can't do that. Please. It's important to Jack." She clutched Rachel's arm. "This was supposed to be a simple dinner party. That's why I had it catered. I don't need this stress right now."

Rachel sighed. "Okay. I'll be there." She gave in because she was going to anyway if she had to watch Violet work herself into a frenzy. Jack should have known better than to ask Violet to host a dinner party right now. But he was probably angling for a promotion and wanted to impress his boss.

"You don't mind sitting next to her at dinner, do you?"

"No. It's fine." She should have come up with someone to bring so she wouldn't have to play Faith's date. But, she had to admit, a part of her was excited about an evening sitting next to Faith. And if she avoided being alone with her, they wouldn't have to talk about the kiss.

"Great. After we get this tree finished, do you want to come over and help me set up Jack's? He hasn't done a thing to decorate the place."

"Of course." Rachel loved decorating for Christmas. In addition to the tree, she had boxes of holiday knickknacks to set out around the house.

"We'll stop and buy an artificial tree and some decorations."

"What? He doesn't have one?"

"He says he tossed his old one when he moved to the condo. He didn't plan to put one up since I had one at my house."

"Why not just move the party to your house?"

"I need to get used to thinking of his place as mine. Besides, you've got to see the nighttime views at his condo. With the right decor, it'll be a beautiful party."

"Then let's go to your house and grab your tree. There's no time like the present to start moving in, right."

Violet smiled. "That's why I love you."

"Before we leave, we'll raid my stash. Then we'll pick up your tree and whatever else we need before we go to his place."

"What would I do without you?"

"You won't ever have to find out." Rachel picked up several ornaments and walked around the tree, already thinking about what decorations she had that might work in Jack's condo. She had some extra strings of white lights. Given the modern style of Jack's place, she thought a gray, silver, and white theme would be classy and festive.

She'd started the day thinking she should try to get out of the party. Now she was somehow immersed in helping plan the evening.

❖

Rachel nursed a glass of white wine and glanced nervously at the door. Of the ten guests, Faith was the only one who hadn't arrived. She smiled at several people as they passed by but didn't engage in conversation. When she heard the door open, she looked over, trying to make her interest appear casual.

Faith appeared in the doorway, carrying a bottle of wine and a Christmas gift bag. Her hair fell in soft waves around her face. When she held out her arms to greet Violet, her deep-red blouse pulled against her breasts in a way that made Rachel blush and turn away. Violet and then Jack hugged her. When she moved inside, Rachel snuck another glance at the door, half of her hoping Faith had brought a date so she wouldn't be tempted, and the rest of her glad she hadn't.

She stayed on the opposite side of the room from Faith as long as she could stand it. She talked to several of Jack's coworkers and even gave her card to a couple of them who expressed interest in finding a condo like Jack's. If she came out of this dinner with a few new clients, she'd count it a win. And if pretending her mind was on business helped her avoid thinking about Faith, then that was a bonus.

She'd just finished chatting with Jack's boss and his wife when Violet called everyone to sit down for dinner. As the couple walked away from her, she felt a presence behind her.

"I've never seen you work a room." Faith's voice so close to her ear raised goose bumps on her skin. "It's sexy."

"I'm not working anything." As Rachel turned, her arm brushed Faith's breasts. She took a step back.

"Judging by the way you've been handing out business cards, if it's not work, you must be looking for dates."

Rachel smiled. "With Jack's boss and his wife?"

Faith shook her head. "Hey, I don't know what you're into. But I'm not judging you." She held up her hands, palms out.

Rachel laughed and grabbed one of them playfully. "You're not, huh? So if I were into something kinky?"

"There are a number of things I would happily try for the first time with you." Despite Faith's teasing tone, her eyes promised there was truth in those words.

Rachel had no problem recalling the image of Faith wearing only her underwear. She'd seen the soft swell of her breasts and the elegant curve of her back. "We—uh, we should go sit. Violet's ready to start dinner."

"After you." Faith's lips quirked and her eyes sparkled.

Rachel narrowed her eyes, annoyed by Faith's amusement, and purposefully reminded her traitorous brain that Faith had been on top of Violet when all those enticing images had been captured. She headed for the long dining table at the far end of the large, open living area. Faith brushed her hand against Rachel's lower back as she passed. Rachel's back tingled, and pleasure bolted up her spine. She closed her eyes for the second it took to gather her composure. If she reacted this way to a caress through her clothing, she was afraid to find out what would happen if Faith touched her skin.

Jack sat at the head of the table, and Violet stood in front of the chair to his left. She gave Faith and Rachel a look, then directed her eyes pointedly at the two empty spaces at the other end of the table.

Rachel hurried into one of the chairs and gave Violet her attention as she made a small speech thanking everyone for joining them. When Violet met her eyes, Rachel smiled politely, as if demonstrating that she could be a good guest. Violet signaled the caterers, and they began setting salads in front of each person.

Thankful for something else to focus on, Rachel picked up her fork and sampled the salad. She sifted through the mixed greens searching for something that looked like plain lettuce. The dressing was nice.

"Do you think this is a mustard vinaigrette?" she asked Faith.

"Did you ask Violet if you could sit next to me?" Faith winked.

"Stop it," Rachel whispered.

Faith glanced around the table. "No one is paying any attention to us. They're all wrapped up in their little groups. We're the two sad single ladies who couldn't find a date for this thing."

"I could've had a date."

Faith's eyes turned serious. "I would have been so jealous of her."

"Faith." It was as if the kiss had allowed Faith to give her the full-court press. And Rachel didn't think she could resist. "We agreed to be friends."

"I'm trying to be friendly."

"I don't talk to my friends like that."

"I'd like to think I'm special."

"I'm sure you do." Rachel returned her attention to her salad, telling herself she wasn't disappointed when Faith took the hint and struck up a conversation with the man sitting to her left.

❖

"This place is amazing." Faith stepped onto the balcony and closed the sliding door behind her. Rachel's elbows rested against the heavy metal rail atop thick panes of glass around the edge of the small patio. She'd seen Rachel sneak away from the party and had given her ten minutes of solitude before joining her. At least once, she thought Jack had caught her glancing out the large windows to check on her.

"I know. I sold it to Jack."

Faith's shoes clicked against the slate floor as she crossed it to lean next to Rachel. The lighting had been designed to cast a muted glow on the floor for safety but not to interfere with the view of the city that Jack had no doubt paid a fortune for. The cityscape would have been breathtaking if she could keep her eyes on it and off Rachel. Rachel's black slacks and black, tailored vest had a tuxedoed air. But her white shirt, left open at the neck and deep into the vee of the vest, emphasized her femininity. The back of the vest was red satin and silky soft; Faith knew from when she'd touched it earlier in the evening. Tonight, her eyes had been made up to emphasize their mahogany depths, and a light tint of gloss drew Faith's eyes to her lips.

"This is one of your million-dollar views." Rachel glanced at her and held her eyes, catching Faith staring at her.

"It certainly is." She didn't hide the true meaning of her words.

"I meant that view." Rachel tipped her chin toward the city before them.

"It's impressive, but I gave up my city vistas for the country. Maybe I'm seeking something else worth looking at." The flirtatious remark came automatically to her lips, at least that's what she told herself to avoid taking her words too seriously.

"Be careful. Someone might confuse your intentions." Rachel turned more fully toward the night sky. In profile, Rachel had a small bump just below the bridge of her nose. The shadow just under her jaw practically invited Faith's lips.

What were her intentions? Rachel had been clear that she wasn't interested in being a one-and-done woman. Why was she still chasing her? Maybe she needed to back off—stop flirting and restore the distance between them.

She sought a more neutral topic. "What are you doing out here when the party is in there?"

"I'm—I need a break from the bride-to-be. God, that sounded ugly."

"No. I get it."

"I didn't mean—"

"Rach, it's okay." She put her hand on Rachel's arm and stroked her thumb against the inside of Rachel's forearm. When a tingle started up her wrist, she pulled away. She'd easily crossed the boundary from comforting Rachel's anxiety to testing her own restraint. "I'm a wedding planner. I understand. Right now, it's Violet's world. And it can start to seem like every time you get together, her wedding is all that's going on. You aren't the first family member to express that sentiment."

"Thanks."

"Sure. Like I said, it happens."

Rachel seemed to be considering her next words carefully. "There's this office Christmas party, and the last several years I've either gone alone or taken Violet as my date."

"And Violet's abandoning you to go on a cruise with Jack." Faith made a joke to cover her confusion. Had she just decided to back off at the same moment that Rachel had opted to move forward?

Rachel gave a nod and raised a brow. "Or I'm tired of it being all about her, as you said, and I'm looking for some fresh company."

Faith smiled and cocked one hip against the balcony rail. "Well, we do seem to be pretty good together at parties."

"So?"

"When?"

"Friday night. Eight o'clock."

Faith made a show of pulling out her phone and checking her calendar. "I'm in. What should I wear?"

"Um—it's cocktail, but nothing crazy fancy. Is that okay?"

"I can pull that off." She would definitely wear a dress, one that would turn heads. If she didn't have a suitable one, she'd use the excuse to do some shopping. Before she worried too much about impressing Rachel, she initiated another sea change. "You seem like the kind of person that has a small number of really close friends instead of a lot of casual friends."

"Is that a polite way of asking why my straight best friend is my go-to date?" Rachel laughed. "I don't have a lot of friends. I have professional acquaintances and Violet and Jack." She tacked on the reminder that Jack was a friend and she was very loyal to him. "You should talk. You don't seem to have a close circle of buddies either."

"I don't. I've always been a bit of a loner. I like a lot of alone time. I have some good friends, mostly that I've met through work."

"Like Casey?"

"Like Casey."

"Are any of them exes?"

"No." She shouldn't take pleasure in the touch of jealousy coloring Rachel's tone.

"Not even Casey?"

"Why are you fixated on her?" Faith straightened but left her hand resting on the railing next to Rachel's.

"Because she's the only friend of yours that I've met. And because she's not only beautiful, but also very sweet."

"Casey's heart has always belonged to one woman."

"How long have they been together?"

"This time? Just a couple of years."

"I'm confused."

"They were together for a long time, since college. Adopted their son together. Then they split up and were apart for a number of years. They decided to give it another shot and eventually got married. But even when she was dating other people, it was clear to me who she was meant to be with."

"That's the most romantic thing I've heard you say. It almost sounds like you believe in forever when it comes to those two."

Faith shrugged. "They still split up and missed out on all those years. It's not fate. It's two women who were willing to try again."

"We're talking about the same thing. Not a fairy tale, but they believed enough in each other to risk getting hurt and are putting in the hard work."

"Then why romanticize it? They're working at it. Most people aren't willing to do that so they throw in the towel and divorce."

"Like your parents."

Faith wasn't up for another discussion about her family history. It wasn't as if she didn't know where her commitment issues stemmed from. "So, what about this office Christmas party? Should I expect a sedate, home-by-ten-o'clock kind of evening? Or is it a wild night of drinking and dancing?"

"Hmm. Something in between. It's my boss, his wife, his boss and his husband, and a bunch of other agents. Other than a few lunches occasionally, I don't socialize with many of them, except at these get-togethers."

"Do they know—will they expect you to bring a woman, you know, as a date?"

"It's not a date."

"You know what I mean."

"Yes. I'm out at work. We won't be shocking anyone."

"Damn." Faith grinned when Rachel scowled at her. "Come on. It would have made the evening interesting. And I've never been anyone's coming-out story. In fact, I'm much more used to women refusing to acknowledge we've been together."

"Have any of your brides backed out of the wedding?"

"A few." She answered honestly, even while she hated what Rachel would assume that meant about her.

"Because of you?"

"Only one." Faith tensed her jaw. "Do you want to hear the whole sordid story?" She'd never told anyone what happened, but she would tell Rachel if she asked. Maybe she considered it penance because now she was ashamed of the way she'd acted back then. Though recounting that whole story would probably mean the end of any chance of something between them.

"No, I don't think I do." Rachel took a step toward the door. "I should probably get back inside."

When Rachel's hand touched the door, Faith spoke. "A part of me was thrilled. A horrible, petty part of me."

Rachel stopped and turned around.

"I don't want to break up any of their relationships. That's not what I'm about. But on some level—someone chose me." Across the darkened space of the balcony, she saw the immediate change in Rachel's eyes and regretted her words. Pity. The last thing she wanted. "Yeah. You're right. We should get back." She brushed past Rachel, shaking her off as she reached for her hand.

"Faith, wait."

She shoved open the door and strode inside. By the time Rachel came in a minute later, she'd already insinuated herself in a conversation with Jack's boss and his wife.

CHAPTER THIRTEEN

Rachel stood in front of the full-length mirror attached to the back of her bedroom door. She'd chosen a charcoal pantsuit with a white collared shirt underneath for the Christmas party. She'd spent yesterday afternoon wandering the women's clothing section in a department store but hadn't seen anything that she loved. So she'd bought a crisp new white shirt and pulled out her best suit.

She'd offered to meet Faith at the party, because she didn't want this to feel like a date. Her boss had arranged to host the party at his country club. Faith insisted that since she had to drive practically right past Rachel's house, she would pick her up. She said she didn't plan to drink much, given her longer drive back home. This way Rachel could feel free to enjoy her evening without worrying about her own transportation home.

Rachel had thought more than she should about their exchange on the balcony at Violet's. Faith seemed content with her lifestyle, keeping everyone at arm's length. Rachel had assumed she chose those relationships because she was unable to commit to anything more. And, on some level, her parents' history of treating marriage like a game explained Faith's attitudes. But that night, Faith had showed her more depth than she'd thought her capable of. She'd never considered that, to Faith, her parents' seeming obsession with tormenting each other translated to a feeling of rejection for her. They had obviously not been one of those couples who divorced and continued to place a priority on their child's needs. Understanding some of why Faith acted as she did still didn't allow Rachel to completely forgive her behavior. But Wednesday evening, for the first time, Rachel had seen regret from Faith, and she wasn't quite sure what to do with it.

The doorbell rang and saved her from examining her need to do anything. She answered the door and was suddenly glad she'd agreed to ride together. She needed to react to Faith's appearance in private, instead of in front of her coworkers. Faith's black dress hugged her body. The rounded neckline and half-sleeves kept the dress classy, while the hem, which ended just above her knee, gave Rachel a sinful view of Faith's sexy legs. A thin silver bracelet with some sort of twisted design encircled Faith's wrist.

"You look nice." Rachel made what she guessed would be the biggest understatement of the night. Faith looked gorgeous. But she didn't want to seem overappreciative.

"So do you. Very handsome." Faith stepped close and flattened her hand against the lapel of Rachel's jacket. "I've wanted to see you in a suit since the day we met."

"Yeah?" Rachel stared at Faith's hand on her jacket, lingering for too long on the hollow between her wrist bone and her hand. Her steel-gray manicure was an unexpected touch.

"Very much." She brushed at a piece of lint that Rachel knew was nonexistent. "Though I will admit there was something extremely appealing about the vest from Violet's dinner." She toyed with Rachel's shirt collar.

Rachel brushed away her hands. "Stop grooming me."

Faith caught her wrist and held it against her chest. "I'm trying to stick to the plan—play this strictly friendly, Rach. So, I shouldn't tell you that since I saw you in that vest, all I can think about is seeing you in *only* that vest."

Rachel sucked in a breath and yanked her hand back. "This was a bad idea."

"Okay. I'll behave. For as long as I can." Faith picked up her keys. "Come on. We both got dressed up. Let's go. I promise to be the perfect, platonic escort."

She'd told Faith she wouldn't be shocking anyone by inviting a woman tonight, but she suspected her coworkers were surprised by Faith all the same.

At the party, Rachel introduced her to her bosses and coworkers. Faith was polite and charming, and by the end of the night everyone she met seemed as captivated by her as Rachel felt. Faith had a way of finding out what mattered to a person and enticing them to talk about it. Rachel mentioned that her boss's wife had spent months planning the party. When Rachel introduced her to Faith, they talked for several minutes about the logistics of putting together an event of that size.

As much as she hated to admit it, with Faith by her side, she had the best time she'd ever had at one of these things. Faith doted on her, while still being friendly with the other guests. She'd asked her to dance, and when Rachel tried to decline, she took her hand and smoothly swept her onto the dance floor. As soon as Faith's arms came around her, she relaxed into her and let herself be led among the other couples. When Faith eased her closer, she rested her cheek against Faith's temple. She wouldn't have admitted it to Faith, but she enjoyed the envious looks she caught from several other guests—men and women.

❖

Faith got out of the car and circled to Rachel's side, but she had her door pushed open by the time she got there. Faith held out her hand to help her out. Rachel took it, enjoying the warmth against her palm. She didn't let go as they walked to Rachel's door.

When Rachel took out her keys, Faith lifted them gently from her hand. "Allow me."

"You know I see right through this gentlemanly act, don't you?" She hated to think she was falling for Faith's usual routine. She'd actually enjoyed the contrast of Faith in a smoking-hot dress acting chivalrous toward her, but she wasn't about to tell her that.

"Do you?"

"You're just trying to get me to let my guard down and invite you inside."

"And you don't want to?"

"That's a very complicated question."

Faith smiled. "I was hoping spending this evening with me might have simplified it for you."

Rachel laughed. "You were hoping the two glasses of wine I drank tonight might do that." She'd been warm and mellow after the second glass but stayed very much in control.

Faith shook her head. She leaned close and said, "No. We'll be amazing together, and I want you aware of every moment."

Rachel's head swam with the implications of those words. Could she ignore what she knew to be true and let Faith make her feel special? Was this how all of those women felt? "Would you like to come in for some coffee before you drive home?"

"That's a dangerous invitation. And one you shouldn't make lightly."

"It's just coffee. You live way out in the country."

"Such a very long drive," Faith purred. She reached around Rachel and opened the door. "After you."

Rachel walked inside, nearly trembling with anticipation. She wanted Faith's hands on her so badly that she scarcely cared anymore about all the good reasons why she should keep her distance. She went directly to the kitchen and turned on the coffeemaker. She dumped some beans in the grinder and grabbed the bag of filters. Faith came up behind her and planted her hands on either side of Rachel on the kitchen counter. She pressed against Rachel's back.

"If you're serious about this coffee thing, I'll drink it like a good girl." She grasped Rachel's waist and squeezed.

Rachel abandoned the coffee prep, turned, and pushed into Faith's chest. She laced her hands behind Faith's neck and pulled her in for a kiss. Faith responded immediately, matching her tongue stroke for stroke. Faith shoved Rachel's jacket over her shoulder, breaking her hold on Faith's neck and trapping her arms at her side momentarily.

They laughed together as Rachel whipped her arms free and dropped her jacket on the counter behind her. She yanked Faith back to her, heady with the taste and texture of her mouth. Faith pulled

Rachel's shirt free from her waistband and fisted her hands in the fabric. She pressed her cheek to Rachel's.

"Stop me now," Faith whispered.

"What?"

"You have to stop me soon, because I can't take much more."

Faith's near lack of control excited Rachel. She knew it was just ego, but she didn't care. "Don't."

Faith tensed for a second, then flexed her hands open and took a step back. Rachel followed, wrapped her arms around Faith's waist, and pressed her mouth against the side of her neck.

"I meant, don't stop."

"Are you sure?" Faith threaded her hand into Rachel's hair.

"God, yes." Rachel eased down the zipper on the back of Faith's dress. When she touched Faith's bare back, she knew she wasn't going to find her self-control.

Rachel slipped the edges of the dress off Faith's shoulder and let it pool at her waist. She unhooked Faith's bra, and Faith shrugged her shoulders out of it. Rachel caught it by one of the plum-colored, lace-trimmed cups. She met Faith's eyes, feeling every bit of the heat that filled them inside her own chest.

"Sexy." She grabbed Faith's hand and tossed her bra over her shoulder with the other. She didn't bother to see where it landed before taking Faith to her bedroom.

She pushed Faith's dress to the floor. Her fingertips felt electric every place she touched Faith, her sides, her hips, the outsides of her thighs as she guided her panties down as well. She knelt in front of Faith, easily ignoring the whisper in her head that she was about to do something very stupid. She didn't care—about consequences, about Violet, or about weddings. She just wanted Faith, and tonight she would have her.

She kissed Faith's stomach, just below her belly button, and Faith rested her hand on the back of Rachel's head. She swept her lips lower, along the crease of her hip and thigh. The scent of Faith's arousal, so close, nearly drew her mouth there, but she wanted to make this last a little longer. She straightened, planted her hand in the center of Faith's chest, and pushed her back onto her bed.

While Faith watched, Rachel stripped off her own clothes. Despite the appreciation in Faith's eyes, this wasn't a striptease. Her one objective was to be naked next to Faith. She tossed each article aside until she stood only in her panties.

She must have hesitated, because Faith said, "You can leave them on if you're more comfortable."

The plain, striped cotton panties weren't the silky, sexy kind Faith wore, but when Faith looked at her like she couldn't wait to touch her, Rachel didn't care. She took them off and got on the bed next to Faith.

Faith reached for her, and Rachel moved over her and straddled her. She bent and kissed Faith. As she eased back, Faith's eyes went to her chest. Rachel looked down and wished her breasts weren't so pendulous. Faith caught the weight of one in her hand and swept her thumb across her nipple, chasing away her self-judgment.

"You're so beautiful." Faith raised her head and caught a nipple in her mouth. Faith's teeth and tongue teased it to a hardened, sensitive point.

She arched into Faith's mouth and moaned. Faith made a move like she wanted to roll Rachel over and take charge. When Rachel pushed her hips down, to hold Faith in place, she felt her wetness paint Faith's stomach.

Whether she was willing to admit it or not, she'd admired Faith's body the first time she'd seen it, and she'd thought more times than she should about what she would do if she ever got her hands on it. She caressed down the center of Faith's chest, purposefully ignoring her breasts for fear of this ending too quickly. She scooted back and ghosted her hands over Faith's stomach and the tops of her thighs, then trailed down her legs. As her fingers touched Faith's ankle, Rachel's face was level with her center. She inhaled the scent of her. When she leaned in, she heard Faith's sharp inhalation. Instead of putting her mouth where she wanted to, she pressed her lips to the inside of her thigh.

"Touch me, Rachel." Faith's tone was demanding, and she clearly expected Rachel to comply.

She rose until her face was even with Faith's and rested her hand low on Faith's belly. "Say it again."

"Touch me."

Rachel stared at her until she seemed to understand. She needed Faith to imprint her name on this memory.

"Rachel," Faith whispered.

Rachel slipped her fingers lower, toying with Faith, teasing her but not giving her much pressure against her most sensitive flesh. She circled, easing back when Faith thrust her hips upward. She bent and let her breath blow across Faith's nipple, then traced its rigid point with her tongue. She fought against her own desperation and ignored her body's clamoring need to have Faith's hands on her as well.

"Harder," Faith demanded.

Rachel smiled. "I understand you're used to control, but that's not how this is going to go." She didn't let up, but neither did she increase in pace or pressure.

When Faith grasped the back of her hair, pleasure spiked and ran down Rachel's spine. She hissed softly, as if releasing a pressure valve that threatened her remaining thread of composure.

She opened her mouth against Faith's neck, scraping her teeth against her skin at the exact moment that she sank a finger inside her. Faith arched and cried out. Rachel stilled.

"God, Rachel, fuck me."

She ignored the command, returning her attention to Faith's breast. She teased and sucked while Faith writhed and tried to force her to move her hand again. Rachel remained inside her, steeling herself against the pull of Faith's muscles as she tried to force her deeper.

"Please." Faith's voice was pure desperation and exactly what Rachel had been waiting for.

She fell into Faith, driving her finger inside her, sucking her nipple and straddling her thigh. She stroked Faith, adding another finger when Faith rasped for more. She thrust her hips against Faith's leg until the pleasure spiraled so tight she feared losing control. She lifted herself away, holding tenuously to her determination to wait. She wouldn't come without Faith's hands and mouth on her.

Instead, she focused on reading Faith's body—pressing harder when Faith's hips surged into her. She kissed Faith hard, and Faith responded urgently, sliding her tongue against Rachel's.

Rachel tugged at Faith's earlobe and whispered, "Ask for what you want."

"I want—"

"Ask."

"Will you give me your mouth?"

Rachel smiled. "You're gorgeous when you give in."

Faith laughed. "Savor it, because it doesn't happen often."

"Oh, I intend to savor it." Rachel slid down Faith's body. She kissed Faith's stomach, then lower, beneath her navel. She slipped her tongue between her folds and touched her clit, smiling against her as Faith jerked.

"Yes." Faith tangled her fingers in Rachel's hair. "Please, don't stop." The desperate edge in Faith's voice told her that Faith feared she might do just that.

She bent and took Faith fully in her mouth, letting her know she was done teasing her. She gave Faith everything her body asked for. She met each thrust, and when Faith tightened her fingers in her hair, she ignored the desire to slip her other hand between her own legs. Faith's hips rolled and jerked, but Rachel continued to stroke her as she tensed. Faith's guttural growl felt strangled, but the flex of her fingers against the back of Rachel's head spurred her to continue licking and sucking until Faith's body relaxed. Even then, she slowed but continued to explore Faith, testing whether she could draw her to another peak.

Faith made a weak attempt to push her away. "I think I died."

Rachel kissed her stomach and chuckled against her skin. She reached up and rested her hand against the center of Faith's chest. "Still beating. Racing, in fact." She couldn't hold back a self-satisfied smile.

"That makes you happy, does it?"

"Immeasurably."

CHAPTER FOURTEEN

Faith woke up with Rachel spooned in front of her. Her chin rested against Rachel's shoulder, and her arm circled Rachel's waist. She feathered her fingers against Rachel's stomach, and Rachel stirred but didn't wake.

She couldn't see the bedside clock, but judging from the sunlight slanting low through the window, she guessed it was still early morning. They'd stayed up late last night, exploring each other, teasing, and talking, then having sex again. Sleeping over wasn't really her thing, but when they'd finished, Rachel had seemed to expect it. When she curled up against her and sighed contentedly, Faith didn't want to leave. So instead of offering her usual excuses for why she had to get home, she'd closed her eyes and pulled Rachel closer.

This doesn't have to be a big deal. Rachel already knew who she was, and she shouldn't have unrealistic expectations. Faith could just enjoy the feel of a woman lying next to her and bask in her memories of last night. She'd thought from their first meeting that Rachel was hot when she was angry. And she now knew that she was as passionate during sex as she was when she was mad. Rachel took control of her like no woman had—in a way she normally wouldn't allow. Typically, she set the boundaries in her encounters and led in the bedroom as well.

Rachel's semi-dominance of her hadn't made her uncomfortable—frustrated, maybe—turned on, for sure. But she'd felt an overwhelming amount of respect and trust underlying the raw sensuality of their time together. Now, she was getting wet again just remembering the way Rachel had commanded her body. And she was oddly excited by the juxtaposition of their carnality last night against the tenderness of waking with Rachel in her arms.

Rachel sighed and stretched, and for a moment Faith worried there might be awkwardness between them. Rachel rolled to her back and met Faith's eyes.

"Good morning."

She didn't sense any tension in Rachel's voice. "Hey."

"So, I don't really know what to do now. I've never had a one-night stand."

"Well, technically, that's not what this was. We've known each other for a few months."

"You know what I mean. I've never slept with someone I wasn't in a relationship with." Rachel tilted her head as if remembering last night, and judging by the heat in her eyes, they were good memories. "It's kind of liberating. Not having any pressure or expectations."

"Oh, I had expectations." Faith grinned. "But you blew them all away. I like it when you take control." She skimmed her hand over Rachel's belly, and her skin twitched in response. "So, I guess you've never had casual morning-after sex either?"

Rachel smiled and rolled on top of Faith. "There's a first time for everything."

Faith flung her arms over her head and gave an exaggerated sigh. "You want to talk about liberating. I never knew it was so easy being a bottom. I'd have done it years ago."

Rachel laughed and flipped the bedsheet over her head as she moved down Faith's body. With no further foreplay, Rachel swirled her tongue over Faith's clit and slipped her fingers inside her. Faith felt Rachel's hum of satisfaction against her flesh when she discovered her already ready.

❖

"Coffee?"

"Sure."

Rachel held up a ceramic mug and a travel cup. "Will that be for here or to go?" Her smile carried no bitterness about the idea that she expected Faith to bolt any time.

Faith glanced at her phone to check the time. She had a meeting with a perspective client, but not for hours yet. She slid onto a stool next to the large kitchen island. "For here will be fine."

"Cream or sugar?" Rachel set a full mug in front of her.

"Do you have skim milk?"

Rachel waved a hand down her body. "Do I look like I drink skim milk?"

"You look gorgeous. I'll take whatever you have that will lighten this stuff up."

Rachel blushed and grabbed a bottle of creamer from the fridge. She brought it and her own coffee, and sat beside Faith.

"I don't have much to offer for breakfast, but I could make some toast if you'd like."

"You have bread?"

"Don't sound so surprised. It's a staple for peanut-butter-and-jelly sandwiches."

Faith laughed. "You eat peanut butter and jelly?"

"Sometimes I get creative and make peanut butter and banana on toast." Rachel grinned. "I told you I don't cook."

"Hence Sharon's need to make enough to send leftovers with you." Faith added a bit of creamer to her coffee.

"Exactly."

"Are you going home for Christmas, too?"

Rachel nodded. "What are your plans?"

Faith shrugged. "My mom asked me to come to Kansas City."

"Are you going? How far is that?"

"Almost a nine-hour drive. And I don't know. They'll be going to her husband's family Christmas Day. I'm not thrilled about making that drive to spend the holiday with strangers."

"If you're interested in local strangers, I'm sure Mom would be happy to have you join us. I'll probably pack a bag and stay for a couple of days, but you could come for as long as you want to, the weekend or just Christmas Day."

She wanted to say yes. She liked Sharon and Sam and could easily imagine how warm and welcoming a holiday at their home would be. Images of sitting down to Christmas dinner next to Rachel, of gathering around the tree to open gifts, and of retiring to the guest room with Rachel came to mind too easily. She could go for the weekend. Between work and her property, when was the last time she'd had a couple of days of leisure?

She shook her head. She couldn't be a part of Rachel's family. That's not what this was. "Thanks. But I'll probably stick close to home. I need a few quiet days by myself to recharge before kicking things back up after the first of the year."

Rachel didn't completely hide her hurt at the rejection, but Faith could see her effort. "If you change your mind, the invitation is open."

"I appreciate it." She didn't want to let the holidays pass without seeing Rachel. "If you don't have plans for New Year's Eve, you could come out to my place."

"Are you having a party?"

A party would be safer. She could scrape together enough guests to provide an appropriate buffer between them. "No. Just me."

"Okay."

Faith lifted her mug and took a careful sip. She regretted that she couldn't accept the invite to the Union family Christmas. But she didn't want to give Rachel or her family the wrong idea. If that meant being alone for Christmas, she would just have to look forward to New Year's Eve this year.

❖

As Rachel pulled her car into Faith's driveway on New Year's Eve, she saw a glow of light coming from the other side of the barn. She got out, leaving the overnight bag she'd packed, just in case, in the passenger seat. She hadn't been entirely sure what Faith's invitation had entailed. By all accounts, two nights with the same woman wasn't Faith's thing. And she'd suggested the evening only seconds after rejecting Rachel's offer to spend Christmas with her family. But she'd brought a bag, hopeful she'd be staying. She wasn't going to push Faith, but she couldn't help but be encouraged by her desire to spend more time alone together.

She rounded the corner of the barn. The patio Faith had been planning outside the barn had been completed. An L-shaped outdoor sectional had been set up under several strings of lights. A fire crackled in a small, round fire pit. A stack of wood nearby provided enough fuel for as long as they needed.

"Hey." Rachel turned at the sound of Faith's voice. Faith carried a bottle of wine and two glasses. "I went back inside for wine."

"This is nice."

"Yeah, well, I'm not really the watch-the-ball-drop type." She gestured toward the house. "If you are, we can go in and turn on the television."

"No. I'm good here."

"Great. Sit. Make yourself comfortable."

While Faith opened the wine and poured two glasses, Rachel settled in on the sectional. She leaned against a stack of pillows in the corner. Faith handed her a glass, then sat down beside her, just on the other side of the pile of pillows. She held up her glass, and Rachel touched hers to it.

"If we get cold, we can go inside. But the fire's working so far." Faith pointed to the back of the sofa. "And I brought out blankets."

Rachel smiled, charmed by Faith's obvious desire to provide a romantic evening. She didn't want to read too much into this setup. But given how they'd spent the night of her office party, she suspected Faith knew she didn't need to woo her into bed. "It's perfect."

"But you'll let me know if you need to go in."

"I will." Despite a bit of a chill in the air, they'd been blessed with an unseasonably warm New Year's Eve. The navy-blue sweater Rachel had chosen to wear this evening provided just enough insulation.

"How was Christmas with your parents?"

"It was nice." *I missed you.* How had she gotten there? Only a month ago, she couldn't stand to be in Faith's company. Then after one night together, she felt Faith's absence so acutely? She and Faith hadn't spoken over the holiday weekend, except for the text she sent wishing Faith a Merry Christmas. Faith's reply of *you too* didn't seem to invite further conversation so she'd left things alone until tonight. "Mom cooked for an army, as usual. If it wasn't for my teenage nephews eating all the leftovers, I would've had plenty to bring you."

"So your sister and her family were in town?"

"Yes. She's an obstetrician and had a patient due last week, so she didn't think they'd make it. But her patient went into labor a week early, freeing her up Christmas week."

"And rescuing that poor kid from sharing its birthday with Christmas. I always felt sorry for those kids when I was in school."

"Right? They never got to have a birthday party because everyone already had holiday plans. Speaking of, did you go see your mom and stepdad?"

"He's not my stepdad." Faith scowled, but then her features relaxed. "Sorry. But the first time Mom remarried, she made me call him Dad. When their marriage lasted little more than a year, I refused to call the next one anything but his first name. And I'm sure I did so with more than a little attitude."

"Teen-Faith was a handful?"

"I was the child of multiple divorces, simultaneously figuring out that I was a lesbian. Between all that and adolescent hormones, those were some rocky years. What about you? What kind of kid were you?"

"I bet you can guess."

"Good kid. Good grades."

"Yep. I was the peacekeeper in my family. I know, predictable."

"I have recently found out, you're not quite as predictable as I once thought." Faith gave Rachel a lingering kiss. "I stayed here for Christmas. Told my mother I had a Christmas wedding to handle. A little white lie to spare her feelings."

"What about your dad?"

"He took his wife and stepdaughter to New York City for the holidays. They're doing the whole Times Square thing tonight."

"You didn't want to go?"

"I wasn't invited." Faith met Rachel's eyes. "Please, don't look at me like that."

"Like what?" It was too late for Rachel to censor her expression.

Faith stood and walked closer to the fire pit. She held out her hands as if she needed the warmth, but Rachel suspected she was gathering her emotions.

"I don't doubt that my father loves me. But he's not very good at splitting his attention. The most important people in his life are the most current ones. It would never have occurred to him to extend an invitation to their holiday plans."

"That's hard for me to hear."

"Why?"

Rachel approached Faith and wrapped her arms around her waist, pressing against her back. "Because it's not how I was raised. And I hate that you didn't have the kind of family life I had."

"I don't need to be pitied."

"It's not pity. It's—" What was it? Why did she want so badly for Faith to know what unconditional love and acceptance felt like?

"It doesn't matter." Faith turned in Rachel's arms. She tilted Rachel's chin up and kissed her. "I can think of better ways to pass the time than rehashing my childhood traumas."

"What do you have in mind?" Rachel traced her tongue along Faith's lower lip. She was more than willing to let Faith distract her.

Faith glanced at her phone. "We have plenty of time before midnight. Let's see how comfortable we can get on that sectional."

Rachel guided Faith backward, until she sat on the sofa. Rachel climbed onto her lap, straddling her legs. She leaned forward, bracing her hands on the back of the sectional. Faith grasped her hips.

"Are you comfortable?" Rachel asked.

"Not quite." Faith wrapped her arms around Rachel's waist and pushed off the sofa.

"Hey." Rachel struggled against her.

Faith lifted her and flipped her onto her back on the sectional. "I can't let you think you're always going to be in charge."

Rachel would have argued, but Faith snuck her hands under her sweater, and suddenly she didn't mind relinquishing control. She buried her hands in Faith's hair and enjoyed the weight of Faith's body on hers.

❖

Faith had just arrived at the hostess stand when someone wrapped their arms around her from behind. Thinking it was Rachel, she turned with a welcoming smile. When she saw Violet, her smile fell a bit, but Violet didn't seem to notice.

"Rachel just texted that she's running late." Violet nodded to the hostess, who had just joined them at the desk. "Let's go ahead and get a table, and she'll be here soon."

They were seated at a small, square table at the far end of the restaurant. Faith chose the chair directly across from Violet, partly so Rachel would have to sit next to her when she arrived. They hadn't seen each other in the week following New Year's Eve. They'd kept in touch through text messages, but Rachel had been swamped at work. She'd been tapped by her boss to help with a new project in their commercial real-estate division. Though she'd mostly handled residential clients, she said she planned to use the project to gauge whether she wanted to make a change in focus.

Faith had been busy working in the barn anyway. As long as they didn't have a cold snap, the concrete floor would be poured next week, so she had to have everything cleaned out, prepped, and ready for the concrete guys. The plumbers were finishing up the day before the floors went in. Faith tried not to think about the things that could go wrong and screw up her timeline, which got tighter by the day.

"I'm getting used to these monthly lunch dates, even if they are just to talk about the progress on the wedding." Violet winked and squeezed Faith's arm. "I think I'm going to miss you after this is all over."

Faith tensed and leaned away from her, drawing her arm back to her side of the table. "Um—Violet. What happened between you and me—"

"Relax, Faith. We both knew what that was. I don't expect anything different."

"You don't?"

Violet smiled, and for the first time since Faith had met her, she saw no hint of flirtation in her expression. "No. I take responsibility for initiating it. But I didn't know you then. I do now. And I regret having thrown myself at you. It was disrespectful of me."

"Disrespectful?" No woman had ever apologized for wanting her before.

"I treated you as if you could offer only one thing. I know now that you have so much more than that to give."

"I do?" She wasn't contributing very much to this conversation, but she felt like with everything Violet said, she was trying to catch up.

"Yes. You're kind and generous. And I think you'd make a great friend. Outside of our professional relationship."

"You—want to be friends?"

"I would be open to that. If you think we can get past our unfortunate beginning."

Faith almost protested. No one had ever referred to sex with her as "unfortunate" before. But while she was still deciding if arguing would send the wrong message, Violet kept talking.

"And I would love it if you can work things out with Rachel. Because she's my very best friend."

Heat crept up her neck. Apparently, Rachel had already shared a bit of girl-talk with Violet. But what did Violet mean by "work things out?" She'd expected that Rachel would keep whatever they had to herself.

"She's not your biggest fan. And that's my fault, too, but apparently she's determined to hold what we did against you."

Again Faith felt like she wasn't completely read in on the current topic. Rachel hadn't told Violet what had happened between them? "I don't know. I thought she was warming up to me."

"You think? God, I hope so. It's been so awkward when we're all together." Violet focused on something over Faith's shoulder. "There she is."

CHAPTER FIFTEEN

Faith glanced toward the hostess stand. Rachel had just paused there when she spotted them. She smiled and waved. As she approached the table, Faith stood to greet her and just managed to stop herself before moving in for a hug. She covered her action by pulling out Rachel's chair for her.

"Hey, it's good to see you again," Rachel said politely as she sat down.

"You, too." Faith let the backs of her fingers brush surreptitiously against Rachel's back as she helped her push the chair in. Violet met her gaze over Rachel's head, and she seemed to be assessing their interaction. She nodded as if agreeing Rachel might be acting more friendly toward her.

As Rachel and Violet exchanged greetings, Faith settled back in her own chair. She studied her menu, content to let the two friends catch up. Rachel's knee nudged Faith's under the table. At first she thought it might be a mistake, but then she did it again, only this time she left it pressed there. Faith slipped her hand under the table and rested it on her knee. Rachel didn't look at her, so she traced slow circles toward the inside of her knee and thigh. Rachel's leg tensed, but her expression barely changed.

The server, a college-aged kid in khakis and a white shirt, arrived at their table with three glasses of ice water. After setting them down, he pulled out a small pad of paper and pen, turning to Rachel first.

"We've only got two menus. Do you want to use mine?" Faith held hers out.

"Don't bother. She always gets the same thing," Violet said.

Rachel glanced up at the waiter. "Southwest chicken wrap and a side salad."

Faith found the wrap on the menu. "Looks good. I'll have the same."

"I'll have the grilled chicken salad, no cheese or croutons, and light Italian dressing on the side." Violet closed her menu and handed it to him.

After he'd gone, Faith took out her tablet. While they waited for their food, she reviewed the wedding checklist with Violet, occasionally adding notes on her progress. Violet had accomplished most of what she'd asked of her. Over the holidays, she had taken Jack shopping for his suit. While there, they'd decided on clothes for the groomsmen as well. Jack had been tasked with telling his guys where to go for a fitting and giving them a deadline to get it done. A frilly dress and a tiny tuxedo had been ordered for Jack's niece and nephew, the flower girl and ring bearer. She and Jack had also decided on a set of invitations. She said they'd been firming up the guest list and would be ready to get them out soon.

"He says his handwriting sucks, and he's out on helping stuff them, too."

"I'll help," Rachel said. "In fact, if you bring your guest list and addresses to my place, we can print out labels and save having to write them."

"Sounds good. Let's make it a girls' night and invite Carly and Marianne to help, too."

"Sure." Rachel seemed less excited about that idea.

"Faith, you should come, too."

"She probably has better things to do than hang out with us." Rachel's detached tone contrasted with the steady pressure of her leg against Faith's under the table.

Faith looked from Violet's hopeful expression to Rachel's closed-off one.

"Rach, Faith and I were just talking about this. You two need to get along."

"We get along fine." Rachel didn't look at Faith.

"Yeah, I thought we had a good time at the Christ—"

"Let's just wait until we figure out when we'll do the invitations. Then we can see who's available."

"Okay." Violet gave Rachel a curious look but didn't question her. To Faith, she said, "What's next on the list?"

Faith ran through several more items until their food arrived. She put away her tablet so they could enjoy their meal. Violet and Rachel spent some time catching up on their holiday activities. Not only were they both close with their own families, but they clearly cared a great deal about each other's. And it seemed Jack had fit into their clan as well. When they'd caught up fully, the conversation turned back to the wedding and Violet and Jack's honeymoon plans.

As they finished up, Faith paid the check, waving off protests from Rachel and Violet. Rachel had a showing in an hour, and Violet had to get back to the store. Faith planned to spend her afternoon working at home.

They stood together and walked toward the front of the restaurant. On the way, Violet excused herself to use the restroom. As soon as she rounded the corner of the hallway, Faith stepped closer to Rachel.

"You didn't tell Violet you took me to your Christmas party." She slid her hand along Rachel's hip, using her body to block the view from the hallway, in case Violet came back.

"No."

"Why not?"

Rachel shrugged. "It didn't come up."

"It did. Just now."

"You know she's all about the wedding right now. I didn't want to distract her from that." Rachel slipped her hand inside the front of Faith's waistband, grabbed a fistful of denim, and yanked her closer. "Besides, it's kind of exciting, isn't it? This little secret of ours."

Faith's stomach twitched as the backs of Rachel's fingers

brushed against it, sending a spiral of sensation outward from their point of contact. "So, for now, this is just between us?"

"Do you mind?"

"Not at all." On some level, whatever this was between them made her nervous. Alluding to something they needed to keep secret felt like an acknowledgment of—what, she wasn't certain—but something just the same. So if keeping it to themselves helped make it feel more casual, less of a big deal, then she was all for that. And if Rachel stuck to the idea of not distracting from the wedding, Faith would be free to enjoy Rachel without examining things too closely for several more months.

❖

"That was exactly what I needed." Rachel rolled off Faith and flopped onto her back on the bed beside her.

"I think that's my line—seeing as I'm the one who just had the orgasm." Faith was slightly breathless.

Rachel chuckled. "Let's just agree it was win-win." She rolled toward Faith, rested her head on her shoulder, and tossed her arm across her stomach.

Faith wrapped her arms around her and gathered her close. She trailed her fingers in circles on Rachel's lower back. "Stressful week?"

"A little. I'm used to a lull in January and February. But since I've been working on this new leasing deal, it's all I can do to keep up with what few residential clients I do have right now." She kissed Faith just below her collarbone. "I shouldn't complain about being busy. But it's been harder than usual to keep my mind on business."

Faith hummed, but Rachel couldn't interpret what the sound meant. Was she agreeing that she was also distracted? Or did she not know what to say because she didn't feel the same way?

"I'm going to get a drink. Can I bring you anything from the kitchen?" Faith eased away and climbed out of bed. She paused long enough to put on a gauzy, light-pink robe.

"No thanks." As Faith left the room, Rachel closed her eyes.

She should take Faith's withdrawal as an answer. Faith had never given her any reason to think this was anything more than physical. Sex with Faith was as amazing as she'd thought it might be, and she often found herself daydreaming when she should have been working. All the same, just because Faith didn't usually sleep with the same woman multiple times, Rachel shouldn't start thinking there was anything deeper there. When she heard Faith come back into the room, she opened her eyes.

"Are you worn out? Or are you feeling adventurous?" Faith stood beside the bed with a glass of ice water in her hand.

"What do you have in mind?"

Faith set the glass on the nightstand, then opened the lower drawer. Rachel rolled over and hung her head over the edge of the bed to look inside. She grinned at Faith.

"Were you thinking about one in particular?"

Faith lifted a glass dildo from among a couple of other types. She held it out and Rachel hesitated. "I don't know how to ask this."

"What?"

"It's bad enough I have to think about sharing you with all those brides. I'm not interested in sharing toys."

Faith's jaw tensed.

"I'm not saying I'm not into this. Just maybe we could get something new to both of us." Rachel grimaced. "Sorry if this kills the mood, but it's how I feel."

"No. It's okay. It's a valid concern." Faith turned the dildo over in her hand. "I've never used this with anyone else. I bought it because I wanted to try it and," she held it up to the light, "it's kind of pretty."

The clear glass dildo had a bright-blue swirl of ridges around the outside. Rachel wrapped her fingers around the shaft, resting them on top of Faith's. "And the glass—it's safe?"

"Yes." Faith narrowed her eyes. "If you plan on being rough enough to break this, you might be too hardcore for me." She transferred the toy into Rachel's hand.

She was surprised by how heavy it felt. Though it looked delicate, it was actually solid. "You want to use this on me?"

Faith's eyes went smoky gray, and when she spoke, her voice was husky. "I do."

Rachel tightened her fingers around the toy, feeling the pattern of the ridges against the inside of her hand. Faith's gaze lingered on her hand, where just the tip of the toy was visible above her fist. "What's the benefit over, say, a silicone one?"

"Hold on."

This time when Faith left the room, Rachel followed. She grabbed a T-shirt on her way out and pulled it over her head. "Whoa. You can't just say 'hold on' and leave the room after bringing out this thing."

In the kitchen, Faith had opened the freezer and was filling an ice bucket.

"Do I need to get drunk for this?"

Faith took the dildo from her hand and pushed it, head down, into the bucket of ice. She glanced at the clock on the wall, then went to the living room and set the bucket on the coffee table. "You don't need to be drunk. But I can certainly pour you a glass of wine while we wait."

"While we wait?"

"Fifteen minutes or so." Faith sat down on the sofa, resting her arm along the back.

Rachel laughed and sat next to her. "And we're just supposed to make casual conversation with a dildo chilling on the table in front of us?"

"Not conversation." Faith angled toward her and kissed her neck.

"I like where this is going." Rachel tilted her head, giving her better access.

Faith lifted Rachel's shirt over her head. "Why did you bother with this?"

"It's weird walking around someone else's house naked." Rachel tugged on the belt of Faith's robe, loosening it. "You're one to talk. You put on a robe earlier."

"Point taken." She slipped it off. "Better?"

"Absolutely." Rachel cupped both of Faith's breasts.

Faith moaned as Rachel's thumbs found her nipples. She closed her teeth on Rachel's earlobe and whispered, "Have your fun. Payback comes in ten minutes."

Rachel shivered. She'd played with ice cubes before and found the sensation pleasurable, but she didn't know quite what to expect today.

Faith guided her back against the sofa arm and moved over her. Faith dropped kisses across her shoulder and down the center of her chest. When Faith pulled her nipple into her mouth, Rachel clasped her head and held her close. She arched as the sensation tugged a thread down her belly and between her legs. She gave control over to Faith and immersed herself completely in every touch and sensation.

Faith slipped her hand between Rachel's legs and teased her until Rachel was about to come. She rolled her hips against Faith's fingers, and just when she began an erratic thrusting, Faith moved her hand away.

"It's time."

Rachel gasped as her body still screamed for the orgasm Faith had delayed. "Could you try not to make that sound so ominous?"

Faith chuckled as she lifted the toy from the ice. "Just relax. I won't hurt you."

She rested the tip of the dildo on Rachel's skin, high on the inside of her thigh. Rachel flinched. She'd known it would be cold, but the icy sensation still caught her off guard. Faith slipped her fingers against her folds and opened them gently.

"Faith." Rachel meant it as a warning, but it came out more as a moan than she'd intended.

When Faith touched the dildo to Rachel's clit, she hissed out a breath through her teeth. After the initial shock, a wave of pleasure rolled through her, not nearly as sharp-edged as she'd expected. Faith rubbed the icy tip against her, increasing the pressure slightly. Rachel tilted her hips, wordlessly asking for more.

"Well?" Faith eased up and acted as if she might pull away.

Rachel grabbed her wrist and held her in place.

Faith's low, sexy laugh vibrated inside Rachel. She slid the head of the toy lower and nudged it gently into Rachel's opening. "Tell me if it's too much."

Rachel nodded and Faith pushed forward. She paused after the head slipped in, letting Rachel acclimate.

"It's strange." Rachel met Faith's eyes, needing both the connection and the communication. Faith's gaze was open and guileless. "You'd think the cold would tighten everything up and be painful, but it's actually very nice."

"Tell me what you feel." Faith eased in a little farther.

"It's deep and full, and both heightening and slowing things down at the same time."

Faith nodded. She lowered her mouth and slipped her tongue along Rachel's clit. The contrast of cold inside her and the warmth of Faith's mouth nearly turned Rachel inside out. She rolled her hips, drawing the dildo deeper.

Faith feasted, bringing heat against the ice inside, until Rachel was so overcome with sensation that she could only surrender.

"Faith. Oh, God, Faith." This time her name was a benediction, pulled from her with each stroke of Faith's tongue and every thrust inside her. She pressed her hand to the back of Faith's head, asking for more pressure against the force building within her. Faith took her fully in her mouth and matched the pace of the glass shaft with that of Rachel's hips.

Rachel continued thrusting, pushing back through the first pulses of orgasm, and she moaned and chanted for Faith not to stop. Faith didn't, and Rachel's pleasure edged up a notch, seizing every muscle in her body. She jerked, her hands fisted at the end of rigid arms. Her every sensory receptor had gone numb save for those centered between her legs, and they were firing on overdrive. She clutched Faith to her, needing the hard press of her to hold her together.

When she finally relaxed back into the sofa, she sighed, more spent than she could remember ever being. Faith rested her head against the inside of Rachel's thigh and eased the dildo out slowly.

"That was amazing." Rachel drew in a deep breath, reveling in the gentle tremors echoing inside her. She threw her arms over her head dramatically. "I only need an hour or so to recover, and then I can return the favor."

Faith rolled onto her stomach, her whole body against Rachel's right leg. When she laughed, the sound vibrated from her chest up Rachel's thigh. "I'm good for now. I—"

"What?"

She sat up and tucked her hair behind her ears. Her sigh held a hint of frustration.

Rachel grabbed her wrist and pulled her back down on top of her. "I was joking about the hour. I'll be ready in a minute."

Faith rolled her eyes and buried her face in Rachel's chest. When she spoke again, her words were lost against the valley between Rachel's breasts. Rachel lifted her chin and met her eyes.

"Was something wrong with what just happened between us?"

"No. God, no. I—just watching you—holding you through that was nearly enough for me. I've never come that close just doing someone else."

"Doing someone else? You're such a romantic." Faith tried to pull away, but Rachel held her tight. "I'm playing." She kissed Faith's forehead. "And I'm thrilled that you enjoyed that almost as much as I did."

She turned to her side, making room, and guided Faith up beside her. Faith slipped a leg between hers, wrapped an arm around her waist, and rested her head on her shoulder. Her body still pulsed from what was possibly the strongest orgasm of her life. She felt even more intensely connected to Faith than sexually satisfied. Maybe she'd only manufactured those emotions, because they'd shared a new experience. But she chose to believe in it for now and deal with the consequences of that fantasy later.

CHAPTER SIXTEEN

Faith stood in the half-finished kitchen in the barn, looking around with pride. The concrete floors had been poured last month, before the weather had turned. It had taken until mid-February, but winter had finally arrived. The kitchen and restroom walls had been framed out. Then she'd waited two weeks for the electrician to upgrade the whole place. Once the drywall was hung and finished, she'd painted the kitchen and both the men's and women's restrooms. She'd installed a commercial sink in the kitchen, and next week the stainless-steel kitchen cabinets would be delivered.

She shrugged her shoulders deeper into her Carhartt jacket. She'd been keeping the barn warm enough to protect the plumbing and give Swan someplace to sleep, but a chill still permeated the large space.

She walked back through the main room, making mental notes of what still needed to be done before the barn was ready to host its first event. While the various tradesmen had been working inside the barn, Faith had dragged her set of mismatched chairs outside, sanded them down, and painted them light gray. She found a dark-gray-and-white striped fabric and reupholstered the seats. The chairs were now lined up inside the barn, and Swan was curled up on one of them. He'd taken to sleeping there, no matter how many times she shooed him away. So she put a folded blanket on the one he seemed to favor. She half expected him to start using one of the others, but he'd stayed true to his preference, though every time she came in, the blanket had been mussed a bit more. He kneaded and pulled at it until it was just so before he lay down on it.

"Hey, buddy." She rubbed her knuckles against the top of his head, and he pushed into them. "I really didn't think this whole barn-cat thing through, you know. I don't think my clients are going to be thrilled about you crashing their weddings."

He purred loudly.

"That's not helpful. You could contribute a bit more to the problem-solving. I might be more inclined to keep you around if you did." She headed for the door. "Okay. See you tomorrow."

Swan stood and stretched, then followed. She stopped at the door.

"It's kind of cold out there tonight. You might want to stay in here."

As she opened the door, he darted through as if expecting her to try to close him inside.

"Swan, get back in here." He stood outside the door and stared at her. She sighed and threw her hands up. "Suit yourself."

She headed across the lawn toward her back door. Swan tailed her, but whenever she stopped, he did, too. She climbed the steps and he scampered up behind her.

"Go back in the barn."

He sat down.

"Stubborn little ass. I should leave you out here to freeze." He'd be okay, wouldn't he? Outside cats knew how to take care of themselves. He'd grown quite a bit since he first started hanging around. He was now long and lanky, and didn't look nearly as fragile. He moved a lot faster and more gracefully. But Faith still saw him at the tiny ball of fluff she'd first taken pity on and started feeding.

She stomped back toward the barn, but he didn't follow. She glared at him and jabbed her finger at the door. He sat down on the porch and ignored her. She sighed and went back to the house. Giving in, she held open the back door. "Okay. Come on."

He hesitated for only a second before strolling inside as if he belonged in her house.

"Don't get too comfortable," she called.

As he moved into the room, he slowed, walking tentatively. He held his tail rigid and straight up in the air. As he advanced, he raised and lowered his head as if looking at everything from different levels. Faith slipped off her jacket and hung it on a hook by the back door. She followed him into the living room and settled on the sofa to watch him explore every inch of the room. He sinuously wound his way under and around every chair and table in the room. Finally he jumped up on the opposite end of the sofa, looked directly at her, and then hopped up onto the back and lay down.

"Oh, hell, no. I'm not vacuuming cat hair off my furniture every day." She glared at him, but he didn't move.

They were still locked in a stare-down when the doorbell rang.

"We're not done here," she said as she went to open to door. She hugged Rachel, then stepped back to let her inside.

Rachel set the sling tote bag she'd started bringing to Faith's on a bench in the foyer. As they walked into the living room, Faith knew the moment Rachel saw Swan. She met Rachel's questioning look with a stern expression of her own.

"I know, I know. I'm getting enough smug looks from him without getting them from you, too."

When Rachel smiled, warmth spread through Faith's chest. She liked the easy banter with Rachel. In fact, she tried very hard not to think about the fact that she'd been enjoying Rachel for two months now—two months longer than anyone else.

"Wine?" She grabbed the bottle she'd popped earlier from the kitchen. When she came back, Rachel was bent over petting Swan and whispering to him. Faith thought she heard the word "whipped."

"One glass." Rachel straightened. "I'm still pretending I'm driving home tonight."

Faith winked and filled a wineglass almost to the rim.

"Whoa." Rachel put her hand over the top of the glass seconds too late.

"You said one glass." Faith filled her own glass halfway. "And you're not going anywhere."

"No?"

"No. We're celebrating tonight."

"What are we celebrating?" Rachel raised her glass. "Other than Swan asserting his dominance over you."

"Funny. You know the list of those who dominate me is getting a little too long."

"I might feel bad about being on that list if I didn't know how much you enjoyed it."

"I really do." She raised her glass. "But tonight, I'm excited because I've booked my first wedding for the barn."

"That's great!" Rachel threw her arms around Faith's neck, spilling some of her wine down Faith's back in the process.

Faith laughed and ducked out of her embrace. Wine had run down her arm, and she wiped it on the front of her shirt.

"Sorry." Rachel set her glass down on the coffee table and grabbed the hem of Faith's shirt. "You should just take this shirt off."

Faith stood still and let Rachel pull her shirt over her head. Rachel's eyes widened when she saw that Faith wasn't wearing a bra. Faith let her look for a moment longer before she grabbed a throw off the back of the sofa and wrapped it around her shoulders.

"Hey, you've been here less than ten minutes, and you're already taking my clothes off. If you're not careful, I'm going to start thinking you're only after sex."

Rachel laughed. "Like we don't both know that's what this is."

Her casual agreement pierced Faith's chest in a way she didn't expect. But she covered and said, "All the same, it's better for my reputation if I'm not quite so easy. Sit down and let me tell you about my new clients."

She sat on the sofa and Rachel settled close to her. As she told her about the couple who had already hired her as a coordinator, Rachel played with the edge of Faith's blanket. They'd expressed an interest in a chic yet rustic wedding. She'd invited them out for a tour, and they had excitedly agreed to book. Both of them had seen her vision, and she'd had no problem promising them a finished venue.

Rachel's fingers slipped under the throw and tangled with

Faith's. "This is great. You've already got a relationship with a lot of the vendors a couple would need. You can probably put together some package deals with them."

"I've been thinking about that. I've already reached out to Casey about doing their engagement photos out here. I'll cover her fees, and my couple gets a trial run with her."

"Good idea. She should have no problem selling herself to them."

"I'd love to book enough that, by this time next year, I'm focusing mostly on events that are here. Though I like being a coordinator, I plateaued in that business a couple of years ago."

"You could try to cultivate a more high-profile clientele. Since you're only in it for the money."

"Why do I hear sarcasm in your tone?"

"I think you have more of a soft spot than you want to admit."

"Whatever. I just need a new challenge." Faith brushed her off. But when she thought about hosting parties out in the barn, she liked the feel of community she imagined those gatherings would have. She could envision having a couple come back to celebrate milestone anniversaries in the very place where they were married.

❖

"This place looks great, Faith." Casey stood in the middle of the barn.

"Thanks. It's getting there." Faith came to stand beside her.

"Do you have many events booked yet?"

"The couple you're shooting today was the first." If today was as successful as Faith suspected it would be, she planned to continue offering the engagement photos as a standard part of her wedding package.

"October wedding, right?"

"Yep. So if you know anyone who's looking, I'm expecting to have everything ready by late summer. I can squeeze in some other weddings before today's couple."

"I'll definitely keep you in mind."

Faith shoved her hands into the pouch of her hoodie. "Do they still want to shoot outside?"

"Yes. It wasn't this cold when we scheduled. But they're excited about getting some exterior shots around the barn."

"I know it wasn't part of the original plan, but I could start a fire in the fire pit if you think you'd like some shots with them around it. Even if you don't get any pictures they like, we can all warm up a little."

"That's a good idea. It'll fit in with their fall wedding theme. Let's try it."

While Casey set up her equipment, Faith started a fire. Then while Casey did her first series of photos, she went inside the house and made a pot of coffee for them.

She carried the coffee and some snacks out to the kitchen in the barn and set them up on the counter, then piddled around in the barn while Casey shot outside. They took a coffee break while Casey set her equipment up for some indoor options. Faith stayed out of the way while they finished the session.

Later, after walking the couple to their car, she returned to the barn. She helped Casey pack her gear and load it.

"I was going over my schedule. We'll be seeing a lot of each other this spring." Casey leaned against the side of her car.

"Yeah. What are we up to? Eight of my couples that you've booked in the coming months?"

"Business is good." Casey grinned.

"That it is."

"Mind if I add you to my list of locations to shoot in? Everyone's looking for rustic these days. I'll take care of everything when I work here. You don't have to play hostess like you did today."

"Sure. No problem."

"Thanks." Casey pushed off the car and opened the door. But she paused before climbing inside. "It's really the least you can do since you've been keeping this place from me."

"What?" Faith exaggerated a look around her. "It's not even finished yet."

"You've owned it for six months now, haven't you?"

"Give or take."

"I could have been using it all this time while you've been slow-walking the renovations."

"Slow-walking?" Faith laughed. "You're right. Well, now you've got the run of the place. Just give me a little notice."

"In case you have company?"

Faith's face grew hot as she remembered how she and Rachel had spent New Year's Eve on the outdoor sectional. She couldn't imagine what would have happened if anyone had walked up on them.

Casey rolled her eyes. "You're such a dog. Hey, you should come over for dinner sometime soon. I know Jacq would like to see you."

"Sure. That sounds good."

"You could bring someone. Are you seeing anyone these days?" Casey's tone indicated she thought she already knew Faith's answer.

She wanted to tell Casey about Rachel. But since they were still keeping things quiet and Casey was shooting Violet's wedding, the situation was complicated. "Nah. You know me."

"I can hope."

"Listen, just because you voluntarily tied yourself to the same woman twice doesn't mean we all have to."

Casey laughed. "I know. We're just boring married people."

Faith didn't think they were boring. But she'd also never had a strong urge to join the married masses. Still didn't, really. Yet she thought about Rachel when they weren't together. And sometimes, when Rachel left in the morning, she wondered what it would be like to spend the day together instead.

Casey must have seen her expression change. "What's on your mind?"

"You guys broke up once."

"Yes." Casey's demeanor remained relaxed.

"Then you got back together. So, how do you know you won't split again?"

"I guess I don't, for sure. It happened before. That's your point, right?"

Faith nodded.

"But Jacq and I have grown. And I trust that we're both committed to not making the same mistakes again. Yet even with our heightened awareness, nothing is guaranteed." Casey paused until Faith met her eyes. "I always assumed you just liked playing the field. Are you really afraid to commit?"

Faith shook her head, though she knew the answer was an affirmative. "It's a long story and involves lessons learned because of the failures of my parents."

"You make your living giving people happily-ever-after. You've met enough people who have figured it out. You're smart enough to realize that your folks' realities aren't everyone's experience."

"Yeah, well, neither is yours." Faith shook away her melancholy thoughts. "If something changes, I'll bring her to dinner. Otherwise, you'll have to put up with just me."

"I knew there was someone on the horizon."

"Don't romanticize it." She folded a little under Casey's probing gaze. "Okay, I've spent some time with the same woman. But she knows I don't do serious."

"You could try."

"No. You don't get it. She knows and she's still with me. That pretty much means she's good with just a physical relationship with me."

"Or she's waiting for you to come around."

"Don't do that."

"What? Give you hope?"

"That's not her. She's practical and doesn't delude herself."

Casey held up her hands, palms out. "Okay. I won't push. But you should take some time to think about whether you want more with her."

Faith spent the rest of the day trying to drive thoughts of Rachel out of her head with the hardest physical labor she could find. But exhausting her body didn't slow her brain. Rachel was the forever type. She'd known that all along. However, for the past three months, Rachel had seemed happy ignoring that part of herself, and Faith had been okay letting her.

She'd wanted Rachel from the first time they'd met. Okay, maybe not the exact first moment, but after she'd put her clothes back on. And sex with Rachel was every bit as good as she'd expected. Rachel wasn't the first woman Faith had been with who was uninhibited in the bedroom. But she was the only one who made Faith want to give more. Before, she'd been satisfied, then walked away easily. In past three months, she'd told herself several times to walk away, but she couldn't stop wanting to be with Rachel.

If this was going to end, Rachel would be the one to call it quits. She stopped in the middle of her kitchen in the process of making a cup of cocoa. She'd poured the hot water over a mix and was stirring it when that last thought flew through her head. Her spoon clanged into the mug and some cocoa spilled over. Swan looked up from his bowl. Then, apparently deciding he wasn't interested, he returned to chewing his food.

"You're really not going to help me with this?"

He crunched as if punishing her for switching him from canned food to the dry stuff.

"I'm not saying I want a relationship. Am I? I like what we're doing now. And I guess she does, too. We don't have to change that." Swan glanced up as if annoyed that now she was interrupting his dinner. "What could a relationship between us even look like? She doesn't want Violet to know she's sleeping with me."

Faith and Rachel, as a couple, would be kind of uncomfortable for their friends—mostly Rachel's—at first. But they would all adjust, wouldn't they? If, in fact, that was what she and Rachel wanted. Was it?

"God, I am not this person." She began cleaning up her spilled cocoa and ended by putting the mug and soaked towel into the sink and walking away. "I am not a woman who agonizes over whether the woman I lo—the woman I'm sleeping with *likes* me back." Wow. She would ignore that little slip.

She should just talk to Rachel about all this. She'd never had a problem being up front about what she was looking for. Just because this time it might not be about sex, she could still be direct.

CHAPTER SEVENTEEN

Rachel stared at the piles on her dining table. Towers of folded card stock, envelopes, and smaller slips of paper took up much of the open area.

"Wow."

Violet smiled in her most charming way. "You promised you'd help."

"Who else is coming?" Rachel opened a bottle of water and offered it to Violet, who shook her head and pointed at the glass of wine she'd already poured, sitting on the table.

"Just us. I—wanted us to have some time together. To talk."

Rachel didn't ask what they were going to talk about. Her first thought was that Violet had somehow found out about Faith. But Violet wasn't the type to hold something like that back until the opportune time. If she knew, she'd have flung it at Rachel the second she walked through the door. Instead she'd set all of this out on the table while Rachel went to get her laptop and took a call from a client.

"Okay. Make a hole." Rachel held up her laptop.

Violet rearranged the stacks until she'd cleared a space large enough for the machine. Rachel plugged in her computer and opened it. Violet had emailed her the guest list already.

"Any last-minute changes before I print the labels?"

"No."

She imported the list of names and addresses in the correct format for the address labels. She'd already made a template with

Violet and Jack's return address—Jack's, actually. She ran to the printer and then came back with sheets of stickers.

"Every envelope gets an invitation and an RSVP card." Violet put one together to demonstrate. "Then a label and a stamp." She'd chosen postage stamps with a scrolled heart design.

"Consider this my RSVP. I'll be there."

"And your plus one?"

"Don't have one."

"You have almost three months to find someone to bring."

"Not looking. Besides, I'll be busy getting you down the aisle and won't have time to pay attention to a date." She didn't delude herself into thinking of Faith as her date. Aside from the fact that Faith would be working at the wedding, Rachel knew that wouldn't be the right time or place to try to take whatever they were to another level. Weddings tended to make the commitment-phobic skittish.

They worked for a while, each taking half the job and passing envelopes. Violet was quieter than usual and finished her bottle of wine rather quickly. Rachel went to the kitchen for another bottle of water.

"Can I bring you anything?"

"More wine?"

She opened another bottle and carried it to the table. "Okay, but you're sleeping here or taking an Uber home." She poured some into Violet's glass, much less than what Violet had been pouring. It wouldn't really slow her down, though. Violet didn't drink often, but when she got her mind set on it, she committed.

Violet pulled her keys out of her purse and dropped them in the center of the table. She drained the glass. "If you're trying to pace me, you shouldn't bring me what you know is my favorite wine." She tipped her fingers toward her glass, asking for a refill.

Rachel complied, then turned the label toward her. She'd grabbed a bottle she already had chilled. "This is left over from the wines we tasted for the wedding selection."

Violet's eyes went flat, followed by a shadow of pain. Rachel sighed and sat back down.

"What's going on?"

Violet hesitated.

"You might as well tell me now. If we wait until you've finished that bottle as well, you'll be in no condition to talk."

Violet sipped again but didn't gulp this glass. She took a deep breath, as if fortifying herself. "I have to tell Jack what happened with Faith."

Rachel stared at the wine Violet swirled in her glass. She might have thought at one time that Violet should come clean. But now she wasn't sure. Jack would be destroyed, and she couldn't stand to see him so hurt. Maybe she'd started to convince herself that she and Violet could live with the deception. A selfish part of her wondered how Violet's confession would change things between Faith and herself.

"I can't start this marriage on a lie."

"I thought you'd decided you couldn't hurt him just to assuage your guilt?"

"There's already a shadow over the wedding planning, though I've tried to pretend there's not. I have to accept that as my fault."

Rachel felt minimally guilty for her role in that shadow. Early on, she hadn't let either Violet or Faith forget what they'd done.

"If it was just the wedding to get through, that'd be one thing. But I can't look at him without thinking about it. I can't live like that for the rest of my life. It will affect our marriage—maybe not now, but someday."

"The wedding is in less than three months. You've had all of this time to come clean and let him get over it, and now you want to tell him?"

"I have to, Rach."

"When?"

"Tomorrow. We're having dinner at my house. That way he can get mad and storm out. He's going to need some space if he's ever going to forgive me."

"Do you think he will?" Violet seemed certain he would, but Rachel wasn't so sure. Jack was a loyal man, but she'd never seen him react to any type of betrayal, so she couldn't predict his reaction. She worried Violet was simply striving for optimism.

❖

Faith opened the oven and checked her roast. It had been in all afternoon, and the house smelled amazing. About an hour ago she'd added potatoes and carrots to the onions already nestled in the moat of beefy liquid surrounding the roast. She'd warmed some crusty bread and wrapped it in a cloth napkin until she was ready to slice it. Rachel should be here soon, and Faith had been testing a conversation in her head all day. She'd done a ton of thinking since speaking with Casey.

She'd always thought that if she ever ended up in a relationship, it would just happen organically. Like if it snuck up on her and all of a sudden there she was, with a girlfriend, she wouldn't have to consciously take the risk. Everything about being with Rachel was easy, except the relationship. They'd entered this with a tacit agreement that it was casual, even when it felt anything but. So, now, if she wanted to change the rules, she'd have to initiate the transition. It wouldn't be easy. And not everyone would understand. But she'd decided to take the risk.

As she was sliding the roast out of the oven, the back door opened. Rachel came in and dropped her bag on the floor. She looked exhausted, and Faith worried that maybe now wouldn't be the right time to have the talk. She could wait until sometime next week, or maybe in a few months, after the wedding.

Rachel stepped into her arms and kissed her. When Rachel would have eased back, Faith held on. She stroked her hand against Rachel's cheek and murmured, "Again."

Rachel complied, smiling against her mouth. Faith deepened the kiss, sliding her tongue against Rachel's lip. She circled her arms around Rachel's waist and thought about spending the next three months pretending this didn't mean anything. She had to know if Rachel was feeling what she was or if she was just happy with the status quo. And she had to know tonight.

Rachel rested her forehead against Faith's shoulder and sighed.

"I've had an incredibly long day and almost begged off to stay home tonight."

"I'm glad you didn't. I want to talk to you about something."

"Me, too. And I figured I should tell you in person." Rachel stepped away from her and fiddled with the silverware she had set out on the kitchen island.

Faith's stomach tightened at Rachel's ominous tone, but she rushed on, intent on getting her thoughts out. "Casey said something last week I haven't been able to get out of my head."

"Violet's planning to tell Jack what you and she did—almost did—whatever."

Rachel's words derailed Faith's determination. Whatever she'd been about to say lodged in her throat. Faith's heart raced, but she accepted the panic blossoming in her chest. She didn't want to hurt Jack and Violet, but she deserved this pain.

"What are we going to do?" Rachel's distress twisted the knife. "Faith, you have to talk to her."

Faith shook her head. "I can't." What could she say? She didn't feel right trying to convince Violet not to come clean. Violet was the only one who could decide what she could live with in her marriage.

"She's going to tell Jack. What if he calls off the wedding?"

"Then I'm out the rest of my fee." The sarcasm cut easily through the nausea churning in her stomach. She was going to lose Rachel over something she'd done before they'd even met.

"This is not funny." Rachel threw her hands up and spun away from her. "I should know better than to expect you to take this seriously. Will you at least talk to him after she tells him?"

"There's nothing I can do." How had the conversation shifted so quickly?

"You can't even pretend you care what happens to any of us, can you?"

Faith struggled with her desire to tell Rachel just how much she cared. But she'd lost the opportunity, and now Rachel was fixed on Violet and Jack's relationship. "Violet spent the last several months trying not to tell Jack. If she's decided to now, it's because she can't live with the secret. I won't be able to change her mind. What do you want me to do? As soon as Jack finds out, I'll be the last person he wants to talk to."

"It doesn't matter what I want. We both know what you're going to do, don't we? Walk away. It's what you're good at." Disappointment flashed across Rachel's face.

Despite their horrible introduction, it hurt that, after everything, Rachel was so ready to believe the worst. Maybe she was alone in her feelings. She supposed she should be glad she'd found out now and not after she'd made a fool of herself by professing her desire to change the nature of their relationship.

She set her jaw and glanced at the door. "Maybe you should be the one to walk. I live here."

Rachel stared at her. Despite the pain now suffusing her gaze, Faith still saw the underlying regret. Rachel was already internally berating herself for getting involved with Faith when she should have known what she was like. Without another word, Rachel grabbed her bag and left.

Faith sighed and collapsed against the counter, dropping her chin to her chest. She would have to check in with Violet tomorrow and see where things stood with the wedding. But for now, she just wanted to feel sorry for herself. She left the roast, covered, on the island and went to the living room. She lay down on the couch, pulled her knees to her chest, and tugged a throw over herself. How could she be mourning something she'd never had and hadn't even known she wanted until recently?

❖

"How did it go?" Rachel asked as Violet opened her front door. But she didn't need an answer. Violet's blotchy skin and red eyes provided ample evidence.

"I guess it's a good thing you haven't sold my house yet."

"Oh, honey."

Violet stepped back from the doorway. "Come on in."

She entered and ushered Violet into the living room. Once

she'd settled her on the sofa, she went to the kitchen to grab a glass of water. By the time she returned, Violet had begun crying softly. She handed Violet a box of tissues and the water.

"What happened?" When she hadn't heard from Violet last night, she'd hoped that was a good sign. Even if it meant they stayed up all night arguing, at least they would have worked it out. She'd texted Violet this morning, and the only reply was a request to come over today. Violet wouldn't provide any more information despite Rachel's follow-up text.

Violet took a moment to compose herself. She blew her nose, then took several deep breaths, but the tears probably weren't over. "He called off the wedding."

"He's just mad. Once he calms down—"

"I hurt him so badly. I don't know how he'll ever forgive me."

"Did you explain why you did it?"

"I tried. He didn't want to hear it." Violet sniffed. "And I can't blame him. If you were with someone and found out they'd essentially slept with someone else, how would you feel?"

Violet couldn't know that it wasn't that hard to imagine herself in that situation. By Faith's own admission, she didn't usually do committed relationships. Rachel didn't think Faith had slept with anyone else in the time they'd been together, but they'd never talked about it. She avoided asking because she didn't want to know. But she had to admit it was a possibility.

Would Faith think she didn't have to tell Rachel if she hooked up with someone because they'd never talked exclusivity? How would she feel if confronted with the reality that Faith had been with someone else while they were together? Betrayed. Hurt. Angry. Just the thought of Faith touching another woman the way she'd touched her made Rachel's stomach hurt. So she had at least some idea how Jack felt. The past was the past, but she didn't want to think it had happened since they'd been together.

"I asked Faith to talk to him, but she wouldn't," Rachel said.

"It's not her responsibility. I did this."

"Why are you so quick to let her off the hook? She was involved."

"I was the one who owed something more to Jack." Violet dabbed at her eyes as tears threatened again.

There was nothing more to say. Rachel sat down beside her and did the only thing she could. She put her arm around Violet's shoulder and held her while she cried.

❖

Rachel stood outside Jack's door, debating whether to knock. She'd shown a condo in a building down the street from his. After seeing her clients to their car, she drove to his place to check on him. Now that she was here, she was nervous. In the two days since Violet had told him the truth, Violet said he hadn't answered her calls or texts. She'd offered to try to talk to him and Violet said no. But how much damage could she do by trying to reason with him or, at the very least, discern where his head was?

She rang the bell. She thought she heard footsteps, but the door didn't open. She assumed what she hoped was a warm, friendly expression in case he was looking at her through the peephole. After what felt like a long time, the door swung open.

"Hey." Rachel entered, but Jack was already walking away from her.

He dropped down onto the sofa and stared out the large windows at the city skyline. Rachel walked to the window and looked out at the balcony, remembering standing out there with Faith the night of their dinner party. She turned and said, "How are you holding up?"

"Did you know?" When he looked at her, his expression was a mix of anger and disappointment. The anger she understood, but the disappointment, which she knew was directed at her, hurt.

She nodded slowly. Giving him anything but the truth would be insulting at this point. Despite her own opinions about Violet's decision to tell him, she had known, so now Rachel owed him honesty as well.

His mouth tightened and he looked away.

"It didn't mean anything, Jack."

"And how do you know that?"

"Because I know Violet. And anyone can see how much she loves you." And because Faith is incapable of a meaningful connection. She kept that venomous thought to herself.

"I don't want to talk to you about this. You clearly chose her side when you decided to keep her dirty little secret."

"She's my friend. I was trying—"

"So am I. Or I'm supposed to be."

"You're right. But I thought I was doing the right thing for both of you."

"Wouldn't you have wanted to know?"

Would she? Probably not. She would have wanted to live in her happy little bubble. But when she thought about finding out later, years down the road, she didn't like that idea either. She would feel like she'd been made a fool of.

"I'm sorry. I really am." She sat down next to him, not sure what else to say.

He dropped his head into his hands, rubbing a big hand through his hair. "What am I supposed to do?"

"I don't know."

"I love her. But I don't know how to forgive this. I think I even understand why she did it. But I can't get it out of my head. I never would have done this to her."

"I know. She does, too." She touched his shoulder but he pulled away. "She didn't tell me what she was planning. I would have tried to talk her out of it. I only found out after the fact, sort of. And it felt like an impossible situation."

He shook his head but didn't say anything.

"She still wants to marry you."

"I need time." He angled away from her and stared out the window again.

She stood. "If I can do anything."

He ignored her. She forced herself to the door, stifling the urge to push. Outside of her family, Violet and Jack were the two most important people in her world, and she wanted to help them fix this. But all she could do now was give Jack what he asked for—space—and hope for the best.

CHAPTER EIGHTEEN

"Mom, are you here?" Rachel closed her parents' front door behind her.

"In the office," Sharon called from the back of the house.

When Rachel's father retired, her mother had taken over his office. She supplemented his pension and their 401(k) by selling various things she'd knitted. Though not usually very tech savvy, she had learned enough to set up accounts on a couple of the online marketplaces. In fact, Rachel suspected her mother could teach her a few things about the Internet now. The agency had an IT guy who handled the website. So email, proofing her own listings, and searching for new ones were the gist of her time online.

Sharon sat behind the aging desktop. The rubber coating on the cord of her mouse was cracked right where it came out of the mouse. Rachel made a mental note to look into upgrading her mother's computer and getting her a wireless mouse—maybe for Christmas.

She sat in the chair on the opposite side of the desk, pulling it closer so she could rest her elbows on the desk.

"Your dad and I were just talking about you. You've been so busy with Violet's wedding, we haven't seen as much of you lately. Speaking of which, we haven't gotten our wedding invitation yet. Didn't you say you two were going to stuff envelopes earlier this week?"

Rachel winced. Violet had come clean with Jack the day after they finished prepping the invitations. After she and Jack argued, she hadn't mailed them.

"What's wrong?" Sharon's clicking stopped, and she gave Rachel her full attention.

"Um, I don't know if you're getting an invitation."

"Well, that's silly. Of course, we are. Have they decided on such a small wedding that we didn't make the cut?" Sharon laughed.

"Violet and Jack argued. There's a chance he'll call it off."

"Couples argue. And they're under a lot of stress right now. I can't tell you how many times I thought about calling off the wedding with your father."

"Mom!"

"You'll know what I mean someday."

"That remains to be seen." She hoped she would someday have the kind of relationship her parents had. Solid, yet clearly full of love. Faith's face flashed in her mind, and she shook her head, trying to clear it. Faith was definitely not the woman she should think about planning a wedding with. She turned her thoughts back to Violet and Jack. "This is a serious fight. I don't want to go into the details, but she kept a big secret from him, and I don't know if he'll forgive her."

"You can't fix this. They have to find their own way."

Rachel quirked her lips in a half-smile. "I know." She couldn't figure out her own love life. But thinking about how to solve Violet's problems seemed somehow easier, though she didn't know why. She couldn't make Jack trust Violet again. And honestly, if Violet wasn't her best friend, she'd probably be on his side. Hell, she was on his side. Violet had acted like an idiot.

"What else is going on?" Sharon gave her that stare that had always seen right through her as a kid. But, as she had then, Rachel attempted a bit of deception.

"That's it. Didn't you know my life revolves around their wedding?"

"I know you better than that."

Rachel laughed. "Yeah? What do you know?"

"We haven't been seeing you much lately."

"You said that. The wedding, remember?"

Sharon narrowed her eyes. "There's more to it. You've had a reason to stay close to the city on the weekends."

"Mom—"

"I'm not mad. Of course, we enjoy you visiting as often as possible. But I want to see you find the person who will make you happy."

"Oh, I don't think that's possible anymore." Rachel shoved her hand into her hair and gave in. Maybe she should confide in someone. She'd been dying to talk to Violet about what was going on with Faith but didn't want to deal with the drama of that. "You remember Faith McKenna?"

"Violet's wedding planner. What does she have to do—oh."

"Yep. We've been, I guess, seeing each other." Rachel folded one fist inside the other and squeezed until her knuckles popped.

"You guess?"

"She's not the serious-relationship type."

"And unless you've changed drastically, you are."

"Yes. But we got involved—physically—and I told myself that didn't matter." She searched her mother's face for judgment but didn't find any. Despite that, she suddenly felt the need to explain her actions. "It's not the kind of thing I would normally do. I mean, I usually get to know a person before—"

"Rachel, you're an adult." Sharon leaned across the desk and covered Rachel's still-fidgeting hands. "This conversation will be easier if we assume I know you have sex and you assume I understand you weren't waiting for marriage."

"Mom!" She jerked her hands back and shoved them in her lap.

Sharon laughed as Rachel's face flushed hot.

"So, this was a casual thing?" Sharon pushed on despite Rachel's discomfort.

"No. Yes. Sort of."

Rachel had seen Sharon's knowing smile before. "You have feelings for her."

"My feelings don't matter, as it turns out. I'm just another wedding-party notch for her."

"I don't think so, honey. Looking back on that weekend before Thanksgiving, I recall the way she looked at you. I don't know her well, but I think it's entirely possible you were different—"

"Just not different enough."

"Well, if she doesn't know how special you are, she's not worth your time anyway."

"That was a very 'mom' thing to say. But it's not that simple." Regardless of how cool Sharon was trying to be, Rachel wasn't about to explain the whole Faith/Violet dynamic. Without that information, Sharon couldn't really give her advice. "But it's fine. I need to figure out how to get Violet and Jack back together and then just get through this wedding. After that, Faith and I can go our separate ways." She stood and walked to a table against the wall, where Sharon had laid out several items she'd knitted. Sharon had photographed them there before posting them for sale. Rachel picked up a multicolored scarf and pulled it through her hands.

"Honey."

"Mom, don't worry. Everything will work out as it should." She replaced the scarf and touched an infant sweater made of the softest yarn she'd ever felt.

"Make sure you let Violet know we're thinking of her. And if she needs anything, you let us know."

"I will." She toyed with the tiny sleeve on the sweater. She'd debated having kids of her own over the years, but the time had never been right, and maybe her urge wasn't strong enough. But she recalled with fondness when her nephews were this small. Jack had talked before about wanting children, and Violet worried she was getting too old. Jack teased that they'd better start practicing now so she could get pregnant soon after the wedding.

❖

Rachel entered the same bar where she'd listened to Stark Raven play. The main room wasn't as crowded as it had been that night. Apparently the advertised Ladies Night hadn't increased their Wednesday-night patronage, though the sparse crowd wasn't bringing down the group of women who had claimed a table close to the door. They talked loudly and laughed even louder. A server traded their empty pitcher for one full of beer.

Rachel was headed for the bar to get a drink when Violet called out to her from a table near the back. She changed course and went that way. Violet sat with Carly and another woman, whose name Rachel couldn't remember, though she'd met her once before. As she took the empty chair next to Violet, both women greeted her. She didn't want to admit she didn't remember the woman's name, so she smiled and said hello back.

"We have margaritas." Violet raised her glass.

A waitress had come over when Rachel approached, and she now hovered nearby. Rachel caught her eye and asked for water.

"Come on, drink with me," Violet whined after the waitress left. "I know you're not one of my bar girls, but you could at least try." When she said bar girls, she gave Carly a high-five.

"Yeah, tonight is about cheering up our girl." Carly touched the rim of her glass to Violet's.

Rachel didn't believe getting drunk was the answer to Violet's problems, but since she was among friends it probably wouldn't hurt her either. Rachel had tried to decline when Violet called with the invitation, but she sounded so down that Rachel gave in. At least they hadn't tried to drag her to a club with thumping music and strobe lights.

For the next hour, Carly and the mystery woman finished drink after drink. Soon, they didn't notice that Violet wasn't keeping up with them. She'd ordered water and alternated between that and slow sips of whatever drinks the other two put in front of her. The more Carly drank, the snippier she became toward Rachel. At first, she thought maybe Carly was just a grumpy drunk, but she seemed to direct most of her vitriol toward Rachel.

Rachel finally blew up after Carly made a particularly nasty comment. "What the hell is your problem with me?"

"Can't take a joke?" Carly's slurred, gurgling laugh annoyed Rachel. Carly lurched to her feet. "I'll get the next round."

"Maybe. If I thought you were joking."

"Lighten up, Rachel. We can't all be as perfect as you." Carly sneered before she walked away.

"She's right," Violet said.

"She's a bitch." Rachel wouldn't accept that Carly had some kind of insight into who she was.

"Yes. She is. But she's not wrong. You've got everything together, and the rest of us can't always keep up."

"I've got it together?" Lately, she'd been feeling more out of control than ever. She hadn't heard from Faith since they'd argued. But her emotions were so twisted up, she wasn't sure what she'd say if she did. Faith had made it clear that she was willing to get physically involved with—well, just about anyone, but she wanted nothing to do with the deeper trappings of personal relationships—her own or Jack and Violet's.

"You have a good job."

"That I'm not passionate about in the least."

"Your family is awesome."

"I'll give you that one." Her mother had called every day since they'd talked to check on her.

"And you're the most stable person I know."

"Ha. I slept with Faith." She was nearly as shocked as Violet when the argument in her head came out aloud.

"What?"

Rachel cringed, but she couldn't take it back now. "Oh, you heard me." She glanced around to see who else might have. No one seemed to be paying them any attention.

Violet stared at her. "When?"

"I took her to the agency Christmas party. That night was the first time."

"The first—how many times?"

Rachel rolled her eyes upward, debating the merits of trying to do the math. "I don't know exactly. It's kind of been ongoing since then."

"You're in a relationship with my wedding planner? And you didn't tell me?"

"Not exactly. I mean, you know her. And it's not a relationship."

"So, recreational sex?"

"I don't know." That didn't fit for her either. But was that how Faith felt? "Maybe. Anyway, it's over now."

"Why is it over?"

"We had a difference of opinion, and she proved herself true to form."

"A difference of opinion? About what went down with Faith and me?"

"It doesn't matter. Let's be honest. Any scenario between Faith and me was bound to run its natural course and end."

Violet shook her head. "I can't get my head around you sleeping with her all this time and keeping it from me."

"We didn't want to distract from the wedding stuff. And given her history with you and with Carly, I didn't want things to be weird when we were all together."

Violet laughed. "Carly will lose her shit when she hears about this."

"No. Carly does not need to know about this."

"You're passing up the perfect opportunity to put her in her place. She's been trying to get a second night with Faith since before her wedding. You've done what she couldn't do."

Rachel shook her head. "I don't need to do that. This is between you and me."

"After the way she's been treating you tonight, you don't want to rub this in her face? You really are a bigger person than all of us."

"No. I just—I don't want to make a big deal. It's embarrassing."

"Your fling with Faith? She's hot. What could be embarrassing about that?"

Nothing. Except she didn't feel as casual as she should, even though anyone who knew about it would automatically assume it was just sex. So she was the idiot who fell for someone who had made it clear from the start that she absolutely did not do relationships.

"Unless it wasn't just a fling."

If she let Violet stare at her for too long she would figure out that Rachel had lost herself. She blew out a breath in a faked display of dismissal. "You've met Faith. What else would it be but sex?"

Violet's eyes shifted over Rachel's shoulder at the exact moment she felt a presence behind her. She knew without looking that it was Faith and that she'd heard what Rachel said. The clean, light scent that was uniquely Faith reached Rachel seconds too late.

Faith bent and put her face next to Rachel's. "Yes. Because I'm completely incapable of anything meaningful." She looked at Violet as if agreeing with Rachel, but the hard edge of Faith's tone negated the delicious chill that usually accompanied the feel of Faith's breath against her skin. Rachel closed her eyes and bit her lip. Shit, her timing sucked.

She turned her head and met Faith's eyes, seeing hurt and something deeper. She looked tired, but not like she'd been working too hard—more a bone-deep weariness. "I didn't mean—"

Before she could figure out exactly what she did mean, Faith straightened abruptly. "I'm getting a drink. Anyone need a refill?" She left without waiting for a response.

Rachel watched the sway of Faith's denim-covered hips until she canted them against a bar stool. God, even being angry at Faith didn't stop her from wanting her hands on Faith's firm ass. Was it any wonder she'd somehow convinced herself she could handle just sex? Faith ordered a drink, and when she pulled some folded bills from her pocket, Rachel could easily recall the feel of her long, cool fingers against her skin.

"Why is she here?" Damn, her libido wanted to drive, and she had never wanted to let it more than at this moment.

"I invited her." Despite Rachel's glare, she shrugged. "To be fair, I didn't know about the sex at the time."

Rachel winced at the accusation in Violet's tone. She was offended that Rachel had kept something from her. Rachel was more twisted up over Faith than she'd thought possible, and somehow Violet still found a way to make it about her. At the bar, Faith tossed back a shot of something and picked up another drink. Instead of returning to where they sat, she struck up a conversation with a couple of guys at the bar.

"You're thinking about leaving, aren't you?" Violet leaned forward as she spoke, forcing Rachel to meet her eyes.

Rachel nodded. She wasn't sure she could be in the same room with Faith without indulging her desire to look at her—maybe touch her. But, if Faith stayed on the other side of the bar, she might be okay.

Violet touched her arm. "Please, don't go. I can't be alone tonight." Before Rachel could point out that she was hardly alone, she started to tear up.

"I'll stay for a little longer." She glanced back at the bar and immediately wanted to take back her words. Carly had slid in next to Faith and stood entirely too close for Rachel's liking. Clearly flirting, she'd angled her body toward Faith and stroked Faith's arm from her shoulder down to her elbow. Faith didn't seem to be making any moves to increase the distance between them. Rachel tore her eyes away and reminded herself that she was here for Violet. She sucked down the rest of her water, then set the glass down too hard on the table. Violet jumped and gave her a curious look.

"I need to use the restroom." She stood and left the table before Violet could offer to go with her. Before she reached the hallway that led to the restrooms, she detoured toward the back of the bar. Last time, she'd seen a door leading off the back patio and onto the street adjacent to the building. She needed some air. She needed to not watch Carly try to charm Faith back into her bed. And she wished that it didn't matter so much to her if Carly succeeded.

❖

"Excuse me. I'm going to say hi to Violet. I missed her when I came in." Seeing that Rachel had left the table, Faith latched onto the excuse to gain some distance from Carly. She hurried away before Carly could follow.

When she reached the table, she found Violet staring across the bar, but she doubted she was actually seeing anything. Surely there wasn't something interesting about the two dudes playing darts over there.

"How are you?" She sat down across from Violet.

"I manage to hold it together in public, until I get home and fall apart." She glanced around them. "Hence, the public get-together."

"Aw, I wouldn't have minded hanging out at your place and letting you break down."

Violet smiled. "See, I knew you'd be a good friend."

"Or I feel guilty." She probably wouldn't admit as much to Rachel, but she didn't mind letting Violet know she understood her part in this mess.

"Rachel said she asked you to talk to Jack and you refused."

"I did."

"And I understand why. But he won't answer my calls or texts. I went to his place, and he won't answer the door. I'm approaching desperation here." Desperate enough to trade on the bit of guilt Faith had just admitted to, apparently.

"I'm so, so sorry, Violet. But you know he won't want to talk to me."

"Probably not. But can you at least try? You're my wedding planner. You said you would handle everything. You're not exactly doing your job if there isn't a wedding, are you?"

Faith pinched the bridge of her nose. Violet's logic was a stretch, but Faith understood her motivation to try. Faith had always justified her actions by saying the brides knew what they were asking for. But after getting to know Violet, she hated to see her in such pain. Faith truly believed Violet was a good person who'd made a bad decision. She clearly loved Jack. Now it was up to him to decide if he could trust her again.

"I'll think about it." She doubted Jack would answer her calls right now. She'd have to come up with a way to see him in person, and that was the last thing she wanted. She'd never had to face a fiancé who had full knowledge of what had transpired. Being around them was hard enough when they were in the dark and she could pretend she had nothing to feel slimy about.

"What's going on between you and Rachel?"

"Nothing." The lie was easier than she'd thought it would be. Maybe she'd been telling it for too long.

"Maybe I wouldn't have picked up on the fact that the two

of you clearly don't want to be in the same room right now, if she hadn't just told me you slept together."

Faith spotted Rachel coming back down the hallway from the restroom. She stopped when she got near enough to see Faith sitting with Violet. She seemed to have a moment of indecision, then detoured to the bar. Since Carly was still there, Faith didn't think she'd linger there long either.

"She said it was past tense, right?" Faith wasn't in the mood to open up, certainly not to Violet. As much as she knew she too was culpable in what happened between them, Violet had acted like she was okay leaving it in the past. Faith had been lulled into thinking she could move forward, maybe become a better person—maybe even good enough for Rachel. Violet's attack of conscience had shot that to hell.

"She did. But I'm not sure I understood why."

"You heard what she said. I'm not relationship material."

"Where do you think she got that from?" Violet sipped from her drink. "You pretty much laid that one out for all of us from day one."

"Yeah. I did."

"Has something changed?"

She looked again at Rachel, who'd just paid for her drink, but shifted uncomfortably in her space at the bar. Rachel glanced at Violet, then at the front door. Faith wouldn't be surprised if she bolted. And Faith wanted more than anything to cross the room and put her arms around Rachel. "For the first time in a long time, I think it's possible."

"Have you told her that?"

"Almost." She'd been about to tell Rachel that she wanted—what? What did she want? To date her? Why did that sound too inane a word for what Faith felt for her? But Rachel had tossed any chance of that aside once Faith and Violet's secret was out. Their friends would find out why the wedding was called off. Things like this never stayed a secret. And Rachel probably didn't want people to know that she was involved with the woman who broke up Violet and Jack.

"What stopped you?"

She wanted to blame Violet. To tell her that her confession to Jack had screwed up everything for them—providing an easy reminder of why Rachel had disliked Faith when they first met. But in truth, the responsibility fell back on her. Rachel had all but asked her to step up, and she'd responded with sarcasm and withdrawal. "I disappointed her yet again."

"I'll admit, given your history with me and with Carly, all of our lives would be easier if this thing with Rachel were over." Violet covered Faith's hand with hers. "But if you and Rachel can make each other happy, isn't it worth exploring?"

"You tell me. You're sitting here heartbroken over Jack. If you guys don't work things out, was it still worth the risk?"

Violet nodded. "Absolutely. I believe Jack is the one for me, but if he's not, someone else is. It won't be easy, but I'll move on eventually."

The concept of moving on after such life-altering love felt like betrayal to Faith, the same kind of disloyalty she'd judged her parents for every time they left one relationship only to hop into another. Maybe, as she'd always thought, love didn't bind a couple together, or maybe they just didn't want to be alone. Or maybe, like Violet, they were able to believe that that next partner could also fulfill them.

She wasn't sure she possessed that kind of blind faith. She glanced once more at Rachel, then stood. Rachel wasn't Violet. And the love Rachel was searching for was the abiding kind. Until Faith was certain she could give her that, she needed to stay away. But she'd started to believe a time would come for them to resolve things between them. She said good-bye to Violet, and as she headed for the door, she met Rachel's eyes. The flash of heat she saw before Rachel looked away gave her hope. She told herself Rachel broke eye contact because she couldn't completely snuff out her awareness.

CHAPTER NINETEEN

Jack," Faith called as she knocked on the door for the third time. "I'm not leaving until you talk to me."

"Go away."

"I can't. I promised Violet I'd talk to you, and you know how she gets." She'd debated whether she should avoid any reminder of her connection to Violet. But she wanted him thinking about Violet, maybe remembering all the things he loved about her.

Her relief when he jerked open the door faded in the face of his anger. She held up her hands in a sign of surrender and hoped he was chivalrous enough not to hit a woman—not that she didn't deserve it.

"Just give me five minutes." His expression didn't change, but he didn't slam the door in her face either. He turned and walked away, and Faith took the still-open door as an invitation to follow. "Violet loves you. You know that. And while you have every right to be mad about this, you know you're eventually going to forgive her. And when you do, you'll be sorry you didn't go through with this wedding."

He stopped at the large windows and didn't turn around. His shoulders hunched as he folded his arms over his chest. "Thanks for your permission to be angry. But I didn't need it. In fact, I don't need anything from you. If Violet didn't make it official, let me. There's not going to be a wedding, hence we no longer require a wedding planner."

"Jack—"

"Take your deposit and—whatever else you got out of this, and leave."

Faith stared at his back and felt horrible. She'd become adept at telling herself she wasn't really hurting anyone, and maybe she hadn't before. But this time she'd devastated Jack, and it hurt her more than she'd expected. She'd risked this moment every time she'd slept with a bride-to-be. Even when Rachel caught her, she'd managed to act like it wasn't a big deal.

"I'm sorry," she said quietly. Maybe it wouldn't help, but she had to attempt to make amends with Jack. She owed that to him, and to herself if she hoped to change her ways. "This wasn't the first time."

He spun around, his surprise evident.

"I'm not telling you this to brag or—whatever. But you need to know that it didn't happen because there were feelings between Violet and me. There's all kinds of messed-up history here that will tell you more about me than about Violet. But let's just say, I'd done it before, and Violet found out." She paused, then took his silence as permission to go on. "You'll have to talk to Violet about her reasons, but let me assure you, there were no emotions attached to what almost happened between us."

"Am I supposed to feel better because she was willing to risk all we have on an emotionless fling?"

"I think maybe she overestimated her ability to deal with the ramifications of satisfying her curiosity. I—I've been with someone she knows, and that person was able to go on and get married, and maybe she thought she could, too. I'm not excusing her or myself." She'd gotten off course and didn't seem to be swaying him anyway. She headed for the door. "I just thought you should know."

"Mission accomplished," he snapped. She paused with her hand on the knob. "So you can move on to your next conquest now. And leave us with the mess you've made."

She nodded. "I did make a mess. But I'm not moving on unscathed either. You probably won't believe this, but I'm not doing this again." She opened the door. "Don't let her go. She made a mistake. But I'm certain if you give her a chance, she'll earn back your trust."

She left without waiting for his reply. She'd said all she could and hoped she'd helped Violet in some way. She'd been soul-searching for herself since Violet had come clean to Jack, but seeing him today had cemented things for her. She might have lost her chance with Rachel. Only time would tell. But regardless, she would never sleep with another client.

❖

"Congratulations. The seller accepted your counteroffer." Rachel smiled as her clients embraced each other.

The Olivers had been married only a month and had been still trying to settle their blended family of five teenagers when he got transferred to Nashville. They'd been living in the two-bedroom apartment his company provided while house hunting. He had been working long hours to acclimate to his new position, and his wife was reaching a breaking point dealing with the kids in such a small space.

"Thank you so much for all you've done." Mr. Oliver shook her hand, then hugged his wife again.

"I just did my job."

Mrs. Oliver shook her head, tears in her eyes. "You did so much more."

Rachel smiled. Truthfully, these past two weeks she'd welcomed the challenge of finding them a new house. She'd reached out to fellow agents, searching for inside information on homes that hadn't been listed yet. Throwing herself into finding a future for the Olivers had kept her from thinking about how badly her life had tanked lately. She hadn't seen or heard from Faith since that night at the bar. She'd picked up her phone to text or call at least a dozen times but hadn't followed through.

She regretted that Faith had overheard her talking to Violet.

With that one comment, what had begun as a disagreement over Faith's refusal to get involved in Jack and Violet's situation had mushroomed into something more complicated.

She and Violet spoke on the phone and texted regularly, but a discomfort that hadn't been there previously underlay their interactions. They avoided talking about Jack, the fate of the wedding, or Faith, which left their conversations feeling superficial and forced. Violet also seemed to be using work as a distraction, and they hadn't gotten together. Violet had texted earlier today and invited her over for dinner. As soon as she wrapped up with the Olivers, she would head to Violet's house.

Rachel reviewed the details of the contract with them once more and promised to let them know when she'd confirmed a closing date. After accepting another hug from Mrs. Oliver, Rachel left them to continue celebrating. Though they'd still be weeks away from closing, at best, she suspected they would go home and start packing immediately.

She stopped on her way to Violet's house to pick up a bottle of her favorite white. She wanted to go home, take a bath, and climb into bed early. Her body was telling her that she was exhausted, but every time she tried to unwind, her mind tortured her with memories of Faith. So, she kept up her residential clients, while also taking on more and more commercial projects. So far, the change in focus hadn't brought the career fulfillment she'd hoped it might, but it had served to help distract her. She'd worked more hours and slept and eaten less than she had in years. On the upside, she'd lost five pounds in two weeks. Maybe she could transition that weight-loss trend to healthy living instead of stress.

She parked in front of Violet's house just ten minutes later than they'd agreed to, pushing all thoughts of a quiet evening at home out of her head. Violet had been keeping to herself lately, and her invitation meant she needed to talk, so Rachel would be there for her.

As soon as Violet opened the door, Rachel held out the bottle. "I brought wine."

"Perfect." Violet grabbed Rachel's arm and pulled her inside.

"I didn't have time to chill it."

Violet took the bottle and waved her hand dismissively. "You know I'm not above throwing a couple of ice cubes in my wine." She went to the kitchen and opened the bottle. When she tipped a glass in Rachel's direction, with a question in her eyes, Rachel nodded. Violet filled two glasses.

"Working late again?" Violet handed over her drink.

"Just delivering some good news." Rachel took a sip of wine. She followed Violet to the living room. Violet curled up in her favorite chair, and Rachel took one end of the couch.

"I have some good news of my own—I hope. Jack and I have been talking. Just on the phone, but it's progress, right?"

"Absolutely. That's great."

Violet nodded. "I think so. I've been one hundred percent honest with him about what was going on with me during that time. Which I think has been easier over the phone than in person."

"Does he seem open to reconciling?"

Violet nodded. "I can tell he wants to trust me. But he needs more time. Hell, I even offered to go to therapy with him."

"He shot that down, I'm sure."

"You know him almost as well as I do." Violet set her glass on a table beside her chair. "I know there's no guarantee that some of this won't resurface later, even if we work it out."

"That's what worries you most."

Violet's expression was confirmation enough. "What if I never truly get him back? Have I ruined both of our lives? And for what?" She dropped her head into her hands. "I'm such an idiot."

Rachel didn't argue, but she didn't feel the need to exacerbate Violet's wounds either.

"What should I do, Rach?"

"Keep talking. It's all you can do."

Violet nodded. She straightened up and swiped at her tearful eyes. "What about you? Have you heard from Faith?"

Rachel shook her head. "And I don't expect to. Have you?"

"I met with her to tell her that, even if we go through with the wedding, I can't continue having her as our wedding planner."

"What did she say?" Violet had just removed Rachel's last chance to be in the same room with Faith.

"She understood, of course. And she gave me back our deposit for her services."

"Why? Extracurriculars aside, she did a lot of work for you." She surprised even herself with her ability to sound flippant.

"She said she couldn't accept it."

Rachel scoffed. "I bet she took Carly's money."

Violet chuckled. "That's exactly what I said. But she said this was different. Then she looked kind of sad and said that *she* was different now."

"And you believe her?"

"I do. I really think she's changed."

"How so?"

"She got involved with you—on more than a superficial level."

"We were sleeping together. That's all."

"You can tell yourself that's all it was, as I'm sure she did, too. But from everything I've heard, you were as close to a relationship as she's been in years."

"Who's your source? Carly?" She wanted to brush off Violet's words, but a twinge in her heart wouldn't let her. She hadn't managed to eradicate the part of her that wanted to mean something to Faith. And unlike Carly, she wasn't interested only in the conquest of "getting" Faith McKenna.

❖

Faith watched the newly married couple move together on the dance floor. When the emcee announced them as Mr. and Mrs., the bride beamed as if she would never tire of hearing those words. Casey snapped a couple of photos. She didn't lower her camera, but Faith sensed a shift in her attention out of the corner of her eye.

"I met with Violet and Jack today to go over their must-get photo list. It's hard to believe it's only a month away. I was surprised you weren't there. Violet said you weren't coordinating their wedding anymore."

"Nope." Faith didn't take her eyes off the dance floor. The groom twirled his new wife, and from his relaxed expression, Faith guessed the dance lessons he'd taken leading up to today had paid off.

"What happened there?"

She shrugged. How could she explain? She hadn't even known the wedding was back on. She was happy if they'd worked things out.

"Come on. You had a contract, right?"

"Not now. Okay?"

"So, they've scaled back the wedding. Same venue but a smaller guest list. They said they've reevaluated who was important in their life. When we were finishing up, the bridesmaids arrived. Who was the one that came to my first consultation?"

"Rachel Union." An image of Rachel in that navy-blue bridesmaid dress flashed in her head.

Casey fired off a couple more pictures. When she spoke again, Faith swore she heard a smug smile in her voice. "One of the bridesmaids, huh?"

"What?"

"When I asked about you, I sensed a ton of tension in the room. I thought at first it was coming from Jack, but when he excused himself to take a call, Violet asked how you were. The only thing I couldn't figure out was which bridesmaid, because they both seemed way too interested in my response."

Faith would have laughed if her stomach wasn't in knots. She hadn't seen Rachel in the month and a half since the night at the bar. Just the idea that Rachel might still be thinking about her made her want to see her. She'd thought at first that she was missing the sex—the very good sex. Rachel was responsive and open, and willing to explore in the bedroom. Of course she remembered their physical connection, but the moments before and after they were intimate caught most in her mind. She liked the way they'd teased and flirted, and the soft conversation—about anything at all—that Rachel seemed to like as they lay in the afterglow of orgasm. Sitting outside by a fire with Rachel on New Year's Eve was possibly the best time she'd ever had with a woman. Rachel understood how her parents' relationships had messed her up and made her clam up in her own personal life. But she only let Faith get away with so much before she called her on her bullshit. She missed all of it, and no matter how much time passed, she didn't think the gut-deep need for Rachel twisting inside her would go away.

"She's beautiful," Casey said from behind her camera.

The newlyweds had separated, and each danced with one of the guests. The bride moved awkwardly with her brother. And though they clearly hadn't danced much together, the smiles on their faces indicated they enjoyed trying. "All brides are beautiful, Casey. You know that."

"I wasn't talking about her." Casey met her eyes. "Rachel."

"How did you know?"

Casey shrugged. "I had a fifty-fifty shot, right? At first glance, Carly is your type. But she's definitely not the kind of girl you'd get all mopey about—"

"I'm not—"

"You have been. Rachel seems like she might challenge you."

She could continue to play dumb, but she doubted Casey would let her get away with it. "She's definitely a challenge."

"She's going to make some woman very happy, someday. Maybe she'll hire me to photograph her wedding."

"Shut up, Casey."

"Don't like thinking about that, huh? I'm guessing you don't want to plan that one." Casey quirked one side of her mouth. "Or maybe you do."

Faith scoffed. "You know I'm not the marrying kind." Though she wouldn't be there to witness it, Faith already knew Rachel would be misty-eyed at Violet's wedding. "But she is."

"So that's it?" Casey put her hand on Faith's arm. "When are you going to see that this stuff you pretend to be so cynical about is real?"

"For you. Not for everyone."

Casey shrugged. "Have it your way."

"It's going to be a long wedding season," Faith mumbled. "How many of these things are we working together this year?"

Casey just smiled, raised her camera, and moved around the perimeter of the dance floor. Faith glared at her back. But she couldn't stay irritated with Casey. She'd always enjoyed Casey's energy, and recently, they'd gotten to know each other better. She'd even thought that next time Casey asked, she might accept her invitation to dinner with her and her wife. She should make an effort to have more friends.

CHAPTER TWENTY

It looks like we need to take it in a bit here." Lola pinched the fabric at Violet's waist. "The dress fit perfectly before. You didn't have to overdo the dieting."

"I didn't." Violet smoothed her hands down the skirt of her dress. "Stress, I guess."

"No worries. We'll fix it up. Let me just get someone to pin this while you have it on. At least we don't have to worry about the length." Lola looked at Rachel. "And with the tea-length, you don't have to learn how to bustle."

"I don't even know what that means."

Violet laughed. "You would have hated it."

"You know how to bustle? How did I not know this?"

"Floor-length dresses often have a train behind them. Even the smallest train can be gathered up and secured out of the way during the reception, so the bride can enjoy herself without tripping or damaging the dress," Lola explained.

"Carly's dress had buttons and ties under the skirt, and each layer had to be pulled up and fastened individually. I'd forgotten about that. You should thank me for picking this dress."

Lola disappeared to the back room to get someone to complete Violet's fitting. Rachel stood and walked around Violet.

"It's really a great dress." She stopped behind Violet and met her eyes in the full-length mirror. "I'm so glad you're getting to wear it."

"All sales are final. I was wearing this dress. I am glad, though, that it will be to my wedding."

"Me, too. I'm glad you and Jack are working things out."

Violet nodded. "I offered to postpone the wedding until he was sure. But he said he loves me and wants to marry me. I don't know if he'll ever truly understand where my head was at then. But at least he believes that I know what an idiot I was, and that I won't let anything like that happen again."

Rachel rubbed her hands together. "Speaking of the wedding, have you two made any progress on the seating chart?"

"No. It's still half-done and sitting on Jack's kitchen counter." Violet had pretty much moved into Jack's place in the past couple of weeks so that Rachel could put hers on the market.

Rachel had questioned whether she might want to hang on to it and just rent it out. But Violet wanted to sell. She didn't want Jack to think she had any hesitations about their life together. So Rachel had handled packing some of Violet's personal items and putting them in storage so she could set the house up for showings.

When Violet told Faith she couldn't finish planning the wedding, Faith had given her the paperwork she had regarding Violet's wedding, including, among other things, the vendor contact information, a checklist, and the schedule she'd been compiling for the day of the ceremony. Rachel, Carly, and Violet divided the tasks. Violet delegated whatever she could to Jack, as well. They'd been working hard, and Rachel had a newfound respect for Faith's profession.

In fact, helping Violet, coupled with her day job, almost didn't leave Rachel time to miss Faith. She probably wouldn't have thought about her at all, if everything wedding-related didn't make her think of Faith. Or if she could go into Violet's store without remembering the day she'd found Faith in the pet-food aisle. Violet had tried to start a conversation about Faith a couple of times, but Rachel continued to shut her out. She'd always been able to talk to Violet about anything. But without Faith in her life, she had an irrational urge to keep her memories of Faith to herself. Eventually, Violet stopped trying. Rachel existed only to get through this wedding and see Violet and Jack off on their honeymoon. Then she planned to take a few days off work, crawl into bed, and completely feel sorry for herself. Until then, she would soldier on.

❖

Faith parked her car at the far end of the parking lot outside of Violet's wedding venue. She rested her arm along the sill of the open window beside her. Violet had gotten the perfect weather she'd hoped for when she booked a location with half the space outdoors. The sky was clear and deep blue. A slight breeze cooled the warmth of the sun and kept the high temperature at a comfortable sixty-five degrees that afternoon. As the sunset painted the cityscape, that number would drop, creating an ideal evening for an outdoor reception.

She leaned her head back against the headrest and exhaled. After everything that happened, Violet would have the perfect wedding day. Faith had never been so regretful about how she'd handled her business. In truth, she was lucky she'd walked away as unscathed as she had. But the incompleteness of the experience still irritated her. Maybe that's why she found herself parked outside the building.

She glanced at the clock on the dash. The reception would have started by now. She regretted not having the chance to see the ceremony. Violet had talked about them writing their own vows. Had they followed through with that? Did Violet cry? And Rachel? Faith was certain she had at least teared up.

Faith's favorite part of a wedding was at the end of the ceremony, as the couple joined hands and was presented as one unit for the first time. That moment always crept through her skepticism about the durability of marriage. Ironically, today, when she wanted most to believe in relationships—that she could be capable of one—she'd missed that.

Before she could get too morose, she got out of the car and walked toward the building. Coming here was probably a bad idea, and if Jack truly didn't want her here, she should respect his wishes.

Plus, there could be a scene. She would try to escape as quietly as she could, but an altercation could damage her reputation. Those were all good reasons to leave. But the devil on her shoulder pushed her forward, whispering that she hadn't been concerned about screwing up her reputation while sleeping with clients, so why should she now.

While planning Violet's wedding, she'd met with everyone from the venue manager to the caterer—not to mention Casey and everyone in the wedding party. She had little hope of getting in and out unrecognized. During the drive here, she'd tried to turn around at least three times. But she'd never been fired from a job. And, while she understood the reason, not seeing a wedding through felt wrong somehow. Maybe she could sneak in, get a look at Violet and Jack, and pop back out.

She'd dressed in black slacks and a black button-down shirt and pulled her hair back in a bun, in an attempt to blend in with the caterers she knew would be moving about the reception. She made it inside and to the elevator undetected. But her plan was blown when the elevator doors opened and the venue manager was alone inside the car.

"Ms. McKenna. I'd been told you wouldn't be here tonight."

Faith had no idea what explanation this woman had been given for her absence, but she doubted Violet told her the real reason. So she banked on a scheduling issue or some other inane excuse and tried to keep her reply just as generic. "That's right. I had a conflict, but I was able to resolve it. And since I started this journey with Violet and Jack, I thought I'd check in on them."

"Certainly. I'm sure they'll be glad to see you."

"Ah—actually, I don't want to take any attention from their special day. So maybe we could keep this between us. I'll just take a peek, then leave them to their celebration."

The woman appeared confused, but she nodded, and Faith just had to hope she would go along. At least until she left. As they exited the elevator, Faith headed for a nearby restroom, purposely going the opposite way as the manager.

Thankfully, she had the restroom to herself. She washed her

hands and dried them. Then, when she couldn't force herself out of the room, she washed and dried them again. As she exited the restroom, she turned down the hallway that led to a side entrance to the reception room. She opened the door slowly, pleased to find a large potted tree nearby. She hurried inside and half concealed herself there.

From her makeshift blind, she had a decent view of the long rectangular table where the wedding party sat. Their guests were dispersed among round tables throughout the room. Dinner had been cleared, and many of the guests already had half-eaten pieces of cake in front of them. Casey and a young man Faith remembered was her art-school intern, each armed with cameras, moved around the room capturing photos of the guests. When Casey turned in her direction, focused on the table about halfway between them, Faith instinctively drew back against the wall. She imagined Casey's expression when she discovered Faith's image in the background in a day or so as she edited photos.

At Casey's request, the bridal party's dinner table had been placed on the wall adjacent to the bank of windows. She didn't want them backlit in front of the windows or squinting into the setting sun. Violet and Jack sat in the center, flanked by their wedding parties. Faith ignored Jack's side of the table, her eyes drawn immediately to Violet's. Rachel sat next to Violet and leaned close to her in conversation. When she tilted her head back and laughed at something Violet said, Faith's chest ached. Despite the dozen conversations taking place between where Faith hid and that table, Faith imagined she could hear the full, sexy sound of Rachel's laughter.

Rachel's dress looked as amazing as Faith remembered. The alterations to the halter top made it hug her breasts in just the way Faith knew they would. She recalled standing in front of Rachel at the bridal shop. She'd slipped her hands over Rachel's shoulders, pretending to adjust the dress. Even today she was amazed she'd been able to focus on anything other than Rachel's warm, soft skin.

Rachel leaned forward and spoke to Jack, then to Violet. She hoped Rachel was able to enjoy this day with her friends without the shadow of all the negativity of the past several months. Faith hadn't been able to enjoy anything since the last time she'd seen Rachel. But she deserved that, didn't she? God, she missed Rachel though. She would crouch behind this stupid tree until her legs cramped if that meant she got to look at Rachel a little longer.

The clink of flatware against glass drew everyone's attention to the featured table. Jack stood and continued to tap the rim of his champagne glass. He looked dapper in his black suit, white shirt, and black tie. He glanced down at Violet, seated at his side, as if drawing courage from her.

"Okay. I'm not used to giving speeches outside of a conference room, but I'm going to give this a shot. This hasn't been the easiest year for us. As many of you know, my schedule is crazy at the best of times, so there was never going to be a good time to plan a wedding. But being here tonight, with Violet, in front of all of you, I truly feel everything was worth it. However, tonight isn't just about a wedding—a ceremony and a reception. It's about the start of our life of commitment together. And whatever trials we've faced have taught me a lot about our relationship," he glanced at Violet, "and about the things we need to do to make our marriage strong. I love you, Violet. And I will for as long as we both shall live."

He turned to Violet, both of their eyes a bit moist. He touched his glass to hers, while everyone else in the room raised theirs as well. Then he leaned down and kissed Violet. As Faith started to turn away, she couldn't help glancing at Rachel again. But this time, Rachel stared back at her. The longing in Rachel's eyes made Faith's heart pound heavy in the base of her throat. She brought her hand to her chest and pressed her fingers against that pulse point, as if feeling the blood rushing there could anchor her. Somehow, she restrained herself from hurrying into the room and pouring her heart out to Rachel.

She should leave before it was too late. But when Rachel flicked her gaze toward the door at the other end of the room, Faith realized it already was. She was lost. Or she had been lost. But the key to her salvation lay in giving Rachel the correct response to the question in her eyes. She nodded, such a small movement in her otherwise rigid-statue stance that she thought Rachel might miss it. But Rachel moved immediately, rising to extricate herself from her chair and then the space around the wedding party's table. She smoothed her hands over her skirt.

Violet said something Faith couldn't hear, but Rachel's murmured response seemed to mollify her. Faith stepped back into the hallway. She followed it around to the door that Rachel had just exited through.

"Can we talk?" Faith blurted louder than she'd meant to. The only other occupant of the hallway, a server passing through, gave her a weird look, but she didn't care.

Without a word, Rachel took her arm and led her to the elevator. Faith's skin tingled under her firm grasp. As soon as Faith stepped into the elevator, she started to speak, but Rachel held up a hand, silencing her.

"Not yet."

The ride to the ground floor took far longer than it should have. Faith shifted her weight from foot to foot and tried to hide the fact that she had to rub her damp palms against her hips. She hadn't been such a nervous mess around a woman since the tenth grade. A light, clean scent Faith didn't recognize wafted in the small space. Faith wanted to ask if Rachel had bought a new perfume for the wedding, but she didn't seem open to casual conversation.

The doors opened, and Rachel strode out and toward the building's exit. When they got outside, Rachel slowed but continued walking toward the bank of the river. The sun had started setting, silhouetting the downtown high-rises against a canvas of blues fading into yellows, pinks, and oranges. Rachel stopped with her back to Faith, staring across the river at downtown.

Faith hung back several more steps than she wanted to, feeling out how much distance Rachel needed between them, despite her desire to be closer.

"Now can I talk?" Faith ventured quietly. Rachel didn't answer for several seconds, and Faith began to wonder if she'd heard her.

Then Rachel shoved her shoulders back determinedly and turned to face Faith. "I overreacted when you wouldn't agree to talk to Jack. And that night at the bar, what you overheard—"

"No. I'm sorry. I wasn't honest with you while we were—involved."

"Oh, God. You were sleeping with someone else?"

"What? No." Faith shook her head. She rubbed her forehead. Rachel thought she could get into bed with someone else? Well, she hadn't given her any reason not to. That's the point she'd been about to make, wasn't it?

"You weren't?"

"No. I—hell, I couldn't think about anyone but you, let alone have sex."

"Then what weren't you honest about?"

Faith drew in a deep breath. "About the fact that I was falling for you."

The shock on Rachel's face would have been laughable if not for the tears that suddenly filled her eyes. "You were?"

"Yes. And that wasn't supposed to make you cry."

"Happy tears." Rachel dragged her finger under her eye, succeeding only in spilling the moisture onto her cheek.

"Yeah?"

Rachel nodded. "I was falling for you, too. And kicking myself for it."

"I'm so sorry. I didn't expect to feel as much as I did for you—and I didn't know how to deal with it." She smiled. "I don't know if I told you, but I don't have much practice at relationships."

The corner of Rachel's mouth rose. "I'd heard that somewhere." Then her expression grew serious. "So where does that leave us now?"

"First, I'm going to kiss you." Faith caught Rachel's face in her hands. She sighed as their lips touched, enveloped in so much warmth that it might as well have been their first kiss. Shutting down the clamoring of her body, she eased back before things got too heated. "Then I'm going to leave."

"What?"

She tilted her head toward the building behind them. "I'm not really welcome in there."

"I can talk to Violet."

Faith shook her head. "It's her and Jack's day. I'll go. But tomorrow, if you're free, I'd love to take you to dinner."

"A date?"

"The first of many, I hope. So let me be clear. I'm not going to be sleeping with or otherwise involved with anyone else. Is that okay?"

Rachel nodded.

She looked again at the venue. "It's going to be uncomfortable for a while. They're your friends."

"They are. And that's why they will eventually be okay with this. Don't worry. I'll convince Jack that I don't plan to let you touch Violet ever again." Rachel looped her arm through Faith's. "Can I walk you to your car?"

"Absolutely."

"You know, Violet and Jack have come a long way together."

"I'm glad. How are you and Jack?"

"We're getting there. He'll probably always believe I should have told him. But he seems to understand the situation I was in, too."

As they rounded the corner of the building by the parking lot, a door burst open. An obviously tipsy Carly emerged, partially supported by her husband. Faith and Rachel hung back while they got in their car.

"They're leaving early," Faith said as Carly's husband drove out of the lot.

"Carly and Violet have been on the rocks, too. Carly has been insufferable lately."

"When is she not?"

"Violet told Jack where she got the idea that you might be open to—anyway, he's not happy with her either. I think she's worried he'll tell her husband. So she's compensating by acting like she doesn't care—like one night with you was worth it."

Faith grinned, then stumbled slightly when Rachel shoved her.

As she righted herself, she wrapped her arm around Rachel's waist and pulled her closer.

Rachel huffed. "She was easier to take when I had you to distract me."

"Yeah?" Faith wondered how often Rachel had thought about the ways they could distract each other since they'd been apart. She'd relived that encounter with the glass dildo in her head a time or two herself.

"Stop smiling like that." Rachel pinched her side, just above her hip.

"Ow." Faith grabbed her hand.

"Seriously, I can't look at her without thinking about you and her together."

"Rachel."

"I'm not even sure I've completely reconciled you and Violet. But I can tell myself you and she didn't really—you know. But Carly—it's like she rubs it in my face without even saying a word."

"She doesn't even know about you and me."

"I realize that. But she's just so indiscreet."

"That's one way to put it." Faith laughed. "It's cute that you're jealous."

"It's not cute. And I'm not jealous." Rachel frowned. "I already couldn't stand her. And when she's always so ready to talk about all the dirty things she did with you, I don't like her even more."

"I'd be willing to bet there's a good deal of embellishment on her part. It was one time and wasn't even very—okay, I don't need to discuss that. What I'm trying to say is, you and I both have a past, and while I know mine is a little more in your face, it's not something you need to think about."

"That's easy for you to say."

Faith had been certain up until this moment that they were both joking. But now, seeing the insecurity in Rachel's eyes, she wanted to reassure her.

"I know." Faith stopped and took both of her hands. "All I can say is, I realize you think about it when you look at her. But since the day we met, I haven't wanted anyone else."

"The day we met, I slapped you."

"You did."

"I think you liked it."

"Oh, honey, there is no part of me that's into being slapped around." Faith touched Rachel's chin with one finger. She held onto one of Rachel's hands as they resumed walking. "While I will admit you are one sexy woman when you're angry, I'd like to focus my energy more on making you happy from now on."

"Starting tomorrow," Rachel said as they reached Faith's car.

Faith opened the door and pulled Rachel with her into the space between the car and the door. "Starting right now." She kissed her again, this time lingering and caressing her tongue against Rachel's. She slid her hands around Rachel's hips, settling them low on her back. Rachel moaned and pressed into her.

"I have to get back," Rachel murmured against Faith's lips.

Faith cradled Rachel's face and kissed her again. "Violet is the center of attention right now. She won't miss you."

"It's Violet. She absolutely will. In fact, there's a chance she's watching us out one of those windows right now."

"Okay. I'll pick you up at six tomorrow."

Rachel nodded, and Faith gave her another quick kiss before ducking inside her car. Rachel stepped back to allow her to close the door. As Faith drove away, she glanced in the rearview mirror. Rachel had walked halfway back to the building, then turned to watch her leave.

Faith felt lighter than she had in months. In the past, the thought that a woman wanted a future with her had inspired panic, but the knots in her stomach had eased when Rachel said, *I was falling for you, too.* She hadn't known she could feel such elation. There was a chance Rachel had feelings for her.

But maybe Rachel had only become involved with her because of her reputation. Rachel had never had a meaningless fling in her life. Was that all Faith was good for?

Tomorrow, though, she had a date. "With the woman I love." It felt good to say it out loud in the confines of her car. But she probably wouldn't tell Rachel on their first date. She tightened her hands on the steering wheel as she repeated the phrase in her head, *first date.*

This was the first time in years that she'd taken a woman out with the intention of building something with her. Well, now she was getting nervous. All the way home her mind raced with ways to impress Rachel.

CHAPTER TWENTY-ONE

Rachel opened her door to a huge bouquet of flowers. Tissue paper crinkled as Faith moved it to the side so she could see around it. A warm flush followed Faith's gaze as she swept it down Rachel's body and back up. Despite Faith's insistence that tonight wasn't formal, Rachel had dressed with Faith in mind. She'd paired a light-blue shirt with a navy pantsuit and debated for only a few minutes before adding the vest under her jacket. Seeing Faith's reaction now validated her decision.

"A three-piece suit? Are you trying to kill me before this date even starts?"

"You like it?"

"Of course." Faith stepped inside and gathered Rachel close with her free arm.

When she kissed her, Rachel's knees nearly melted. Faith kissed her like she wanted to push her inside, close the door, and take her right here in the foyer. Rachel wrapped her arms around Faith's neck, completely in for whatever she wanted. Then Faith slowed, her lips becoming more patient, as if she were gathering control. When Faith released her, she couldn't hold back a murmur of disappointment.

"Sorry. I got carried away."

"No need to apologize." While she loved the idea of Faith unable to control herself, she was charmed by Faith's obvious desire to set a tone of respect for their first official date.

"Those are beautiful." Rachel took the flowers from Faith. "And so are you. I'm sorry I didn't say so sooner." Faith's black jersey wrap dress was belted at the waist. The skirt hugged her hips, then fell in folds to just above her knees. Rachel's fingers itched to undo that belt and see what she had on underneath. That was the pitfall of already having slept with your date. She wanted to skip the formalities and take Faith to her bed. Instead, she focused on the minutiae of the evening.

"Come in for a minute while I put these in water." She led Faith to the kitchen, retrieved the scissors, and held the flowers over the sink while she snipped the end of each stem. "Would you grab me a vase out of that corner cabinet?" She nodded toward the lower cabinet nearest the refrigerator.

"Sure." Faith bent and Rachel had to pull her eyes away. Wondering if the fabric covering Faith's butt felt as soft as it looked wasn't exactly how she'd planned to distract herself.

Faith straightened and turned around, and Rachel didn't focus her attention back on her task fast enough. Their gazes locked. Rachel jerked toward the sink and had just snipped the next stem when she heard Faith curse under her breath, followed by the sound of shattering glass. The vase now glittered in pieces on the floor around them.

"Don't move," Faith said. "You don't have shoes on." Rachel had left her shoes by the door, intending to slip into them as she left. "Where do I find a broom?"

"Hall closet. There's a dustpan, too."

She stood still while Faith picked her way carefully over the minefield of glass. Faith winced when pieces crunched under her shoes. As she returned from the hallway, she swept the bits she tracked with her back into the kitchen. She handed Rachel the dustpan.

"I'm sorry. Was that a valuable vase?" Faith brought the trash can closer to them.

"Not at all. Don't worry about it." Rachel bent and held the dustpan against the floor so Faith could fill it.

They worked together until the mess was disposed of. Faith apologized again, and Rachel brushed off the accident. Rachel grabbed another vase, filled it with water, and put the flowers in. She slipped into her shoes and they headed out the door.

In the car, their conversation was stilted, and Faith wrung both hands against the steering wheel. She pulled into a spot in the lot outside the restaurant and shifted the car into Park. Rachel dropped her hand on top of Faith's on the gearshift.

"Hold on." She caressed her fingers against the back of Faith's hand. "What are you so nervous about?"

"Don't laugh."

"Okay."

"Do you know how long it's been since I've been on a date?"

Rachel laughed and Faith glared at her. "I'm sorry. But you are the same woman who flirted with me shamelessly until I went to bed with you, right?"

"That's not quite how I remember it."

"I didn't think you were lacking in confidence."

"Sure. When it comes to flirting and sex, I'm all good. But this," she gestured between them, "this is important. It's the first step toward our future."

"When you put that much pressure on it—now I'm nervous, too." Rachel laced her fingers into Faith's. "Tonight isn't a typical first date, though. We've known each other for eight months. Even if tonight is a disaster, I'll still answer the phone if you call me for a second date."

"*When* I call you for a second date."

Rachel smiled, happy to see some of Faith's confidence returning. "Let's go in there and have a nice dinner. Then you can take me home, and maybe I'll make out with you in the car before I go inside."

Faith's smile was much more relaxed. "You're not going to invite me in?"

"I don't want you thinking I'm the kind of girl who has sex on the first date."

Faith laughed. "I already know you're not."

"If I have to play hard to get again just so you won't stress about tonight, I will."

Faith slid her hand from under Rachel's, then trailed her fingertips up Rachel's arm. "You can try." She brushed the side of Rachel's neck, smiling when Rachel leaned into her touch. "But we both know it won't be as easy as it once was."

Rachel closed her eyes and sighed happily.

Faith pulled her hand back, and when she spoke, the cocky edge had returned to her tone. "Let's go eat. Then we'll see about that make-out session you promised me."

"Promised?" Rachel got out of the car and waited while Faith circled to her side. "I think I said *maybe*."

"Right. But I know what you meant."

❖

Faith awoke to the ringing of her cell phone in the next room. She scrubbed the heel of her hand against her eye, then turned over and found Swan staring back at her from the other side of the bed. As soon as she'd started letting the damn cat into the house, he'd acted like he owned the place. He'd claimed a spot on the bed at night. He ate his meals in the kitchen next to the fridge. And he only ventured out to the barn anymore when he was following her out there. He was a social dude for a cat. Would getting him a buddy keep him from trailing her around so much? But she didn't want to cross the line between reluctantly owning one cat to purposefully getting more. And since she hoped to open parts of the property to the public at some point, she didn't want too many cats running around.

Last night, Rachel had been true to her word, leaving Faith sitting in her car in Rachel's driveway after a heavy make-out session. She could tell Rachel had been as worked up as she was and both respected and cursed Rachel's discipline.

She pushed back the covers and got out of bed. After a brief stop in the bathroom, she went to the kitchen to retrieve her cell phone, which she'd left charging on the counter. She had one missed call from Rachel. She dialed Rachel back right away.

"I decided not to wait for you to call for a second date," Rachel said as soon as she answered.

"Right. Because it's already been eight hours since I dropped you off from our first one."

"Clearly you're dragging your feet."

"Then I appreciate your initiative in correcting that oversight on my part."

"So, do you want a second date?" Rachel's voice carried a tease of promise.

Faith stretched languidly. "I do."

"How about now?"

"Now?"

"I happened to be in the neighborhood, and I thought you might want to have breakfast with me."

"There's nothing in my neighborhood but my house."

"Right. That's why I was in the area. To bring you breakfast." Just then the doorbell rang. "Are you going to let me in?"

Faith opened the door to Rachel holding a large bottle of orange juice in one hand and a paper bag in the other.

Rachel held up the bag. "My favorite breakfast tacos from a truck near my house. They're not so great with coffee, so I opted for juice."

"Come on in." Faith took the bag from her and led her to the kitchen. Her stomach growled as the aroma of spicy sausage and egg drifted to her.

She set the bag on the counter and turned to pull Rachel into her arms. As soon as she touched her, breakfast was forgotten. Rachel barely had time to slide the juice bottle onto the counter before Faith crushed her mouth to Rachel's. Rachel buried her fingers in Faith's hair and matched her kisses.

Faith slipped her hands under the hem of Rachel's T-shirt and stroked her sides. She moved her mouth to the edge of Rachel's jaw and down her neck. She bit her lightly, then said, "How do you feel about sex on the second date?"

"My first showing isn't for two hours," Rachel said as she pushed Faith toward her bedroom.

"Perfect. My whole day is free." Faith backpedaled, keeping her hands on Rachel until they reached the edge of the bed. Swan stood and stretched. "Beat it, Swan." He hopped down and indignantly left the room.

They undressed each other quickly and slid into bed together. Faith moved immediately over Rachel. She caressed her stomach while she kissed her shoulder, her collarbone, and down the center of her chest. Then she gave in to every urge she'd suppressed during their date the night before.

"Faith," Rachel murmured, guiding Faith's head to her breast.

Faith sucked and lightly bit Rachel's nipple until Rachel's hips moved restlessly against her stomach. She lifted herself away from Rachel and moved to her side, pleased with Rachel's disappointed moan. Rachel went with her, rolling slightly to her side. Faith pushed her hand between them, slipping through Rachel's wet folds. Rachel's eyes slid shut for a moment, and the pleasure on her face echoed and spread through Faith's chest.

"I love touching you." Faith found and stroked Rachel's clit as she understated her emotions. Surely, their relationship was too new for the depth of feeling raging through her. So instead of full disclosure, she fell back on what she knew and concentrated on pleasing Rachel completely.

Rachel tilted her hips, and Faith took the cue and pushed inside her. Rachel moaned. Faith kissed her, pouring everything she couldn't say into the play of her lips on Rachel's. She stroked her tongue against Rachel's, then drew back to suck her lower lip, all while pressing and thrusting inside Rachel.

Rachel's body took her in, drawing her deeper as she added another finger. She braced her thigh behind her hand and let Rachel set the pace. The sight of Rachel, head tilted back, riding her hand, might have been enough to get her off with just a touch or two. Rachel wrapped her hand around the back of Faith's neck and tugged as if she, too, couldn't get close enough.

"God, yes. Please, there." Rachel's voice was as tight as her body, her motions becoming quicker and more erratic. The sheer beauty of this moment swamped Faith. She wanted all of Rachel more than she'd ever wanted anything in her life.

Faith covered her near sob with a moan of encouragement. Rachel squeezed her eyes shut and bit her lip as she approached orgasm. Faith curled her fingers and pressed her thumb against Rachel's clit.

As Rachel hovered so close to release, Faith let herself go as well. "I love you."

Rachel's eyes flew open as she crashed over the edge. She grasped at Faith's back as her body went rigid. She cried out, and Faith continued to thrust, drawing every bit of pleasure from her orgasm.

"That was dirty," Rachel rasped as she relaxed back against the pillow.

Faith sighed and dropped her head into Rachel's neck. She kissed Rachel's damp skin and lifted her head. She met Rachel's eyes with her heart and her gaze completely open.

"Faith?" Rachel searched her face, and Faith smiled as she didn't even feel her old instinctive urge to shut down.

"It wasn't dirty. It was the most honest I've ever been with you. Or anyone."

Rachel cradled her face in her hands and kissed her mouth. "I love you, too."

❖

"Can you believe this day is finally here?" Rachel squeezed Faith's upper arm enthusiastically.

Faith warmed at the feel of Rachel pressed to her side. "I think you might be more thrilled about their wedding than they are." She nodded toward the bride and her bridesmaids as they climbed out of the three cars that had just pulled into the area designated for the wedding party. Faith had created separate parking in one of the front pastures for guests, and that area would soon be filling up as well.

"You can play cool all you want, but I know on the inside

you're jumping up and down like a little kid, too. It's your first event here. It's okay to show your excitement."

"Our first event," Faith said. She turned to Rachel and took her hands, relishing this quiet moment with her before they spent the next several hours making sure the first couple to get married at Faithful Union Farms had the happiest day of their lives. Faith recalled the tears that welled in Rachel's eyes when she had suggested the name for the venue. She'd wanted to honor the property's history as a working farm, though she had no desire to restore that purpose. But even more importantly, she'd hoped Rachel would understand the depth of her commitment by including both of their names in the title as well. "You've worked just as hard for this day as I have."

Rachel kissed her lightly on the lips. "I didn't realize how much I would enjoy working on this wedding."

During the last five months, as the date for the first wedding at Faithful Union approached, Rachel had helped Faith finish getting the barn and surrounding property ready to host its first wedding. Since Rachel still carried a full client load at her agency, Faith handled her usual part of the wedding planning. But in the evenings and on the weekends, they worked on the farm.

"Why? I thought you had a lot of fun helping plan Violet's."

"Parts of it were extremely pleasurable," Rachel purred, having also perfected the tone that had skyrocketed Faith's arousal in the last five months as well.

"Do you know how many hours we have until I can get my hands on you properly?" Faith squeezed Rachel's ass and took some satisfaction in watching Rachel's evil grin fall away. "I'll go show the girls to the bride's dressing room. The guys should be here in a bit, and you're in charge of them."

"Got it." Rachel kissed Faith's cheek. "Casey is already here someplace. She wanted some shots inside before the guests starting arriving."

Faith intercepted the bridal party as they finished loading their arms with dresses and totes, no doubt carrying shoes, underthings, and hair and makeup supplies.

"Hello, ladies. Here, let me get this." She carefully lifted the bride's gown from her. "If you'll all follow me, I'll get you set up in one of our rooms. The fridge in there is stocked with water and other drinks. If there's anything at all you need, please let us know."

She showed them into the room and reviewed the first part of the schedule, telling them how much time they had to get ready. She'd just left them in the room when she ran into Casey in the main reception area.

"How's it going in there?" Casey asked.

"They just got here. I told them you'd be dropping by to get some shots of them getting ready."

"Good. I'll give them a bit." Casey played with the settings on her camera. "Everything looks great, Faith. It's going to be a beautiful first wedding. You've done an amazing job."

Faith spotted Rachel at the far end of the barn, fiddling with some of the flowers around the cake display table. "It wasn't just me."

Casey glanced across the room, then met Faith's eyes with a cocky grin. "I told you she'd make someone a great wife, someday."

"Yeah, okay. Let's not rush things." She played Casey's comment off. But Faith had no doubt that she wanted to marry Rachel someday.

Being in a relationship had been a learning experience for Faith. The past five months hadn't been all smooth sailing, but Rachel was the only woman she wanted to figure it out with. Once they'd decided to date, Faith found that Rachel wasn't one of those women who would let her get away with anything and just go along.

"It's good, though, right?" Casey asked.

"It's awesome."

"She's a great girl. Jacq and I really like her." Casey had invited them over for poker night a couple of times in the past five months. Faith had been surprised to learn that Rachel was fairly good at bluffing and could read Faith almost every time.

They'd been so busy all summer that Faith liked to steal a quiet night in with Rachel when she could. But she also loved having Rachel by her side when they were out together. And she found a degree of comfort she'd never expected in having someone to go home with her every night. Well, most nights. Rachel still had her own place, but she spent many nights at the farm. In the beginning, Faith had used the excuse that they had a ton of work to do on the venue. But before long, she found she didn't need an excuse. She wanted Rachel with her, so she asked her to stay.

❖

Rachel watched the bride dancing with her father and swallowed against the lump in her throat. Weddings didn't usually affect her like this. She'd been less emotional at Violet's. But the barn looked so beautiful, and she felt invested in how it had all turned out. The ceremony had gone smoothly. The caterers were great. And Rachel took some pride in helping create this day for the happy couple.

She glanced across the room and met Faith's eyes. Faith's radiant smile mirrored how Rachel felt inside. She'd seemed more passionate about this wedding as well. Maybe because it was the first at Faithful Union. But Rachel thought there was more to it. She'd seen a renewed spark in Faith that she wanted to attribute to Faith's love for her and how much fun they'd had working side by side.

Faith circled the group of guests on the dance floor and stopped at Rachel's side.

"The DJ has this covered for a little while. Come take a walk with me?" Faith held out her hand, and Rachel placed hers in it.

They slipped out the side door, onto the same patio where they'd spent New Year's Eve. Guests had been in and out that door earlier, but for the time being they had the space to themselves. Faith glanced at the sectional as if she, too, was remembering that night, but she led them past it toward the house. They sat on the steps to the back porch, out of earshot, but where they could still see the barn if someone came looking for them.

"What a great night, huh?" Faith's right shoulder and the outside of her thigh touched Rachel's.

"It is. I didn't realize how hectic these things could be for you, though. I feel like I've been going nonstop since sunup."

"We have."

"Does it feel different since it's your venue?"

"It does."

"Are you okay?"

"Yes." Faith cleared her throat and tapped her own knee nervously. "I actually wanted to talk to you about something. I debated waiting until later, after the wedding was over. But I looked across the room, and you were so gorgeous, I couldn't wait any longer."

"Okay." Rachel covered Faith's hand and laced their fingers together. "Go ahead."

"I wanted to make sure you know how happy I've been these past several months. Since we met, my life hasn't been the same. If you told me a year ago that I would be looking forward to sharing my life with someone, I wouldn't have believed you. But now—I just can't imagine anyone else being by my side. So tonight, I planned to ask you—I mean, if you wanted to—I think you and I—"

"Are you trying to propose?" Rachel was half joking, but Faith seemed so nervous, she wasn't sure.

"Ha, no." Faith grabbed Rachel's other hand and rushed to continue. "I'm going to propose to you. Just not on someone else's wedding day. Don't worry. I'll make it special."

Rachel laughed. "And I'll say yes."

"Not yet. You wait until I ask."

"So what was your big speech leading up to?"

"Two things, really. First, unless I'm mistaken, you've taken to the venue and event-planning thing. If you're interested, I'd love for you to become more of a partner in the business going forward. If the venue is as successful as I'm hoping, I'm going to need help, and I really liked working with you on this one. I already have some things booked in the next year, and with just a few more events, you could cut back on real estate or leave it altogether if you wanted to." In addition to her wedding-planning clients, she had booked several weddings and an anniversary at the farm in the next year. She'd also been talking to a guy about hosting his family reunion.

Rachel didn't even have to think about it. "I'd love that."

"Great. Secondly, I'd like you to move in with me. I want you here with me when I go to bed and when I wake up in the morning. It's silly for us to maintain two separate households."

"If you'd told me on the day we met that I would ever hear you ask me that—"

"You wouldn't have slapped me?"

"No. I'd still have done that." Rachel grabbed Faith's jacket lapels, pulled her close, and kissed her. "I love you so much."

"Is that a yes?"

"Absolutely. I would love to live here with you and Swan."

"What?"

Rachel tilted her head toward the kitchen window, where Swan lay on the sill looking out at them.

"You only like him because he sleeps on your feet and keeps them warm. Between you and that cat, I'll be outnumbered."

"Are you taking it back?"

"Never."

"Then, yes. I'll move in with you."

Faith kissed her again, slipping her hand along Rachel's neck in a possessive gesture. "Do you think we could sneak inside the house and get a quickie in before we're needed out there again?"

"No." She was tempted, but getting caught having sex during their first wedding wasn't the reputation she wanted for their venue. She smiled to herself as she thought *our venue.* "But let's get through this wedding. Then, when everyone's gone, we can christen the barn."

"Again?"

"We've never had sex in there after a wedding. That makes it new."

"You'll get no argument from me." Faith stood and pulled Rachel off the step. "Let's go take care of this couple. Then we can start planning the rest of our lives."

About the Author

Erin Dutton resides near Nashville with her wife but will gladly jump at any opportunity to load the dogs up in the car or RV and travel. In 2007, she published her first book, *Sequestered Hearts*, and has kept writing since. She's a proud recipient of the 2011 Alice B. Readers' Appreciation medal for her body of work.

When not working or writing, she enjoys playing golf, photography, and spending time with friends and family.

Books Available From Bold Strokes Books

A Lamentation of Swans by Valerie Bronwen. Ariel Montgomery returns to Sea Oats to try to save her broken marriage but soon finds herself also fighting to save her own life and catch a murderer. (978-1-62639-828-3)

Between Sand and Stardust by Tina Michele. Are the lifelong bonds of love strong enough to conquer time, distance, and heartache when Haven Thorne and Willa Bennette are given another chance at forever? (978-1-62639-940-2)

House of Fate by Barbara Ann Wright. Two women must throw off the lives they've known as a guardian and an assassin and save two rival houses before their secrets tear the galaxy apart. (978-1-62639-780-4)

Planning for Love by Erin Dutton. Could true love be the one thing that wedding coordinator Faith McKenna didn't plan for? (978-1-62639-954-9)

Sidebar by Carsen Taite. Judge Camille Avery and her clerk, attorney West Fallon, agree on little except their mutual attraction, but can their relationship and their careers survive a headline-grabbing case? (978-1-62639-752-1)

Sweet Boy and Wild One by T. L. Hayes. When Rachel Cole meets soulful singer Bobby Layton at an open mic, she is immediately in thrall. What she soon discovers will rock her world in ways she never imagined. (978-1-62639-963-1)

To Be Determined by Mardi Alexander and Laurie Eichler. Charlie Dickerson escapes her life in the US to rescue Australian wildlife with Pip Atkins, but can they save each other? (978-1-62639-946-4)

True Colors by Yolanda Wallace. Blogger Robby Rawlins plans to use First Daughter Taylor Crenshaw to get ahead, but she never planned on falling in love with her in the process. (978-1-62639-927-3)

Undercover Affairs by Julie Blair. Searching for stolen documents crucial to U.S. security, CIA agent Rett Spenser confronts lies, deceit, and unexpected romance as she investigates art gallery owner Shannon Kent. (978-1-62639-905-1)

Unexpected by Jenny Frame. When Dale McGuire falls for Rebecca Harper, the mother of the son she never knew she had, will Rebecca's troubled past stop them from making the family they both truly crave? (978-1-62639-942-6)

Canvas for Love by Charlotte Greene. When ghosts from Amelia's past threaten to undermine their relationship, Chloé must navigate the greatest romance of her life without losing sight of who she is. (978-1-62639-944-0)

Heart Stop by Radclyffe. Two women, one with a damaged body, the other a damaged spirit, challenge each other to dare to live again. (978-1-62639-899-3)

Repercussions by Jessica L. Webb. Someone planted information in Edie Black's brain and now they want it back, but with the protection of shy former soldier Skye Kenny, Edie has a chance at life and love. (978-1-62639-925-9)

Spark by Catherine Friend. Jamie's life is turned upside down when her consciousness travels back to 1560 and lands in the body of one of Queen Elizabeth I's ladies-in-waiting...or has she totally lost her grip on reality? (978-1-62639-930-3)

Taking Sides by Kathleen Knowles. When passion and politics collide, can love survive? (978-1-62639-876-4)

Thorns of the Past by Gun Brooke. Former cop Darcy Flynn's heart broke when her career on the force ended in disgrace, but perhaps saving Sabrina Hawk's life will mend it in more ways than one. (978-1-62639-857-3)

You Make Me Tremble by Karis Walsh. Seismologist Casey Radnor comes to the San Juan Islands to study an earthquake but finds her heart shaken by passion when she meets animal rescuer Iris Mallery. (978-1-62639-901-3)

Complications by MJ Williamz. Two women battle for the heart of one. (978-1-62639-769-9)

Crossing the Wide Forever by Missouri Vaun. As Cody Walsh and Lillie Ellis face the perils of the untamed West, they discover that love's uncharted frontier isn't for the weak in spirit or the faint of heart. (978-1-62639-851-1)

Fake It till You Make It by M. Ullrich. Lies will lead to trouble, but can they lead to love? (978-1-62639-923-5)

Girls Next Door, edited by Sandy Lowe and Stacia Seaman. Best-selling romance authors tell it from the heart—sexy, romantic stories of falling for the girls next door. (978-1-62639-916-7)

Pursuit by Jackie D. The pursuit of the most dangerous terrorist in America will crack the lines of friendship and love, and not everyone will make it out from under the weight of duty and service. (978-1-62639-903-7)

The Practitioner by Ronica Black. Sometimes love comes calling whether you're ready for it or not. (978-1-62639-948-8)

Unlikely Match by Fiona Riley. When an ambitious PR exec and her super-rich coding geek-girl client fall in love, they learn that giving something up may be the only way to have everything. (978-1-62639-891-7)

Where Love Leads by Erin McKenzie. A high school counselor and the mom of her new student bond in support of the troubled girl, never expecting deeper feelings to emerge, testing the boundaries of their relationship. (978-1-62639-991-4)

Forsaken Trust by Meredith Doench. When four women are murdered, Agent Luce Hansen must regain trust in her most valuable investigative tool—herself—to catch the killer. (978-1-62639-737-8)

Letter of the Law by Carsen Taite. Will federal prosecutor Bianca Cruz take a chance at love with horse breeder Jade Vargas, whose dark family ties threaten everything Bianca has worked to protect—including her child? (978-1-62639-750-7)